THE GORGON CURSE

THE EMPOWERED SERIES
BOOK 3

The Gorgon Curse
The Empowered Series Book 3
USA Today Bestselling Author
Heather Young-Nichols

heatheryoungnichols.com

Also by Heather Young-Nichols

Rules of the Game

Kissing the Player

Wanting the Player

Winning the Player

Moonstruck

Moonstruck

Moontouched

The Empowered Series

The Gremlin Prince

The Goblin War

The Gorgon Curse

Shadow Coven

Haunted Magic

Cursed Magic

Stolen Magic

Fated Magic

Forever 18

Forever Grayson

Forever London

Forever Lennox

Heavy Hitter

Pushing Daisies

Daisy

Van

Bonham

Daltrey

Mack

Courting Chaos

Cross

Ransom

Booker

Dixon

Finding Love

Making Her Mine

Making Him Hers

Harbor Point

Love by the Slice

Love by the Mile

Love by the Rules

Gambling on Love

Highest Bidder

Highest Stakes

Highest Reward

Holiday Bites

All I Want

All of Me

The Fallout Series

Last Good Thing

Last First Kiss

Last Chance Love

With J.A. Hardt

Bound by Magic

With Amelia J. Matthews

Dirt on the Diamond

After Office Hours: Seducing the Professor

Chapter One

"Do you think you can manage that, Sloane, sweetie?"

I ground my teeth together so that the words I wanted to say remained inside me. If they came out, I'd lose my job and that would bring with it a whole slew of problems.

"Sure," I told my asshole boss, who tended to give me instructions like I was a toddler. All because he didn't think women knew how to take direction or do the simplest tasks without his wisdom.

Fuck that guy.

It was restocking, not rocket science. I could do it as I'd been doing for the last two years.

At least he disappeared back into his office so I could restock the coffee without him overseeing.

I hated him and at this rate, I would hate my life along with him.

Working in a coffee shop wasn't the dream, but I wasn't allowed dreams. Growing up in foster care meant I'd take whatever I could get and hopefully better my situation as I went. Aging out wasn't how most people imagined. They didn't pin a dollar to your collar and wish you luck. Or at least, my system didn't. I had people to call if I got in trouble or needed help, but it was never enough help. College would be free for me, sure, but I hadn't been the best student and college brought another slew of problems.

No. I preferred being on my own, even if I had to deal with a sexist ass of a boss.

It was nothing I hadn't dealt with before.

So I spent my day stocking up on everything we needed to make sure we could make the coffee and give every customer the jolt they needed. I was an expert at this point and could make their venti sugar-free iced caramel macchiato with skim milk and light caramel drizzle half-caff in my sleep.

It was all just so... boring.

Did I expect an exciting life? No. Not really. One thing foster care did well was teach you how to manage expectations. My expectations were perfectly managed and since so many others had it a lot worse than me, I hated myself for complaining.

Still... was a little excitement too much to ask for?

That Friday, I was out to dinner with a friend I'd made in foster care. She'd aged out the same time I had and we'd been in several of the same homes together. We promised we wouldn't lose touch and scheduled this monthly dinner—our one splurge—to make sure we had time to catch up and remind ourselves that we weren't in this alone.

"So what're you going to do?" Rhea asked after I'd told her about my boss... again. Rhea was gorgeous with her honey-blonde hair and coppery eyes. I didn't know where she'd gotten that combination—neither did she—but it worked. She was also tall like a model, whereas I... just wasn't.

I shrugged. "What can I do?"

"There are other jobs," she countered. Rhea had gotten lucky and started as a receptionist in a dentist's office, which paid so much better than slinging coffee. I just keep applying to various office work, hoping something could work out.

"I know." I sighed. "And if he calls me 'sweetie' one more time, I might stab him or quit. I'm not sure which."

She snickered. "Quit. Don't stab him. I hear prison is the worst."

Her parents were both in prison, which was what had landed her in the system. Neither would give up rights and no one worked very hard to force them, so Rhea was a lifer like me. No hope of adoption. At least she knew who her parents were, however shitty. I didn't even know my parents' names.

"Maybe I should do something fun," I said while pushing my fork through the mashed potatoes. I'd eat them and if I didn't, I'd take them home. We learned early to never pass up food. Then I sat up straighter. "Yeah. Maybe I need to do something fun."

Rhea furrowed her perfectly shaped eyebrows. "Are you saying being here with me isn't fun?"

"I'm not saying that," I countered quickly, to which she laughed. "I'm saying I need to do something I haven't done before. Just... something."

Her eyes widened and she sat up straighter. "What about a road trip?"

"Yes!" I'd said it too loud, but I couldn't have cared less. A level of excitement that I'd never experienced before filled me. There wasn't much in my life to be excited about. "A road trip. I have the car."

"And it's a great car."

I shrugged. It was what I could afford and it looked fine, ran well. What more could I ask for?

"Do you want me to go with you?" she asked with excitement at the prospect, but also hesitation.

"No, Rhea. No. I think I need to do this myself."

"Are you sure? I can take the time off."

Last year, Rhea had met a guy at a party. Two months later, the positive pregnancy test had appeared. That might've been the scariest moment of either of our lives. But Charlie had stepped up, moved Rhea into his apartment, and they'd been together since. Once the baby had shown up—a girl —they'd both fallen in love with her and each other. It was a struggle. They were young but were doing everything they could to make sure their daughter didn't ever end up in the system.

And I was backup. Even if something happened to both of them, I'd take their kid. In no world would that adorable little girl grow up the way Rhea and I had.

"No, Rhea. You and Charlie are saving up for a house. I know this. I'd never ask you to take the time."

"You didn't ask," she countered. "I offered and I've never been anywhere, either. It's not like it'd be a hardship to get me to go. Charlie would take care of everything."

I reached across the table and set my hand on top of hers. "I know he would. You found yourself a great guy, but no. I'm not derailing your plans." When she opened her mouth to argue, I said, "Besides, I think this is something I need to do myself. Prove that I can."

Her mouth snapped shut. That was another thing about growing up the way we had. We often felt the need to prove things to ourselves.

"Well, if you change your mind..." She'd drop everything to be there for me.

I wouldn't change my mind. Something inside of me was urging me to go and go alone.

Over the last two years, I'd lived cheap—sharing a tiny apartment with Rhea until last year—and put aside every penny I could. Sometimes, I picked up side jobs to earn a little extra. Having money in the bank meant there was some security.

It was the only reason that I could quit my job for a short road trip. Now, I'd just have to hope I got another when I returned.

Quitting was hard. It wasn't something I was made to do, but my boss made it a little easier. He was an asshole I didn't want to work for, anyway.

So when he said I couldn't have a few days off, I quit.

Excited apprehension raced through me as I left the coffee shop.

This was a new adventure. Probably the only one I'd have in my life and I was going to enjoy it.

That night, I grabbed my phone and called Rhea, putting her on speaker as I looked at my closet.

"Hey," she answered, though I could hear the baby laughing in the background, causing my stomach to clench. She had this beautiful little family and if I didn't love her the way I did, I'd be jealous.

"What do I take on a road trip?" I put my hands on my hips, though she wouldn't see it.

"Uh... I assume whatever you'd need if you were home. But I've never been anywhere, so I'm not sure." Something scratched against the phone. "Charlie!" After a pause, she asked, "What should Sloane take on a road trip?"

"Pants," he answered, making me roll my eyes. "My sister forgot to take pants once."

I sighed. "I know that, but how much? One small bag?" Because one small bag was all we ever took from home to home in the system. And sometimes it was a garbage bag.

"I'd take more," he said. "When are you leaving?"

"Tomorrow morning, I hope."

"We'll be right over."

Then Rhea said, "I guess we're coming over."

While snickering, I said, "See you in a minute."

They didn't live far, so it wouldn't take long. Probably the most time would be spent packing baby Claire up.

Five minutes later, there was a knock on my door. Their little family was on the other side.

"Keys," Charlie said, holding his hand out to indicate it wasn't a question.

"Uh..." I grabbed my purse then handed him the keys. "What're you doing?"

"If you're going on a road trip, I'm going to make sure your car can handle it. I'll probably change the oil because I know you're shit about getting it done."

I furrowed my brows. "How did calling my friend to ask what I should take on a trip end with you checking out my car's roadworthiness?"

He scowled then walked away while Rhea, holding three-month-old Claire, stepped inside.

"You should've known this was going to happen," she said as she marched over to my room. "As soon as you called me. You knew. He'd want to check your car out when he found out you were leaving."

I shrugged. I probably should've known that, given that Charlie treated me how I assumed he'd treat a little sister. I'd never been a sister, so I didn't know how all that worked.

"Now." Rhea set Claire on the bed and turned to me. "Let's get you packed."

We spent an hour making sure I had everything we thought I'd need. Since I didn't have an actual suitcase, we packed two duffle bags and a backpack. I wasn't going to be gone long—a couple of weeks if I was lucky—and Rhea said she'd take care of my apartment, get the mail and check on it basically since I didn't have any pets or plants, but she didn't want me to find myself needing anything.

Then we packed a bag of snacks from my kitchen. It wasn't a lot, but there was no reason to buy snacks on the road when I had a few I could take.

We'd just finished when Charlie came through my door.

"All set. You'll be fine. I did put some new tires on because you needed them." He gave me a pointed look. "As I told you two months ago."

I smiled. He had told me that, but I couldn't

afford them right then. Until this trip, taking any money out of savings had been forbidden. New tires was going to hurt the trip fund. "How much?"

He waved me off. "Don't worry about it. I'm going to work on my boss's old Ford truck for free." His boss owned the garage where he worked but couldn't do the work himself anymore.

"I can't ask you to do that, Charlie." I shifted my weight from one side to the other as the hair at the back of my head stood on end. His generosity made me uncomfortable, mostly because I wasn't used to it. In my world, people didn't do something for you unless they wanted something in return.

"You didn't." Then he motioned to Rhea. "You ready to go?"

"Yeah. Claire's going to want to go down for the night soon." She picked her baby up then came over to me. "Make sure you call. A lot. Or at least text. I feel like a worried mother sending her baby off into the world."

I chuckled while Charlie snorted. "It's kind of the same thing. I will call or text every day unless I don't have signal." She was about to protest. "But I'll make sure to let you know as soon as I'm somewhere I have it."

Her face fell likely because she knew it was the

best she was going to get. Rhea pulled me into a hug and Claire wrapped her arm around me too.

I was going to miss that kid.

After they'd left, I was standing in the middle of my apartment, rethinking everything.

I'd never gone anywhere before. You'd think that since I'd moved around a bit to and from foster homes, I'd have been used to this. But this was different.

I wouldn't see my apartment for a while and I didn't really have a plan. Going on the road with just my intuition seemed like a bad idea.

Yet everything inside of me said it was what I needed to do.

The next morning, I loaded up the car and got ready to leave early. I couldn't sleep anymore and there was no reason to wait. I was heading north. The Upper Peninsula was beautiful in the pictures I'd seen, so that was where I was going.

And drive I did. Until I hit Mackinaw City. Before getting out of my car, I used my phone to do some research. I'd heard about the island. The fact that there were no cars there was intriguing. Then I saw the cost of the ferry ride and *noped* the fuck out of that.

Instead, I spent the day roaming the city. It was

very touristy, but I was fine with that, given that I'd never been a tourist before. The fudge was delicious and there was something about the humidity in this area that made it the perfect place to make fudge. Or that was what the person in the fudge shop said.

After grabbing dinner at the Dairy Queen, I sat at a table outside and scrolled through my phone. The day was almost over, so I'd need to spend the night, but everything I found in Mackinaw was too pricey for me. Could I technically afford it? Maybe. But the thought of paying that much for a single night's stay made me nauseous.

Then I discovered motels in St. Ignace were much cheaper. It was just across the bridge.

The Mighty Mac, as it was called a lot. Michiganders were proud of this bridge, but I was on the beach looking at it and my palms began to sweat. When I looked up the cost to cross it, I found that someone would drive you across in your vehicle if you needed them to. It was an extra ten dollars. I decided that I wasn't going to spend the extra money.

I could do this.

It was only five miles.

What could happen in five miles?

So I strapped myself in my car and steeled myself to cross the Mackinac Bridge.

At first, it wasn't a big deal. Just a normal road, then we got to the suspension part and the fact that I was in the left lane because the right was too close to the edge for me. The left lane had grates instead of cement. I'd bet you could see down to the water and the thought of those grates breaking terrified me.

My hand slipped on the steering wheel because my palms were so sweaty. The moment I could, I changed lanes. Having concrete below me was reassuring. One at a time, I wiped my hand down my shorts.

I was glad when the crossing was over. The motel I found was just on the other side of the bridge, so I got there and settled, taking a shower before falling backward onto the bed. I could sleep just about anywhere.

In the morning, I headed out again. This vacation was going to be a lot of time in my head and I wasn't so sure it was the best idea. But I was already here, so I wasn't going to stop.

Again, something was pulling me north. Then west.

There was a time that I went an hour without seeing another car. Every time I came across a gas station, I stopped and filled up because I worried there wouldn't be another one.

People lived up here, so that was a dumb thought, but still. It made me feel better.

After going west for a while, I turned north again. There was nothing up here. What was I doing?

According to my GPS, I was heading toward the Keweenaw Peninsula, which looked like the northernmost point of the Upper Peninsula.

Why? Why was I going there?

It was like my car had a mind of its own because I didn't specifically want to go here yet knew I had to.

None of this made any sense.

I passed a broken, dirty sign that read *Phoenix*. Who knew there was one outside of Arizona? And I kept going.

The woods got thicker and I came to a skidding stop when I saw another sign that warned me to keep out.

Yet it didn't say why.

So what did my dumbass do? Got out of the car and started looking around.

The hair on my arms stood on end. There was an electrical feel to the air. It was like I'd just licked the end of a nine-volt battery, which I thought almost everyone had done when they'd been kids. The breeze skittered across my skin, nipping at it like a bug.

Should I leave?

Yeah, of course, but did I? No. I wanted to figure out why this was happening and why I felt like I needed to be here.

Chapter Two

There was something very weird happening here.

The air... wasn't right. The feel... was off.

When I heard a sizzle in the air, not unlike bacon frying in a pan, I knew it was time to go. Whatever was happening here, I didn't want any part of it, and fuck the universe if it *wanted* me to be a part of it.

It was like I was fighting against myself. Something telling me I had to be here, but my brain wanted me to run. I'd never experienced anything like it before.

The battle raging inside me, I also didn't understand. But I also wasn't about to be the girl in the horror movie who went to check on the noise, only to be killed in the most ridiculous way. If instinct was telling me to go, I was going to go.

After hurrying back to my car, I started it up and slammed it into drive.

It was so stupid to come here. So stupid to think the universe had some plan for me. Me. A foster kid who didn't even know her parents' names.

I hit a big bump, which was a warning to slow down. In my hurry to get out of here, I was going to ruin my car. Where would I be then?

When I took a right, my lights flashed over something on the path.

An animal. It had to be. I wasn't very big and it was moving a little, clearly injured. That was when the animal looked up and it was... a young woman.

Jesus.

What the hell was a young woman doing out here? Every horror movie scenario that I knew flashed through my brain, given that there was a young woman, maybe my age, battered and broken in the woods in the middle of no fucking where.

Fight or flight? Fight or flight?

Instinct told me to flight, to leave this place and not look back.

But would I be able to live with myself knowing that I'd left this poor woman here probably to die?

No. I wouldn't live with that. So I slammed my car into park and scanned around us. The young woman... I thought she was blonde, though it was hard to tell in the dark and with her... injuries. Was someone chasing her?

When I didn't see any movement around us, I slowly opened my door, ready to slam the thing shut again if I needed to. Again, nothing happened, so I got out of my car and looked over at her. The car was still between us, but she'd gotten closer.

"Hey, are you all right?" I asked. What a stupid fucking question, given that she was clearly not all right. Once I got out to the road and had cell service, I'd find the nearest hospital. The closer she got to me, the worse it looked.

With an arm wrapped around her stomach she said, "Fling." Well, that made no sense. She made no sense.

She was trying to answer, but nothing that made sense came out. I couldn't understand it at all. Then she teetered on her feet and shook her head like she was shaking off death itself as she stumbled around the car toward me.

No. She was coming right at me and when she almost got to me, her legs gave out, causing me to lurch forward to catch her.

We needed to get her out of here. My heart was pounding so hard that I was sure she could hear it.

Hell, I thought the entire country could hear it. Blood *whooshed* in my ears as I worried about what had happened to her, if we'd get out of here before whatever had done this to her came back, or if she'd die in my car.

She was trying to help hold up her weight, but it didn't work. Luckily, I was strong.

"Stay with me," I told her, out of breath from holding her as I dragged her to the other side of the car. Her eyes became small slits and I couldn't imagine she could see much. As I got closer to the car, she pushed her feet harder.

When I dropped her into the passenger seat, she let out a groan, but it was guttural, as if that movement alone caused so much pain, she couldn't even call out. Or she was too injured to vocalize.

She wasn't very big—my size, maybe—as she sunk back into the seat like it was the best mattress in the world. There were bruises along her arms. A black one with red filling in the center. She was bleeding and I'd guess from her reactions that she'd broken some ribs.

Something—or someone—awful had done this to her.

I hurried around to the driver's side of the car and pulled my door shut before quickly hitting the locks. At least we'd have that defense and I'd run over anything that got in our way at this point.

I gripped the steering wheel so hard that it turned my knuckles white. "I'm going to get you to the hospital." Just as soon as I could get some cell service to figure out where that was.

"No," she gasped, her first clear word since I'd found her. Her throat was rough, given how jagged the words sounded. "Home."

She had to be delirious. Her injuries weren't exactly the kind of a thing a first-aid kit could take care of. "I can't take you home. You need a doctor."

"I need home," she insisted.

I glanced at her then back to the road, trying to decide what to do here. The right thing would be to take her to the doctor. A trauma center, actually, looking at her more closely. But I didn't know this area and didn't have service to GPS a hospital.

How would I find one? If this woman could help me, it'd be easy, but everything about her said she'd only lead me to her house.

I glanced back and forth as I drove the car back out of the woods. "Are you sure?"

She nodded slowly and closed her eyes.

"All right, then," I said under my breath.

Maneuvering out of the woods was harder than

driving had been on the way in. I chalked it up to having a possibly dying woman in the car with me and the fact that we were in a thick forest in almost total darkness and I had no idea where I should go. When I'd come in, there had been some light. Not a lot. Even though the sun had been out, the thick trees had blocked most of it.

The woman lay back, and though it was hard to tell, she kept her eyes open as she told me when to turn left or right.

There was still nothing and I had no idea where she was leading me. This was probably the stupidest thing I'd ever done.

Then a large house with darker siding came into view. It that looked so out of place in this area. I don't know if I would've called it a mansion, but it was huge.

"This is it?" I asked, glancing over at her. Her head sort of nodded once. "I didn't think there was anything out here." That was more to myself.

She gave me what I thought was meant to be a smile, but it wasn't much.

This area was deserted. Even the things I'd read online said that this area of the Keweenaw Peninsula had been mostly abandoned after the copper mines had dried up. People didn't live out here. There were no jobs... no prospect of anything unless you wanted to be totally off-grid, living like a mountain man.

As soon as I brought the car to a stop, the woman groped at the door to find the handle to get out.

"Let me help you." I hurried over to her side of the car to help her out. While trying to be gentle didn't really work and seemed to frustrate this woman more, I didn't want to hurt her.

She wrapped her arm around my shoulders as I wrapped mine around her to help. The small, dragging steps she took made the walk take forever, but I was fine with that. Her injuries were so severe even with me only glancing at her and not knowing the extent, I just wanted to get her to the door before she died.

When we got to the door, the blonde woman raised her hand and pointed to tell me that she'd like me to open it. I swallowed hard, steeling myself for whatever I might find on the other side. If we could just get inside, I could pass her off to her family and get the hell out of here.

Rhea was going to be so pissed at me for even stopping to help. But so far, this wasn't a trick. No one had tried to grab me to sell me on the black market.

So far.

Oh, shit. Hopefully, her family wouldn't think I'd done this to her. She hadn't talked much yet, but maybe, inside, she'd be able to.

As soon as I'd hoisted her into the house, we were in a larger entryway, filled with people, each having their own, intense conversations. Some sounded angry. Others concerned.

What the hell had I just walked into?

I opened my mouth to say something when a loud gasp rang out and the room fell silent.

A large man with dark hair lurched forward and wrapped my charge up in his arms. I stumbled back from the suddenness of the movement and because I was no longer holding more than just my own weight. His strong arms would be more than enough to help her.

Hopefully, there was a doctor here.

He started to walk her away, but she pushed him gently as her eyes searched for something else. Someone else.

When they landed on the man across the room with brown hair and bluest eyes, he stepped forward but didn't come closer to her. His face was tight with anger... maybe worry. I didn't know these people, so it could've been anything.

Though she leaned more heavily against the man

who'd first grabbed her, she cleared her throat, as if she were trying to be strong.

The blonde glanced at him then back to me, but before she could get a word out, an absolute mountain of a man stepped forward with everyone's eyes on him. He was clearly in charge, yet no one was rushing to get this young woman to the hospital.

It wouldn't be long before she absolutely faded out.

Chapter Three

That mountain of a man called out orders as if he were the general of this odd little army filling the entryway. He wanted things done and he wanted them done now. Then he hurried over to where the dark-haired guy was holding the wounded woman up, which was way closer to me than I would've liked.

I didn't know what was going on in this place, but I knew that I wasn't part of it and was holding my breath waiting for them to blame me for what happened to this woman since I was the one who had shown up with her.

All of this happened in seconds.

"Fern," the man bellowed. "Do everything for Alyssum that you can."

A small, redheaded woman turned to the man holding the blonde, whom the leader had referred to as *Alyssum*. "To my office," she told him, making it clear that was an order.

"Wait," Alyssum croaked, which made everyone stop as she grabbed my wrist. She hadn't been very far from me to begin with.

Speaking sounded so painful for her. Almost as if she had the worst case of strep throat ever. As she stood there, her eyes scanned over everyone, like she was looking for just the right person. Then her eyes stopped as she croaked out, "Jensen." It was barely audible.

This man pushed through the crowd and in any other situation I would've called him *dreamy*. He was tall with brown hair and the most brilliant, blue eyes. So blue, they were almost unnerving.

Alyssum squeezed my wrist tighter as I looked from her to him and then back. I wasn't sure she knew she was holding on to me so tightly and my stomach dropped at the reason why. Was she trying to make sure no one in this room was going to kill me? Eat me alive? Throw me out on my ass?

A conversation passed between the two of them. One that no one else would hear, but maybe others who knew them would understand. My heart pounded against my chest and if this didn't stop soon, I was liable to pass out.

"I've got her," he said, but she didn't let go of me. "Alyssum. I've got her. Nothing will happen. You need to get yourself healed."

Finally, my little blonde protector—at least here in this house—released my wrist so that the big guy could carry her away.

Now I was alone. I didn't know why having the tiny blonde with me had made me feel safer than I did now, but that was the case, nonetheless. Maybe because this was her family. Now, I wasn't an expert in families, of course, but this seemed super dysfunctional and fucked up.

Not a single person asked her what had happened when she'd walked in the door bloody and battered. Almost as if they'd expected it. Almost as if they'd seen it before.

If that wasn't my sign to get the hell out of there, I didn't know what was.

Slowly, I started backing up toward the door. They were all rushing off to do whatever the mountain had told them to do and not a single one was paying attention to me. I could do this. Get in my car and get the hell out of here.

Right as my hand wrapped around the doorknob, the dreamy man said, "I'm Jensen."

I released the knob and let my arms fall to my sides, but I didn't say anything.

"I'm Jensen Burkhardt," he said again, reaching his hand out to shake mine. I was an awkward hand-shaker, but I took it, anyway. "What's your name?"

"Sloane," I told him, but I didn't give my last name. The less information I gave right now, the better.

"Do you know Alyssum?" he asked. I shook my head but didn't say anything. "Where did you find her?"

My gaze left him to focus on the two men hurrying through the foyer. Jensen turned to glance at them. Then his eyes were back on me.

"How about I get you somewhere less public?" he asked. I raised an eyebrow.

Since I hadn't been born yesterday, I wasn't about to go anywhere with him. Though that argument went out the window since I'd stopped for Alyssum in the first place.

"I'm not going to hurt you." He took a step closer with his arms folded over his chest loosely so that it didn't look threatening at all. "Even if you weren't under Alyssum's protection, I wouldn't hurt you."

I swallowed hard and then nodded. If I had trusted my instinct to get me here, I might as well keep doing that and my gut was telling me he was all right. That I didn't need to fear him.

He waved for me to follow, so I did as he headed to the stairs.

"Is she... your sister?" I asked.

He snorted as he started the climb. "God, I hope not." There was an inside joke in there somewhere.

"So this isn't her family?"

We reached the top of the stairs and he took me to the left. "It kind of is," he said. "Let's get inside and I'll explain what I can."

Down a second hallway—how freaking big was this place?—he stopped at the first door and opened it. We stepped inside to find a room that was decidedly... masculine. There was a large bed in the middle and a lot of room all around.

"Is this your room?" I asked.

"Yes," he admitted. I was about to run out the door when he quickly added, "I only brought you here because nobody will come in."

I stopped. Our eyes locked and as startling as the blue was, I could see the truth he was telling.

"OK." Then I shut the door so no one walking by

would hear us. "So that woman was Alyssum?" He nodded. "This is *sort of* her family?"

He nodded again. "The big guy barking orders? That's her dad, Ash. But she's not blood-related to anyone else who was down there that I know of."

"And you're not her brother?" I moved over to sit on the nearest chair. My knees had been shaking since I'd found Alyssum in the woods.

"No. I'm her..." His jaw tightened then released. "Friend. Before we keep going, and I swear I'll explain what I can and won't lie to you, where did you find her?"

"I was in the woods and she was just... there."

"Why were you in the woods?"

I shrugged. "I don't know. Something drew me up here. I'm on a solo vacation just... experiencing things." Though telling him I was alone might not have been my smartest move.

"Would you like a bottle of water?"

"Yes, please," I said so quickly. The moment he'd said *water*, I realized how parched I was. Maybe it was the adrenaline coming down.

Jensen went over to the mini fridge, grabbed a water, then came back over and set it on the table. I swear I downed half of it.

"OK, so you were in the woods. You saw Alyssum?"

I nodded. "I was coming around a bend and she was there. I thought she was an animal at first but soon realized she wasn't. She looked so hurt that I couldn't just leave her there. I wanted to take her to the hospital, but she said to bring her home."

"Yeah," he agreed. "They can do more for her here than at a hospital.

"How is that possible?" I set the bottle back on the small table harder than I needed to. "What's going on here? Why does the air feel weird? How in the hell can regular people take care of a woman I'm pretty sure is about to die?"

"The air feels weird to you?"

My mouth opened and then closed as if I were a fish out of water. *That* was what he'd gotten from what I'd said?

"Yeah. It felt creepy as hell in the woods. Like... electric, but maybe not in a good way."

"That's... interesting."

"Jensen, I'm trusting you here. What's going on?"

He sat on the edge of his bed and sighed. "That, I can't tell you. We'll have to wait for Alyssum."

After blinking twice slowly, I thought he hadn't heard me. Wait for her? That woman was too messed up to come back from this. "She's going to die, Jensen."

He shook his head quickly. "No. She won't. Trust me on that."

Well, we were at an impasse, then. I wanted to know what was going on and he wasn't going to tell me. I supposed the only thing left for me to do was leave.

When I pushed to my feet, he said, "Where are you going?"

"Uh... anywhere but here." Then I started for the door, but he slid in front of me. I supposed the flight part of *fight or flight* was about to make an appearance.

"You can't leave."

I raised my eyebrows, then he held up his hands.

"If you try to, I don't think you're going to get very far. I mean, would you please not leave? At least not until you talk to Alyssum?"

"That's... going to be a while."

He shook his head. "It'll be sooner than you think." He wet his bottom lip and ran a hand through the already messy brown hair. "Look, I'm kind of new here too. Just a little while ago, I was in New York living my life. Now I'm here. Just...

she's going to be so pissed that I couldn't get you to stay."

That was something to consider, given that I also wanted to make sure she was all right. That had been the entire point of all of this.

"Fine," I finally said. "I'll stay, but as soon as I see she's all right, I'm gone."

"Fair enough." He sighed in what felt like relief. "I'll go check on Alyssum." He scratched at his jaw. "You should stay here. Don't roam around the house without me. The bathroom is through that door." He pointed to the other side of the room at a door that could've been a closet but was apparently, an attached bathroom. "Do you have a phone?" I nodded and pulled it out of my pocket. After he took it from me, he tapped away. "I'm putting my number in here. If you need to leave this room, call or text me first."

All of this was scaring me and honestly, making me want to stay in that room alone even more. Once Jensen left, I was going to lock the door so quickly.

He headed for the door then turned back around. "Do you need anything from the car? If you're staying here tonight?"

Oh, right. Yeah. "There's a duffle bag in the backseat."

He gave me a nod. "I'll bring it up here in a little bit." Then I tossed him the keys because right now, I just wanted him to go.

Once I was alone and the door was locked, I let out a long sigh and pulled my phone out. There were only three contacts in there. Rhea, Charlie, and now this guy Jensen. Intending to send Rhea a text to tell her everything that had happened, my thumb paused over the first letter.

Rhea would insist I come home if I told her. Or make Charlie march up here to get me. No. It was better if I waited until I really understood what was going on. Then maybe I'd tell her. Instead, I sent the same text that I did every night per our agreement.

That I was in for the night and all was good.

It was weird being in someone else's room. I wasn't sure what to do, but then there was a knock and I realized more time had passed than I thought.

Jensen was standing there with my bag over his shoulder and a tray of food in his hands.

"I brought you something to," he said as he came inside. "Wasn't sure what you'd like so there are some choices." After setting the tray on the table, he set my bag on the bed.

"Don't you need your room tonight?" I asked him.

He shook me off. "Nah. I'll be down the hall if you need me, though."

"Thanks for bringing this." I waved my hand toward both my bag and the food.

He nodded then left the room so that I could lock the door again, though he hadn't offered up any information on how Alyssum was doing.

I'd just have to wait.

In the morning, I was sitting in the chair at the table by the window when there was a knock on the door. I'd undone the lock after I'd gotten dressed in case Jensen needed to come in here. Right now, I was just staring out at the back yard.

"Sloane, right?" Alyssum asked as she came carefully into the room and sat on the edge of the bed. "I'm Alyssum."

How in the hell... That woman was close to dead yesterday. Now she'd just walked into the room I was staying in. How was that possible?

"Yeah. That guy Jensen told me your name." I paused for a moment before continuing. "What he didn't tell me is why I can't leave. Though he made it abundantly clear that if I tried to, I wouldn't get very far and indicated you'd kick his ass if you woke up and I was gone. Which brings me to... How are you walking around? When I found you, I thought you'd die before we got here and now you look like you only had the flu, as if you weren't bloody and broken twelve hours ago. What is going on here?" I'd thought of some of this all night but hadn't intended to ask them all in one breath.

Alyssum smiled, but even that movement looked like it hurt. "OK. Let's start over." An even bigger smile pushed at the corners of her mouth, but everything about the way she was holding herself told me that she was still very hurt. I recognized the signs. "I'm Alyssum Bracken."

I sighed. "Sloane Reagan." I was a couple of inches taller than Alyssum, though I didn't think either of us would qualify for any tallness records in height. I was usually the one who made others look taller. Otherwise, we were roughly the same size, though I thought I was thinner, whereas she had far more muscle.

The one compliment I had gotten most of my life was that my face was perfectly symmetrical, which, apparently, is a marker for beauty. Whatever. Alyssum's face had some bruises shading her pale skin.

"I need to ask you a couple of questions first, but then I'll tell you what you need to know," she said. I nodded because this was what I had expected. "What were you doing in the woods last night?"

"Nothing," I answered quickly, but she raised an eyebrow. "Fine." I sighed. "Driving. Trying to have an adventure. It's stupid because it's just the Upper Peninsula, but I haven't really been anywhere. I've seen pictures and thought it'd be beautiful up here. One of the websites mentioned a lighthouse not far away so I kept driving. I wasn't *doing* anything."

Now she smiled again as if there were something familiar about what I'd just said. "Where's your family?"

"I don't have a family." I bit my lips together. That was a stupid thing to tell her. I might as well have said *It's fine to murder me and dump my body in a barely concealed grave. No one will look for me.* "Great. Now you know you can kill me and no one will come looking."

Alyssum snickered then sucked air between her teeth as she held her ribs.

"Ouch," she muttered. "No one's going to kill you. That's why I made sure Jensen kept an eye on you. I don't want you hurt. You saved my life."

"What happened to you?" I asked.

"Car accident. Because you helped me and you've made it this far up here on your own, I'm going to trust you. I don't trust people, so this is a big deal. Please don't make me regret it." She took in a deep breath and shook her head slightly, like she wasn't sure she believed she was about to say something. "We're gremlins."

This time, I laughed loudly. "Gremlins."

Gremlins were these weird, little creatures from an '80s movie. The only thing I remembered was something about not feeding them after midnight. It wasn't like I'd watched it. But it didn't matter. Because gremlins weren't real.

"Yup." She rolled her eyes. "I mean, no. Not really. But humans seem to understand that term better than to say we are Gremalian. We aren't human and we have the ability to control energy. It's why I've healed quickly. Copper enhances our powers and helps us heal."

Healed so quickly? Had she? Alyssum was still in a ton of pain and was holding herself in a protective way. The way I'd seen one of my foster mothers carry herself after a knockdown drag-out with the foster dad, which had resulted in a new home for me the next morning. I'd also carried myself like that at one time to try to keep anyone from knowing what had happened.

And I didn't have a better explanation for why

she was as improved as she was. She should have been in a hospital, hooked up to machines. Not sitting here talking like this.

Yesterday, I could barely understand her.

"I'm supposed to believe this?" I finally asked.

I'd believe a lot, but this...

Alyssum shrugged as the corners of her mouth turned up. "You don't have to. But it is the truth and I can prove it."

Prove she was a gremlin? What the hell was I about to see?

But I immediately regretted not telling Rhea everything last night.

Chapter Four

Gremlins weren't real. There were very few things in this world that I was absolutely sure of, but that was one of them.

They couldn't be.

If what she was saying was true, then this world included supernatural creatures that mere humans didn't even know existed.

Ghosts? Sure, why not?

Aliens? Absolutely. It made sense.

Gremlins? No way. Besides, what did gremlins do, anyway? Wreak havoc, as far as I could remember. Or what was the word? Gremalian? I didn't know what that even meant.

"First, why don't you have any family?" Alyssum asked while I was still trying to figure out what kind of loony bin I'd walked myself into and how I'd be able to get out of here.

After swallowing hard, I told her. "I've been in foster care as long as I can remember. When I aged out two years ago, there wasn't anyone who cared enough to stay in touch. Which is how I ended up in the woods. I was tired of working. Of only surviving. I wanted to live." And I didn't want to tell her about Rhea. If these people were crazy, I didn't want her and her little family dragged into this.

Then I sighed. "So can you prove what you say? That you're a... gremlin?"

Alyssum snorted and then nodded, but nothing followed it. She looked around the room, her eyes narrowed as if she were actually trying to figure out how to prove it to me while I stood there waiting, knowing there wasn't a chance in hell that she'd be able to prove being a gremlin.

She bit into her bottom lip and then the bedroom door opened and Jensen came through. Alyssum released her lip and waited for him to get all the way inside.

"How's it going in here?" he asked, watching Alyssum and never looking at me, though I felt that the question was for both of us.

Without answering, she said, "You need to show her your power."

His head cocked to the side and his eyebrows rose high. Clearly, he hadn't known she'd been going to tell me what she had. The fact that he didn't ask, *What power?* or *What the hell are you talking about?* meant that he wasn't surprised at that part. Just the telling me part.

Did that mean they could seriously be gremlins? That meant he had to be one too and now I really had to get out of here. Except... part of me was curious. I was looking for adventure. What could be more adventurous?

Even if I considered for a moment that I'd had a terrible accident, maybe driven off the Mackinac Bridge, and was currently dreaming while in a deep coma. I didn't think that was the case.

"Jensen," she continued, "I can't do it without setting my recovery back. Please. I trust her."

That... I doubted, but I had proven that I wasn't going to run or freak out, I supposed.

Nodding, he said, "OK."

Jensen lifted his hand, pointing a finger at the lamp closest to me. A blue spark shot from his finger to the lamp, causing the lightbulb to brighten. More and more until I thought it would burst. Then it did, sending little shards of glass out toward the lampshade.

I moved closer and noticed that the plug was lying on the floor, so I bent over and picked it up.

"Holy shit." I jumped from the chair as the same adrenaline from last night shot through me. It might've been for a different reason, but it was the same stuff. "I mean... Holy shit." Then I let the plug drop from my fingers.

There were so many questions to ask that I couldn't organize them. My mouth opened and closed rapidly with little sounds but no words coming out.

Alyssum chuckled. "Let's go talk some more."

"I'll clean up the glass," Jensen offered, but he didn't sound happy about it. Maybe it wasn't the cleaning up that he was irritated with, but the fact that he'd broken the lightbulb in the first place.

I supposed... they were gremlins. Or "Gremalians," as Alyssum had called them. Whatever they were, I still needed more information.

"Let's go to my room," Alyssum said once we were out of Jensen's. "It'll be more comfortable for me. I'm still healing."

"I have so many questions." If she let me, I'd ask them all.

"I'm sure you do."

Alyssum led me back out the way Jensen had brought me in, but she turned down the other hallway then stopped at the first door on the right. This house was like a maze to me, though I was sure I could make it to the front door if I needed to.

Now... I wanted to stay. I wanted to know more about what was going on here. Curiosity may have killed the cat, but I hoped to hell it wouldn't kill me.

Alyssum's room wasn't what I had imagined. Not that I'd spent a lot of time imagining it. If someone had asked, I would've said that even though she'd shown a toughness not usually found in nature, I'd bet her room was pink and frilly. Over-the-top girly.

It wasn't. Clearly, this was a woman's room because there was a softness that wasn't present in Jensen's, but it was just... a room. Everything in it appeared to have a function. She didn't have a wall of dolls or anything. Not that I thought she would because someone who'd been as hurt as she had been yet still talking had to have some strength.

Wait. Was that the Gremalian thing?

"OK." Alyssum blew out a slow breath as she situated herself on the bed. "I'll answer your questions now. Then she pulled her legs under her blanket and patted the bed beside her. I supposed I was going to sit.

"Are you all right?" I asked her as I kicked my shoes off then climbed onto her bed, carefully folding my legs beneath me so I didn't jostle her too much.

"I will be." She glanced at me, giving me a small smile. "It's a Gremalian thing. Well, a Gobel thing too."

"None of those words make sense to me separately or put together."

Alyssum snorted. "No. They wouldn't, would they? I'll explain. Let me answer your original questions first." She took a drink from the bottle beside her and winced like it stung going down. Shaking the bottle gently, she said, "I'll explain that, too."

I swallowed hard. Did I even remember the questions I'd asked her in Jensen's room? Turned out, it didn't matter. She did.

"You can leave," she told me abruptly, but not meanly. "I don't want you to because I'm grateful you were there in the woods when you were, but no one will stop you. I'll make cure you get out of here safely, but I feel... I don't know. Kind of a connection to you. It's probably weird to hear that."

It was, but I felt a connection or something to her and this place too.

"You wouldn't have gotten far last night because everyone was on high alert," she explained. "That's why he said you couldn't leave and I would've kicked his ass if I woke up and you were gone because I'll never be able to thank you enough, but I at least wanted to thank you in person." Her eyes met mine. "Thank you, Sloane. You could've kept driving and left me there. Most would have, given the situation, but I would've died. I wasn't anywhere near copper."

"Copper?" I asked. "It heals you?"

I nodded. "That's why we live in copper country. Humans think the copper ran out. In reality, we ran the humans out. There's still copper here, though it's not in great supply, which is why there's been a battle for it for longer than I've been alive."

"A 'battle'?" I asked. "With whom?"

"The Gobel." She snorted. "Humans would probably call them 'goblins,' but they're a lot like us. Just different powers."

I rubbed my hand over my forehead. All of this was overwhelming. "So that's why even though you were basically dying last night, you're fine today?"

She shook her head. "I'm not fine. I will be later today, but yes. It's the copper that's healing me. And this." She tapped the bottle she'd been drinking from. "It's a copper-infused something. I don't know. I think Fern told me, but I can't remember right now. It's my mother's concoction to heal from the inside."

I furrowed my brows. "Your dad was the mountain man giving the orders yesterday?"

She giggle but nodded. "Yeah. He's the leader of our people."

"Was your mother there?"

Her eyes darkened as she sadly shook her head. "My mother was recently killed in this battle we have going with the Gobel."

"I'm sorry," I whispered. The only thing I could think of worse than not having a mother was losing the one you had and loved. I had no idea what I was missing out on while Alyssum had had her mother's life ripped from her.

"What about you?" she asked. "What about your life and family? You said you grew up in foster care..."

It wasn't as good of a story as hers, but I told her, anyway. I told her that I didn't have family and I kept Rhea out of it for now. Told her that I'd grown up and aged out of the system. All of it. Well, almost all of it. I didn't get into the details of my sad story because they were sad and I didn't feel the need to share them.

"So, you walked into a war." She swallowed

down more of the healing liquid before offering me a bottle of water. I took it and drank down a good bit before she continued. "My best friend is a Gobel. They can control nature, which is what happened before you found me yesterday."

Apparently, this best friend… Aric had been taken after a battle. Taken by his own people, but still taken and they were pissed that he'd been helping the Gremalians in the us-versus-them scenario they'd had going on.

She wanted to go after them, but Jensen hadn't. So she'd done so with Aric's brothers. One was the guy who had helped her when we'd come in last night.

I'd never keep all the names straight.

"So humans think the land up here is abandoned?" I asked.

"Yes. That's what we want them to think. It's surprising that the electricity in the air didn't chase you away."

I narrowed my eyes. "That's what I was feeling when I got here?" She nodded. "It was creepy, but not enough for me to leave. I thought it was the universe telling me I need to be here." I told her then laughed at the idea.

"Maybe it was," Alyssum said more seriously.

"So what now? What's going to happen to me now that I'm in the place where humans aren't supposed to be?"

"Nothing," she said quickly. Too quickly.

"Alyssum, this whole thing only works if we trust each other. I'm trusting you to not fry my ass or let someone kill me. Please don't make me not trust you." Because she wasn't telling me the truth.

She sighed out a long breath. "Normally, when on occasion, a human does come up here, security... blips their memory so they don't remember being here."

"They're going to erase my memory?" I blinked three times as I considered that. "Do I want them to do that?"

"No." At least she was being honest. "It doesn't always work well."

Well, that sounded awful. "Then don't let them do it to me. I'm not going to tell anyone anything. I don't have anyone to tell." Except Rhea and I wasn't going to do anything to put her in danger.

"We won't let it happen," she promised. "But you have to listen to me while you're here. If I say to come back here, you need to do it. There are people on both sides who won't hesitate to kill you if you get in the way. I'm not trying to scare you. I just don't want you getting hurt."

Like she had. That was the right time to change this subject. I was in danger in here, sometimes, and that was enough to make me want to run. But this was the most interesting thing to ever happen to me and I wasn't ready to go.

Plus, there was something about Alyssum, about this place, that I wanted to know more about.

"Tell me what you want me to do." Because I wasn't a fool and I'd do it to keep myself safe for now.

"Nothing major. Just sometimes things come up and I'll tell you it's safest in our room."

"'Our' room?"

She nodded. "I figured you could stay in here."

"Listen." I swung my legs over the side of the bed and stood. "If there's that much danger—"

"There's not. Not really. I've just never had the kind of friend who would stay over and I thought it'd be fun. Plus, that means I'm close by to answer any questions that come up." She rolled her eyes. "And they will come up because there are people on both sides who are idiots."

"All right."

"So, you'll move your things in here at least until all of our people know you're in Delaware so they won't get freaked out. Oh. And don't roam around by yourself a lot until then either. Don't need to spook someone."

Right. Spooking a Gremlin would be bad. I wasn't comfortable enough to do much without her or Jensen with me right now anyway. That made it an easy thing to agree to.

Speaking of Jensen...

"What about that Jensen guy?" I asked her. Her cheeks pinked and she didn't look up at me. "Things seem tense between the two of you."

She snorted and slid back further into her bed. "It's complicated right now."

Alyssum's eyes drooped. We'd been talking for a long time and she was still healing. I hadn't slept much last night, either, because I'd been in this place and hadn't known what had been going on.

"If you were in Jensen's room overnight, where did he go?" she asked, once again laying herself down even more.

"Not sure," I told her. It wasn't like the guy had cleared his schedule with me. "He said he would be down the hall if I needed him, but I locked the door and stared outside the entire night."

Alyssum nodded, like she knew exactly where that meant he had been. I hadn't done any exploring to find out which rooms were near his, so I was clueless. I had assumed that he'd be somewhere close, so if I sent a text, he could be there quickly. But I hadn't asked. Hadn't wanted to know, actually.

"Well, I'm going to need to nap." She patted the other side of the bed. "You should too. Around here, we get sleep whenever we can."

That sounded like a good idea. As hungry as I was, I was more tired than anything else. A few hours sleep was just what I needed.

Once we woke up, I'd ask for food. After all, if I was just pitted into the middle of a gremlin-goblin war, I had to be rested and fed.

It wasn't like I'd be fighting, but I still wanted to be ready for anything.

Chapter Five

THE NEXT MORNING, my stomach thanked me for feeding it. I'd had snacked on what Jensen had brought me but things had been busy and I didn't want to bother anyone. Alyssum woke up feeling better than ever. One hundred percent, she said. So she took me downstairs, where we had cereal because neither of us could wait for anything to cook. It was the best cereal of my life.

That was where she told me that I was welcome to anything in the house, whether she was there or not. By now, she figured that word had gotten out and I'd be safe even without her or Jensen, though she said I should still be with one of them whenever possible.

When Jensen came into the kitchen as I set my

bowl in the sink, he brought with him a tense air. I didn't know what was happening between the two of them, but it was for sure something. Alyssum hadn't told me too much about her and Jensen, but I could feel it.

When their words became terse, I slid out and headed back up to her room.

Jensen obviously wanted to take care of Alyssum, but she was resistant. If that didn't scream exes, I didn't know what did.

Her room was where she found me. Sitting on her bed staring out the window. The countryside here was gorgeous, full of green treetops as far as I could see. It was a stark reminder that we were in the middle of a forest.

"What's wrong?" I asked as she paced around her room.

When she'd gotten dressed this morning, she'd put on a pair of jeans and a T-shirt. I was wearing shorts because I'd packed light but was also wearing a T-shirt. She was rocking boots while I was wearing a pair of socks. I'd pulled my hair up into a bun, but hers was down in beautiful, blonde waves.

"Nothing." But then she sighed and stopped pacing for only a second. "I'm cagey."

Once she'd begun crossing the room again, I said, "I can tell."

"The guys aren't back yet," she said and I knew she meant that guy Aric's brothers. "I'm going to have to go without them."

"You're leaving?" I asked quietly.

"If the guys aren't back soon, yes."

Well, if she was leaving, I'd go with her and for that. I needed different clothes. There had to be a reason that she was wearing jeans in the middle of summer looking like a tiny, badass fighter.

"I'll go with you," I said as I hopped off the bed and grabbed my bag to look for better gear. Alyssum was already shaking her head, so I told her, "You can't go alone."

Alyssum grabbed my arms and pulled them away from the bag I'd set on the end of her bed. "I appreciate the offer, Sloane, but really, you could get hurt."

"I'll be careful."

She sighed, making me feel like a little kid who was being obstinate. I might not have known much about this world, but I was in it and she was my friend. I'd go to help her. "No. I just... I can't be worried about you while I do this, OK?"

I cocked my head to the side. "You know I hate you, right?"

She giggled as a smile broke the serious look on her face. "No, you don't."

There wasn't going to be any fighting this. I dropped the jeans in my hand and sighed. "Fine. You're right. I don't." Alyssum didn't want me to go so I wouldn't get hurt. But there'd been a time that staying here in this house was enough to hurt me. Or at least enough for her to fear that I'd be hurt. She'd delayed her own treatment to ask Jensen to make sure that I would be taken care of. "I'll be safe here, though, right?"

"Sloane," she said, stopping in front of me. "Things are weird with Jensen and me right now, but he promised me he had you. Which means he's got you. Do what he says and everything will be fine. My dad will also take care of you." Then she snapped her fingers. "Oh, there's a man named Flint; you can trust him completely, and Sage, one of the fighters who protects my dad. I don't get along with Sage well, but he's a good person when it comes to security, OK?"

I swallowed hard then nodded.

My confidence in what she was telling me was low, but again, following my gut had never steered me wrong, so I would continue to believe it. And it was telling me that I could trust Alyssum. So far, everything she'd said was right.

No one had tried to hurt me since I'd been here, though I got the impression she didn't think anyone would. Only that if security or other Gremalians didn't know a human was around, they might respond in a way she didn't want them to.

Once Alyssum had left me, I didn't know if she'd left the house or just the room. Still, I stayed here for a while and walked slowly around her room, trying to imagine her life.

Alyssum was the daughter of her people's leader. I supposed that was a lot like being the president's daughter in the human world. Did that mean people followed her around, wondering what she was doing? She didn't seem to have Secret Service-type protection, but then again, she could control electricity, so would she really need it, anyway?

Still, it had to be an immense amount of pressure. And while I didn't know the whole story, she'd said her mom died because of the war. Just not how and that it'd been very recently. How she was still functioning... I had no idea.

There were all of these questions I had that I didn't have time to ask Alyssum. But she mentioned a library in conversation and that Jensen might have slept there the night I'd been in his room. The library was where the information was, so it was time for me to go exploring.

Stepping out of Alyssum's room by myself for the first time was weird. I hadn't been alone in the public areas and worried that someone might wipe my memory at any moment. Which was ridiculous.

The first door I opened was a bathroom. Good information to have, I suppose. Alyssum's and Jensen's rooms both had one attached, so I hadn't needed to know where any others were, but now that I did, I'd remember it.

The second looked like an unused bedroom. A guest room, maybe. But if they had guest rooms, why would I need to stay in Alyssum's? Other than her wanting to protect me, I supposed. I'd stay there, anyway.

That was how it went. I'd open a door and find that it wasn't what I was looking for. Then I opened Jensen's bedroom and it hit me. I should've started there. If the library was close to his room, had I started there, I'd already be in the library.

So I went around the corner and opened the first door I came to and voila! It was the library.

Quickly closing the door behind me, I hurried

into the room, hoping that no one would interrupt me. I didn't know if I was supposed to be here or not, so it was better if no one knew.

The library had dark-wood accents and an unlit fireplace in the middle. It reminded me of the old structures and a lot of the books fit the aesthetic. Old.

Where to begin?

As I looked through some books, I realized that all I wanted was to know everything. A big ask, I guess. But this was another world with its own politics and customs.

I was in there so long that my stomach growled. At first, I ignored it, but then it reminded me that I'd already done that for a long time and this time, it wouldn't stand for it.

Snickering, I left the library to go to the kitchen, where I made myself a sandwich. I was sitting, eating my sandwich when Alyssum's dad came in, causing me to pause with a chip halfway to my mouth.

Her dad gave me a nod as a greeting then began pulling out everything I'd just put away. I guess he was hungry too.

At first, he made his sandwich in silence. Then as he cut the thing in half, he asked, "How are things going here?"

"Good," I said automatically, then I realized I

still had a bite in my mouth. I chewed and swallowed it quickly. "Good," I said again more clearly.

"Alyssum show you around?"

"Not really." Did he know she'd left? I wasn't going to mention it unless he did.

"Exploring on your own?" he asked. I nodded. "Good. I've made sure everyone knows you're here, so you shouldn't have any trouble. I wouldn't leave the grounds, though."

"OK." Mr. Bracken was a large man up close. He'd been huge in the foyer, but I thought that maybe I'd made him bigger in my mind because that situation had been scary. But no. He was huge like a big teddy bear. A big, scary teddy bear.

"Alyssum was protective of you." He was talking about when we'd first gotten here.

"I think because I helped her," I told him. "She didn't want someone tearing my head off or zapping me after I stopped in the woods." He took a big bit of his sandwich. "Was it really a car accident?"

He nodded as he swallowed. "Not with another car, but yes. From what the Bramble brothers told me, yes."

"So they hit a tree?"

"You could say that." There was no humor in his voice. Everything he said was very matter-of-fact.

Then I remembered that he'd recently lost his wife—assuming they were still married—and it made sense. Not that this was a humorous situation at all. "Alyssum told you about us?"

"She did. She had Jensen show me what you can do." He raised an eyebrow. "Well, maybe not everything you can do, but he made a lightbulb explode with electricity, even though the lamp had been unplugged. It was to prove that you're gremlins."

He furrowed his brows and looked at me, so I raised a hand. "Sorry. Gremalians. And she told me about the Gobel and what's going on. She had to so that I wouldn't hightail it out of here."

"That's good." He took a drink of the water he'd grabbed. "That could've been bad for you and Alyssum's lost enough." He put the bottle back down then sighed. "Her mother was recently killed. Part of this fight with the Gobel. I think Alyssum's been pushing that all down and I'm worried it's causing her to make some choices that aren't the smartest."

"She seems pretty thoughtful to me," I said quietly and for the first time, the corners of his mouth ticked up. I'd bet he was gorgeous when he actually smiled.

"I don't know that anyone has ever described my daughter that way. She's impulsive. Stubborn."

"Does she get that from you or her mom?"

He snorted, but it came out like a sigh. "Me, unfortunately. The kindness, wanting to protect you, that's her mom."

"I'm sorry your wife died," I told him because it was the right thing to do.

"Me too. I worry that my family is a target because I'm making the decisions. At least with the Brambles and Jensen with her, I know Alyssum will be protected. Any one of those men would lay down his life for her."

"Then there's nothing to worry about, right?"

"Right." Mr. Bracken narrowed his eyes and watched me, like he was searching out my soul or some deep, dark secret I was hiding. Then he said, "I don't think a normal human could've withstood the electricity in the air to get this far up here."

I bit into my bottom lip and shrugged. "Maybe I'm not a normal human."

He grunted but continued eating his sandwich. Finishing in record time, he said, "That's what I'm wondering." Then he left the kitchen.

I sat there... confused. What the hell was he talking about? That was when I remembered that the last thing I'd said was that maybe I wasn't a normal human. I'd meant I was weird, not... anything else.

Now I couldn't wait for Alyssum to get back so that I could tell her.

After lunch, I went back to the library. There was nothing else for me to do and my instinct was telling me not to leave. I could go. Head home. Go back to my normal life, but that wasn't what I was supposed to do. The universe didn't want me to do that and don't ask me how I knew because I had no idea.

I was alone in that room when the sound of my phone ringing took about twenty years off my life. I gasped out loud at the noise then shook my head. I was such a good not-normal human that the sound of a phone scared the crap out of me.

Rhea's face lit up my screen. I'd only been texting her, so this time, I answered.

"Thank god," she said after I greeted her. "I was beginning to worry someone had taken your phone and was only pretending to be you. I needed to hear your voice."

I snickered. "No. It's me. I've just been busy."

"Doing what?"

My heart sped up. Lying to Rhea wasn't something that I normally did, but right now, I couldn't tell her the truth. At least not the total truth.

"Making friends. Having an adventure. There are some places up here that don't even have a signal."

"I don't like it," she said and I could practically picture her pouting. "You should always have a signal. Charlie thinks you've met someone and eloped."

Now I laughed. "Fat chance of that happening. I did meet someone and she's nice, but I don't think we'll be eloping any time soon."

"So no one's taking advantage of you?"

I snorted. "Have you met me? Foster care taught us both how to not be taken advantage of. How to read people and get out of situations. You don't have to worry about me, Rhea." I trailed my fingers across the spines of some books as I slowly walked along the shelf.

"You're enjoying yourself?"

That was the question, wasn't it? Was I enjoying myself? I supposed I was. Not every moment, but being here and getting to know these kinds of people even existed was such an experience, how could I not enjoy it?

"Yeah. I am. It's been fun." I swallowed hard. "It's like seeing a whole new side of the world."

"I love this for you, Sloane. Now the question is,

when are you coming back? You've been gone forever."

Now I had to laugh. I had not been gone forever. "I've been gone days, Rhea. Days. You knew this was going to be a couple of weeks. It hasn't been one."

She sighed. "It feels like forever."

My eye caught a book with a copper trim. There was nothing on the spine to indicate what the book was, but the copper spine meant it was something special. Alyssum had told me enough about their use of copper for me to know that I needed to look at this book.

As Rhea talked about the new things Claire was doing, I pulled the book out and opened it. In beautiful scrolling—handwritten, it read, "History of the Gremalian People." Then underneath it read, "As seen by the women behind the leaders."

Oh, *this*, I had to read.

"That's all awesome, Rhea, but I have to go. I'm sorry. I'll call you later." Then I ended the call without waiting for a reply.

The history of Alyssum's people as told by the women behind the leaders? That meant Alyssum's mom had to have had an entry in here. She was a woman behind a leader.

Anyone could've come in to find me, so I hurried

out of the library and back to Alyssum's room, where I could dive into the books.

I don't know how long I read, but every bit of it was interesting, even the boring stuff. Things about expanding the city. Mentions about a Gobel attack and the stress their leader was facing. The dates on this went back quite far, which meant the battle with the Gobel went back, but Alyssum had said that she thought both sides had been lied to, though she hadn't elaborated.

Whatever it was, I wasn't going to judge the Gobel just yet.

As I sat there, Alyssum hurried into the room and shut the door, turning the lock.

"Hey," I said, but she didn't look at me. "How did it go?"

She shook her head, dust flying off it onto the floor. Or dirt. Her clothes were marked up as well and now all I wanted to know was what happened but I wouldn't have the chance to ask. "I need to shower." Then she ran off to do that.

I didn't know what had happened while she'd been gone, but something definitely had.

And I was anxious to find out what.

Chapter Six

After changing into a more comfortable pair of shorts and a T-shirt, I started making my way to the basement. I'd never been down there, but Alyssum had told me where to go. They were doing some training that she thought I'd want to see and it'd be better than sitting in this room any longer.

I appreciated that she wanted to keep me safe, but being in that room was starting to drive me crazy. Suddenly, I wished that I had packed more clothes, but given that I hadn't known I'd be in a house with gremlins and goblins, watching them train, there'd been no way for me to prepare for that.

Even though I'd started venturing around the house on my own, I still moved quickly and as quietly as I could through the open part of the house.

No one had stopped me on any of my outings on my own, but that didn't mean they wouldn't.

I was hurrying alone when two men stepped in front of me, though they clearly didn't see me. They were headed the same direction as I was. They were talking, though for the life of me, I couldn't make out what they were saying.

One was tall with dark hair with wide shoulders and he carried himself with a confidence that I didn't see much. It wasn't cocky. It was confident.

The guy next to him was also tall, though thinner. Everything about him said he was younger. Not quite as confident in the way he carried himself and when the taller man reached over and mussed his hand through the other man's hair the way you would a little brother, it told me what I needed to know. These were brothers. But Alyssum was an only child, so who was this? And why were they headed to the same place I was?

We were in the kitchen, about to go through the door Alyssum told me to take when the taller one glanced over his shoulder, noticing me for the first time.

And... time... stopped.

He was beautiful. Dark eyes taking me in and probably trying to place me, given that I would be a strange face to most people here. I'd met almost no one. Then he stopped walking and turned to me.

His face was kind, but he was looking me over as if trying to decide whether I were a threat or not.

"Hey," he said, his deep voice echoing to my core. It was like when I'd first come up here and felt the electricity skittering over my skin. *He* was doing that to me.

Was he a Gremalian like Alyssum? That would make sense, especially with the electricity thing they could do. Was he testing me?

"Hi," I squeaked out, then I shook my head. This man was making my knees weak just by standing in front of me. That didn't mean I had to let him know that.

He cocked his head to the side. "Do you need something?"

After quickly wetting my bottom lip, I shook my head. "Alyssum told me to meet her in the basement."

His face changed. Softened. Like he was no longer trying to decide if I was a danger or not. "Right," he said. "You're the woman who found her in the woods?" I nodded but couldn't take my eyes off him. Heat started creeping up my chest. This was so embarrassing. "Well, thanks for that. She means a lot to me. I'm Aric and this is my brother Laken."

The kid next to him snorted. He looked to be around fifteen or sixteen and the two were quite obviously brothers.

"I'm Sloane." My throat was so dry, those words almost hadn't come out.

"We're headed to the basement, too." He waved his hand. "Come on. I'll show you where it is."

Once he had his back turned to me, I mouthed *what the fuck* because me suddenly turning into a sixteen-year-old girl seeing the quarterback for the first time wasn't it. That wasn't me. Apparently, unless I saw the hottest man known to the universe. Or... goblin? He was a goblin, I thought. Alyssum had told me about her friend Aric, but her description had done him zero justice.

Following him was hard, but at least neither of the brothers turned to look at me again, so they wouldn't see me berating myself for the way I'd acted.

They took me down the stairs and down the hallway. It was long with doors on either side and seemed to go on forever. At least as big as the house, but I thought down here might be bigger. They stopped at the first door on the left.

"You made it," Alyssum said as she came over to me and grabbed my wrists in a loose grip. "I see you've met Aric and Laken." I nodded but pinched my lips together, causing her to smile. "Trust me. I know."

Though I wanted to ask what she was talking about, I kept my mouth shut. This wasn't the time or the place.

"OK," she continued while fighting a smile. "You stay back because I don't want you to get caught up in anything. We'll be focusing on Laken, so you should be fine. But we have to get back on the same page for this to work. You can of course leave if you feel... anything weird."

I furrowed my brows. "'Feel anything weird'?"

She nodded. "On the very slim chance that we can't control it, I don't want you sucked up in it."

"Got it. If I feel weird, I'm out of here." Though the fact that I involuntarily wanted to keep glancing over at Aric already had me feeling weird.

As I settled back against the wall farther away from them, Aric spoke to his brother. He talked about what was going to be happening. I didn't understand it all, but apparently, Alyssum and Jensen could suck power from others.

"It's fine," Laken snapped. "I'm not worried."

Aric snorted then grabbed a chair and pulled it back toward me. Once he'd stopped, he pointed to the chair to offer it to me, but I shook my head. My nerves were too on edge for me to sit right now. So he dropped into it and sat next to me as if it were the most natural thing in the world.

Which it was. People sat next to each other all the time. Hell, I sat next to strangers at the movies sometimes.

The only problem here was that he was affecting me in a way that I wasn't affecting him.

I watched as Alyssum and Jensen shook out their hands, then she slipped one of hers into one of his. The waiting was rough. Waiting for something to happen. Watching Laken like a hawk to see... anything.

Nothing happened.

Alyssum pulled her hand back and cracked the knuckles then slipped it back into Jensen's. He barely held on to her and their fingers weren't intertwined. It was like they were both there, but not really wanting to be.

"That's it?" Laken taunted. "I hardly felt anything."

"Laken..." Aric's deep chuckle startled me. "You're gonna regret that."

I snickered because he sounded so much like an older brother. One who both wanted the younger one to be careful but also to learn a lesson.

Jensen and Alyssum shook their hands out again, only this time, Alyssum grabbed his aggressively, linking their fingers and squeezing him hard enough that it looked like he had no choice but to hold on.

Energy spiked in the room. It was a slow build and I didn't know why I felt it. The hair on my arms stood up, but it wasn't unpleasant.

For me.

Laken fell to his knees in agony. All emotion was gone from his face as he braced his hand on the floor, breathing raggedly, as if that were all he could do.

Holy shit, that looked awful.

Alyssum yanked her hand from Jensen and slowly, Laken's breathing evened out. The color came back to his face. He looked... alive again.

"What the fuck was that?" Laken yelled.

Aric jumped to his feet, hurrying over to be next to his brother. "Sucks, doesn't it?"

"Yeah, it sucks. What was it?"

"It's what we"—Alyssum waved a hand between Jensen and her—"can do together. I'm sorry."

"'*Sorry*'?" He roared, but he turned it on his brother. "How could you do it, Aric? You're a sadist.

How could you have sex with her knowing she can do this to us?"

My mouth dropped open in surprise. Of all the things I could've guessed had been about to come out of that kid's mouth, that wasn't one of them. Not only that, but I was completely confused. Alyssum had been with Jensen, I thought. And now I was the friend lusting after the guy she was really with?

Or wait. Was that old? Did that happen before she'd gotten with Jensen?

I had so many questions that I put a hand over my mouth, hoping to shield the surprise.

Aric roughly grabbed the back of his brother's neck and dragged him to the door. As he pushed Laken through the door, Aric's jaw was hard as granite and his nostrils flared slightly in anger. One thing foster care had given me was a fantastic ability to read people and the situation.

Laken didn't try to come back inside. But Aric was leaning against the wall next to the door with his arms crossed over his chest.

This was obviously news to Jensen as well. His blue eyes were hard like ice and his entire face was stone.

"He's lying, right?" Jensen asked quietly, though

given Aric's reaction, it was clear Laken had been speaking the truth. "Just lashing out?"

"Jensen..." Aric sighed and ran a hand through his hair.

Jensen shook his head then left the room quickly, not waiting for an explanation. Though how could they explain?

Things had just gotten so messy and I didn't have all the information, but I sure as hell wanted it.

Alyssum turned to me, opened her mouth to say something, then shook her head and slowly left as well, which meant Aric and I were alone in this training room.

"So, that was fun," he said, his voice making me jump. We'd been silent for too long. He stood but still had his arms folded across his chest.

"You say *fun*. I say *messy*." I swallowed hard, not sure what else to say. I didn't know everything that had happened. What had unfolded in front of me had left Jensen hurt, for sure. Which led me to some conclusions, but I wouldn't say those because I didn't know what had happened.

He snorted. "Yeah. I guess it was. And you get all the dirty laundry on day one."

I shook my head. "It's not day one for me."

He bit his bottom lip quickly then let it go. "Yeah. You're right. It's not."

Silence hung between us and I wasn't sure why he was still here unless he wanted to make sure I got back up to her room all right... or he was open to questions.

"I'm just confused," I told him as I awkwardly shuffled a little closer. "Alyssum told me that you're her best friend."

"I am."

"And Jensen's."

He closed his eyes for a second. "I am. Or I was. I guess we'll see how that turns out later."

"Right. Now, I'm no friend expert, given that I only have passing friendships that don't last except for one, so I could be totally off about this... Is that how friendship is supposed to work?"

Clearly, I knew it wasn't. Friends didn't sleep with their best friend's woman. Or even ex-woman, if Charlie was to be believed. Yet here we had a some kind of three-way dynamic and I'd be lying if I said I didn't really, really want to know what that was.

"It isn't," he finally agreed, which just opened up more questions. "How about I tell you about it as we walk you slowly back to Alyssum's room?"

"Why slowly?"

"It's not a short story."

Hopefully, that meant he was going to spill all the beans. I nodded then followed him out of the room.

"I met both of them in New York," he started. "I went there to find Jensen just like Alyssum did, only I got there first. The idea was that whoever could get him on their side would win. It's dumb."

"'Win'?" I asked.

"The war." Which was what I had thought he'd meant. Aric stopped in the kitchen and asked, "Do you want a drink?"

Not really, but I said, "Sure" so that he'd keep talking.

After handing me a bottle of water and taking one for himself, he sat at the table, so I took the seat across from him.

"I wanted him on my side to stop the war," he told me. "I was tired of seeing people on both sides be killed or injured. Alyssum wanted him on hers to win the war. In New York, she and I came to an agreement. To hopefully stop the fighting."

"That didn't seem to work." From what I could tell, or had been told, a war was still coming. "I've overheard some things," I confessed. "Not that I understand any of it."

He nodded. "It hasn't worked yet, but the three of us became friends. And Gobel, once we become your friend, it's hard for us to stop being your friend. It's almost a mate-for-life thing without the mating. It takes a lot for us to break a bond."

That was... intriguing, but there was more to it.

"It sounds like more than friends," I told him. "I've talked to Alyssum some. I was under the impression that she was with Jensen, though not right this minute. They'd broken up the night you were taken?" Though my words sounded more like a question. I was clear on what Alyssum had told me, but people sometimes opened up to you more if you sounded unsure.

"They are." He winced. "Or were. I'm not sure what's going on with them right now, but assume they'll make up." Aric sighed then took a long drink. "The night I was taken—the night you found Alyssum—she wanted to go after me right away. So did my brothers. Jensen didn't. That caused a problem and Alyssum can sometimes jump without thinking."

Yeah. It sounded like she could, given that they might've had sex since then and it'd been days.

"So you think they'll get back together?" I asked. He nodded. "But you two dated first?"

His dark eyes met mine. "Not exactly. For the briefest moment, she dated us both in New York, but it was always going to be Jensen. We both knew it."

"So what your brother said..."

His lips pressed together as his features tightened then he rubbed the back of his neck. It wasn't directed at me, I didn't think, though I *had* just pried into something personal.

"I'm sorry," I said before he could answer. "That was way too personal for me to pry into. You don't owe me anything."

He held a hand up to stop me from saying anything else. "I don't owe you an explanation, but I want to give you one. You were there for it. No. It didn't happen in New York. It was when she got me out of there."

My eyes widened in surprise and my mouth formed an "o."

"Not my best moment," he confessed. "It was a mistake and didn't mean anything."

"Then why do it?" I asked, as if his answer meant something to me. Was I attracted to him? Hell yes. An hour ago, I'd been falling over myself and acted like a complete fool in front of him because of the way I was drawn to him. But this was messy and I usually tried to stay away from messy.

"It was a release." He shrugged. "Getting out of there was rough and we were full of adrenaline... It was like we were just happy to be alive."

"Makes sense." Sort of, but I wasn't about to tell him that I still had questions. I'd pried too much already. Then I pushed up out of the chair and put the bottle in the sink. They used reusable ones. "I should go find Alyssum. When she left, she looked like she could use a friend."

"Yeah." He stood too. "I should probably go talk to Jensen."

I snorted. "Your task sounds less fun than mine."

After shaking his head, he said, "I don't think either sounds fun. If my brother would've kept his fucking mouth shut, neither of us would be dealing with this."

Just as we turned to go up the stairs, I told him, "I don't know. It sounds like maybe *you* should've kept your mouth shut."

He furrowed his brows as my heart raced. That had sounded so bitchy. "What?"

"That was harsh," I told him. "What I meant was you had to have told him, right? If you hadn't, he wouldn't have known to be able to out you."

"Ah." He nodded, then we turned down Alyssum's hallway. "You're not wrong, but I didn't tell him. I was talking to my older brother and he overheard. Or was there. Whatever, but you're right. If I'd kept my mouth shut, we wouldn't be here."

We stopped at Alyssum's door, though I didn't go right in. "Why did you want to explain it to me?" I asked. There was something about being here that was making me want any information I could get. Maybe it was because this was an entirely new world and I wanted to know everything about it.

He took a deep breath then let it out slowly. "I don't know. There's something... different about you. I can't explain it."

"Wait." I stood up straighter, though the height I reached was still so much shorter than he was. "Did we become friends? Are you now bonded to me?"

His low chuckle made me believe that everything would be all right. That I hadn't overstepped to a point that he was going to walk away and put his walls up.

"Maybe," he finally told me. "I don't know, but there's definitely..."

"Something," I finished.

"Yeah."

"I look forward to figuring out what that is."

"Me too." His voice was low, deep... so strong that it was like his words could touch me.

Before he could affect me anymore, I slipped into Alyssum's room and closed the door.

I'd never had that kind of reaction to a man before, yet now that I had, I was a little desperate for more of that feeling.

Chapter Seven

THAT NIGHT, we'd spent in her room and Alyssum was quieter than normal. She was polite, we had dinner just the two of us but she was reserved. Then Alyssum was gone the next morning, yet she didn't say exactly where. There was one person who would for sure know. That was, if he hadn't gone with her. The unfortunate part was that I had no idea where his room was. Only Jensen's and I'd heard him in the hallway earlier talking to someone and assuming that Aric was going wherever Alyssum was.

As I turned the corner toward Jensen's room, not intending to go there, but more wandering to see if I could hear anything in the hallway that would lead me to Aric, I slammed face-first into a hard wall of muscle and stumbled back.

"Are you all right?" a deep voice asked after he'd grabbed me, making sure I didn't hit the ground. When I looked up, I found one of Aric's brothers with his eyebrows pinched in concern as he watched me.

He had the same dark hair and eyes as Aric

"Yeah." I stepped back so that he'd release me. "I'm all right. Sorry. I was... lost in thought."

Aric's brother gave me a small smile. "That's all right. I should've been looking out."

After blowing out an embarrassed breath, I said, "You're... Stone?"

He nodded. "And you're Sloane." We hadn't met yet, but Alyssum had given me a rundown of the brothers who were here in the house after I'd met Aric and Laken. "Where are you headed? You look a little lost."

"I am." There was no point in denying it and he could help me find his brother. "I'm looking for Aric, actually, but have no idea where his room is or if he went with Alyssum this morning."

Stone's grin grew wider. "He didn't. I'm headed to his room now. I'll show you."

He walked away with me hot on his trail, taking twice as many steps as him. How nice it must've been to be tall and have long legs.

"How do you like it here?" he asked.

"Uh..." That was a tricky answer. I wasn't sure I did like it here the way a person usually meant when they asked the question, but I also didn't want to leave yet. "It's... different."

He snorted. "I bet."

When we were near Jensen's room, Stone slowed and opened the door not far from his. "Aric," he said as soon as he opened it. "Someone's looking for you."

He continued into the room while I remained outside. If that room was full of his brothers, I didn't want to intrude.

Then Aric appeared in the doorway wearing jeans and a black T-shirt while his hair was sexily disheveled.

"Hey," he said, leaning an arm against the door jam. "What's up?"

"Do you know where Alyssum was going today?" I asked. When his eyes narrowed slightly, I added, "I mean, you don't have to tell me. I'm just curious. She said she had to go, but I had to stay here. Not a big deal if you can't tell me."

His face softened as one corner of his mouth rose almost imperceptibly. "Do you want to go outside?"

Outside? I hadn't been out there since... I'd

gotten here and I was beginning to lose track of the days. "Yeah. I'd like to go outside."

I'd been in the house because that was where Alyssum had said it was the safest. I'd be safe here and had no idea if that included the outside of the house, but if Aric came with me, I had no doubt.

Aric shut the door behind him, then we began our walk through the house.

"They have a really beautiful garden here. Alyssum's mom designed and maintained it, I believe."

"You believe?"

"Yeah." He held a door open for me, one that led outside, but we'd barely made it down the stairs. I'd assumed we'd have to go out the front or out the kitchen because that was how houses usually worked. "I don't know everything about this place."

We stepped out into the bright, morning sun and walked down a path that led to a beautiful, private garden. There were bushes that were trimmed and a lot of flowers lining the path. There had to be someone who took care of this every day.

"Wow," I said as he led me over to a bench in the shade. It felt good to have the breeze on my face. "This is impressive."

"It is." He turned, folding one leg under his other

so that he was facing me. "So, you wanted to know where Alyssum is?" I nodded. "She and her dad plus Jensen went to talk to my people. The Gobel. To see if they can work something out to end all of this fighting and hopefully, it's an agreement that doesn't involve me punished for treason."

My eyebrows shot sky freaking high. "'Treason'?"

"Yeah." But he smiled, which I didn't get. "Working with the Gremalians isn't exactly sanctioned."

"So you and your brothers might be... what? Imprisoned?"

"Nah. Me, they'd probably put to death because I started the whole thing. My brothers would be much less severely punished because... it doesn't matter. They'd be all right."

I sat back harder against the bench and began picking at my fingernails.

Aric... dead. I really didn't like that idea. All because he wanted to end the fighting between his people and Alyssum's. That did not sit well in my chest. I swallowed hard.

"Would they really do that?"

He sighed a frustrated breath. "Yeah. They would. It's why Alyssum wanted to get me out of there the night I was taken and not wait for Jensen to make a plan."

"Yeah," I said quietly. "That makes sense." A silence hung between us before I asked, "So is it dangerous that they're going now?"

"It is, but you saw what Alyssum and Jensen can do together in the basement. What they did to my brother. They'll be all right. Her dad isn't going to let anything happen to her and they have their best with them."

"You're not their best?"

He chuckled and the sound was a relief. "I am one of their best, though I'm not really theirs, but I couldn't go—otherwise, my people would grab me up because the Gremalians will be seriously outnumbered."

As I nodded, I decided that I needed a break from that kind of talk. Maybe this was something normal that they lived with, but it wasn't normal for me. "So you're the bad boy in this situation?"

Now he released a full laugh. "I guess you could say that." But then his dark gaze settled on me. "Do you like the bad boy, Sloane?"

My heart hammered against my chest. Did I like the bad boy idea? No. Not at all. "Not specifically," I told him. "I saw a lot of so-called bad boys in foster care, but all they'd do is either get you arrested or get you pregnant. I didn't want either." Finally, I looked back up at him. "But there are always exceptions."

My heart did not slow down and I felt the need to donkey-laugh right there as he looked at me. That sounded an awful lot like flirting and if I were being honest, I hoped he took it as such. There was something about Aric that I couldn't explain, but this intense attraction had hit me the moment I'd seen him. Now, maybe it hadn't for him, but that didn't affect what I felt.

"Good to know," he said quietly, then he cleared his throat. "Does what I told you happened between Alyssum and me bother you?"

I furrowed my brows as I tried to reason out why he'd ask me. What would it matter if it did bother me?

"No," I told him honestly. "It's not really my place to be bothered, is it? It doesn't affect me. Neither of you were in relationships, right?" He adjusted his weight uncomfortably. "Or maybe you were?"

"No." He shook his head to emphasize the point. "No relationship, but she'd just broken up with Jensen. Doesn't that make me a bad guy?"

"No," I told him honestly. "If there was a 'bad

guy' in that situation, it'd be her. *She* was the one who had just broken up with someone, but they were broken up. I'd bet Jensen sees that sooner rather than later, too. People make mistakes." My eyes widened as I realized what I said. "Not that I'm saying what you did was a mistake—"

"It was," he told me. "And I agree. They'll figure it out." After wetting his bottom lip, he continued. "In the interest of being honest, I should say that I had spent some time with Alyssum's friend Dahlia, but we weren't together. It was just—"

"Passing time?" I asked, hoping that was the case. Why? I didn't know. It didn't make sense. It wasn't like a goblin and human could be anything, right? Actually, I didn't know how that worked.

"That's a good way of putting it." He watched me longer than he needed to. So long that I had to look away before I did something really stupid.

Having him this close made my insides turn to Jell-O. Luckily, it was warm outside, so if my face was pinking up, I could say it was the heat, but it wasn't.

It was Aric.

"You should show me your power," I told him. "Jensen showed me his." I cringed. That sounded bad. "I assume Alyssum's is the same, but she was injured and said it'd tap her energy."

"Sure." But I would've sworn a smile played on his lips. This man... was going to be the death of me, if a person could die from being too turned on.

He stood then waved his hand for me to do the same. After leading me farther into the garden near a section of flower, he put on a hand on each of my shoulders, causing my muscles to jump and tighten, then gently guided me until I was standing in the middle of the flowers.

Then he stepped back.

He moved his hands and at first, I didn't think anything was happening. And then, the flowers bloomed bigger, the colors turned brighter, and they grew until they were as tall as I was. Suddenly, I was surrounded by bright, colorful, flowers. And I had no idea what kind they were.

I laughed as I moved through them. When I came back, I couldn't take my eyes off of what he'd done. "This is beautiful."

"It is," he whispered closer to me than he had been, but when I glanced over at him, he wasn't looking at the flowers at all.

Hot lava rushed through me, making my skin

burn, but it was a pleasant burn. My breathing came quickly. He was looking at me.

"So you control flowers?"

He might've smiled, but there was no less intensity in his dark eyes. "Nature. Comes in handy if you have to wrap a tree around someone."

"I can see that," I said quietly as he reached out to cup my cheek and ran his thumb over my skin. Slowly, he moved toward me.

This was that delicious moment before someone kissed you for the first time. It was torture, but the best kind. If I had wanted to end it, I would've grabbed the back of his head to bring him to me, but I didn't want to end this moment. You never got it back.

"They're back," someone yelled from the house. It sounded like his little brother, Laken.

Aric closed his eyes and sighed. "Fucking Laken."

Which made me giggle.

The moment had passed or been ruined, but what Alyssum was doing was more important and we had to go back in there.

When I'd thought you never got that moment back, I'd been wrong. At least for Aric and me, hopefully, we'd have a second chance.

Aric slid his hand down my arm, wrapping his fingers around mine when he got there then led me back into the house. He stopped in the foyer, where we all knew Alyssum, Jensen, and her dad would be coming in, but I released his hand and hurried up the stairs.

Hiding in her room was what I was used to, but I felt Aric's gaze on me the entire time I retreated.

I had no idea how much time passed before Alyssum burst into the room and hurried to her closet, pulling out a duffle bag.

"What's going on?" I asked as I watched her.

"Dad is sending us away," she explained. I was game for anything at this point, so I moved across the room to grab my bag. "No. Us. Me and the guys."

The guys? That meant Jensen and Aric. Aric was leaving and I was... I didn't know what I was going to do. "Why?"

"So we aren't killed."

I took a step back as all of the air in my lungs rushed out of me. Aric had said he could be killed by his people. Was this it? No. I wouldn't believe that.

"This is dangerous," she continued. "Running. It's how Jensen's parents died, but I guess it's our only option."

Only option? That seemed unlikely, but now my

arms and legs felt like they were vibrating and all I wanted was to run with them. Not just because Alyssum was my friend, but Aric... "Where are you going?"

She swallowed hard. "I can't tell you. I'm sorry."

What did that mean for me? As worried as I was for them, I'd spent a lifetime having to look out for myself. I couldn't stop doing that. "So, I stay here with your dad?"

"Do you want to leave?" she asked. "You can. We're not holding you prisoner, but Dad would have to make sure you got out of the area safely. He'll do it if I ask him."

Well, that was the last thing I wanted to do at this point. In a matter of days, this place had felt more like home to me than anywhere else that I had lived. Including my apartment. That was in second. "I don't want that," I said quickly. "I'll stay, but maybe I need to find something to do."

"Good. I don't want you to go, either. Hell. *I* don't want to go." She threw things into her bag quickly then turned back to me. "Hey. What about Fern? Ever been interested in medical stuff? You could work with her." She gave me a playful grin. "Make yourself useful."

"Oh, ha ha. Yeah. I think that'd be cool." After

all, I'd rescued her. Maybe it wouldn't be a bad idea to learn how these things worked in her world.

"All right, then."

Alyssum gave me a quick hug and reminded me that her dad would make sure I was taken care of. Then she thanked me again for saving her life in the woods that night.

After she was gone, I was alone in her room.

Not for long. I hadn't moved an inch before there was a knock on the door. Aric slid through before I could answer.

"Alyssum told you?" he asked as he quickly crossed the room. I nodded. "I guess this is the only way."

"That's what she said." I blew out a nervous breath. "She also said it's dangerous."

The corners of his mouth turned up. "Are you worried about her, or me?"

"All of you," I answered honestly. "But yes. I'm worried about you. There's so much..." I shook my head, knowing that there wasn't time. "I can't explain it, but—"

"You don't have to." He pushed his fingers into my hair and I rested my hands against his chest. "I get it."

Then that moment from the garden... the one

that I'd thought we'd get back... turned into the quickest second of my life as he pressed his lips to mine.

I melted right into him.

His mouth was warm and wet. He controlled this kiss, parting my lips so that he could slide his tongue between my lips. Pushing up onto my toes, I slid a hand around the back of his neck to where his hair met skin.

This right here... the best kiss of my life. I'd thought my knees had been weak before, but it was nothing compared to this.

All too soon, he broke the kiss then pressed his forehead to mine.

"I have to go," he whispered.

"I know."

"I wish my brothers were staying in case you need anything."

I nodded. That would be nice. As of now, it would just be me. "I'll be fine. I feel like I'm well-protected here."

"Yeah." He said it, but it didn't sound like he fully believed it. "It'd be too dangerous for you to come with us."

"I know," I told him quietly. "I'll be fine."

Though there was no way for me to be sure.

He dropped a quick kiss to my forehead then turned and walked away, leaving me standing in Alyssum's room, alone.

I thought about running after him to watch them go but decided against it. Knowing they were going was plucking at my nerves enough. Watching... I didn't think I could handle.

It wasn't until the room became claustrophobic that I left it. Since it was just early afternoon, I headed to the kitchen, hoping having something to eat would settle my stomach. I had a bad feeling about them leaving. Alyssum had said it was dangerous and that was all I could think about.

As I sat there nibbling on my sandwich, people passed through the kitchen barely noticing me. Who was I kidding? It seemed like the Gremalians noticed everything. Like when I'd been walking behind Aric right before I'd first met him. I now had no doubt that he'd known I'd been there.

They just didn't say anything to me.

There were so many questions that I wasn't going to ask.

Instead, I'd find Fern and begin learning how to heal the people I had come to care about should the need arise again.

It was all I could do.

Chapter Eight

"THEN YOU ADD this copper to soak," Fern told me as she dropped some metal into the pot and stirred.

Fern was about my size with the cutest red hair and honestly, I'd been told that she had worked as a healer with Alyssum's mother, but she didn't look much older than Alyssum and me. I was twenty and Fern looked like she could maybe be my older sister.

"You soak metal in this and then people drink it." It was hard to not cringe and show exactly what I thought of that idea. In my head, this would taste like metal and nothing else. Not exactly appetizing.

"You can't taste it," she told me, but I still had my doubts. "You can have some when it's done if you're curious. I don't think it'll do anything for you since you're human."

As I continued to stir, there was suddenly a question that I was desperate to ask and she was the only one I could. Alyssum's dad—that would be ridiculous. He was busy trying to save his people. Alyssum and the guys had left yesterday and while I had their phone numbers, I wasn't sure I was allowed to call or if they had their phones on them at all.

"Fern." She glanced up at me from her to-do list. This morning, she'd told me we had a lot to accomplish because she wanted to be fully stocked on everything at all times. Never knew when someone would get hurt. "How would I know if I wasn't fully human?"

She furrowed her brows and pressed her hand against the list she was holding. "Do you think you're not human?"

"No. Not necessarily." Focusing on the amber liquid in the pot made me less self-conscious about this conversation. "It was something Aric said," I confessed. "That it's weird a human like me could stand the electricity surging up here. The part meant to keep humans out."

"That *is* odd." She leaned against her desk, almost sitting on it, but her feet still rested on the floor. "Did it not scare you?"

I shrugged. "*Scare* isn't the right word. I definitely felt... something. But it didn't give me a bad feeling."

She thought about that for a moment, then said, "Well, it's the first time I've heard of that, but we don't have any reason to think you're not human, right? We can sense Gobel because they're our natural enemy, but we can't necessarily sense every supernatural creature."

There were still questions to be asked, but I decided to leave it at that for today. Mostly because there was no reason to think I was anything other than a regular, fragile human.

Yesterday, I'd worked the afternoon with Fern. She felt that I was a quick leaner and that was the first time I'd ever heard that. Let's just say my foster care experience hadn't been the most encouraging.

Then today, we'd worked until lunch, and she'd explained why they thought copper healed them the way it did. Now, it didn't always work. Such as the case with Alyssum's mom. She'd been killed here in the house—the foyer, to be exact—and Alyssum had found her. Even with the copper they'd had around, it hadn't been enough. Her wound had been too deep, her bleeding too fast. Maybe if someone had been there to hold pressure to slow it down while the copper had worked, but no one had been there with her.

My heart broke for Alyssum all over again. She was nineteen and had already seen too much.

Then this afternoon, we'd worked on elixirs and copper packs. It was like their own first-aid copper kit. But then we were also going to be packing regular first-aid kits.

Why?

Because not every wound was bad enough that a fighter would want to stop and wait for the copper to work. Some just needed a Band-Aid and would heal on their own. Also, like with Alyssum's mom, some might need to use human ways to slow things down while the healing happened.

It was a lot to learn and when I went to Alyssum's room after dinner, I was basically ready for bed. Because I didn't want to act like a ninety-year-old going to bed at seven, I took my time taking a bath, getting myself ready, and I even grabbed a romance to start reading.

That was too much. It was putting me to sleep, so I finally snuggled down into the bed and gazed out the window. This area of Michigan was so beautiful and if I hadn't known better, I would've sworn that I could see sparkling water in the distance. Mostly, I thought about Aric, Alyssum, and Jensen. No one had told me that they'd arrived in New York all right.

That was the hardest to deal with. My worry about them. Alyssum had said it was dangerous and there was no way for me to get an update.

Until my phone rang.

I snatched it off the side table so quickly that the power cord yanked out of it and hit the floor. I didn't care.

When I saw that it was Aric, my heart leaped in my chest as I sat up and pushed my hair behind my ears to make myself presentable as if he'd see me. It was a regular call, not a video call.

"Hello?" I answered.

"Did I wake you?"

"No," I told him as I folded my legs beneath myself. "I was staring out the window and swear I could see water with the moon sparkling off of it."

"You probably did," he told me, but he was talking quietly, which made me think that everyone was around him and suddenly, I also felt a little left out.

Which was insane.

"Lake Superior is huge," he added.

"That's true." I nibbled on my bottom lip, as I was suddenly nervous. It was like I was back in high school or hell, middle school. "So you all made it all right?"

"Yeah." He let out a tired sigh. "I can't tell you exactly where we are, though. Ash knows if you want to ask him."

"Of course." I shook my head, like I expected him to see it. "I didn't think you would."

"Laken's been freaking out since we left, though."

"Why is that?" If we were going to stay on the phone, my feet would fall asleep in this position, so I scooted back so that I could lean against the headboard with my legs stretched out in front of me.

"He's never really gone anywhere," he explained. "His whole life has been in Phoenix, obviously Delaware, and then some of the small towns around us."

"Yeah. That would be kind of scary." I knew what going to new places was like.

"But you moved around a lot, right?"

"Yeah. Sometimes I'd stay in a home for a long while, but the older I got, the shorter my stays became." I swallowed hard. Hearing his voice calmed my nerves and I wasn't sure that I wanted him to have that effect on me. "I don't think everyone wants to deal with teenagers."

"Were you a troublemaker?" There was humor in his voice as he asked the question.

That meant I was suddenly telling him about me as a teenager. I hadn't been a troublemaker. I hadn't had the luxury of being a troublemaker. Cause trouble and *boom*. New home. But me telling him all that meant that I got to ask about him as a teenager.

Let me just say... Aric *had* been a bit of a trouble-maker. His mom sure had had her hands full. At least it had been all normal teen stuff. Sneaking out. Getting caught with a girl. Things like that.

Before I knew it, we'd been on the phone an hour when he said, "I have to go." At least it didn't sound like he wanted to.

"I should probably go to sleep," I told him. "Fern is a taskmaster, but I'm learning a lot."

"Goodnight, Sloane." The deep rumble in his voice made it feel like he was right there beside me.

"Goodnight, Aric." But I waited for him to end the call.

As comforting as talking to him had been, sleep was still hard to find. My brain wouldn't let go of the memory of his voice and I wished like hell he was here so he could kiss me again.

Aric called me the next night and the one after. We spent about an hour on the phone talking about all the things you normally talk about when you're getting to know someone. I hated that he wasn't here, but those phone calls were almost better for learning about a person. You had no choice but to share and there was almost an added bit of anonymity to it, given that he couldn't see me as I spoke.

That was what my days were like while they were gone.

I'd work with Fern, eat, take some walks in the garden, then talk to Aric at night. With them gone, nothing had happened here that I was aware of. It was calm. Almost serene, as far as I was concerned.

My text and calls to Rhea kept her worry at bay. Even if I was going to be longer, at least she knew I was all right. She'd watch the apartment as long as necessary. Even if I didn't have anything living in the place, the neighborhood meant that I wanted someone to be seen coming and going and I didn't want the mail to stack up. She didn't have to go every day but maybe every few days.

Then on the fifth day of them being gone, I was walking toward the infirmary after grabbing a bite to eat when I heard Ash yelling from his office.

"This wasn't supposed to happen!" he yelled, causing me to stop in my tracks and press myself against the wall so no one would see me. "They've got my daughter."

My mouth filled with acid as my heart dropped.

They had to have meant the Gobel.

The Gobel had Alyssum.

"They're working on it," Sage told him, then something slammed against Ash's desk. I couldn't see into the room from my vantage point.

"They need to work harder." His words were strained. "They need to get her back."

"They will," Sage said more quietly. "Those men love Alyssum. They're not going to let anything happen to her."

A *thump* came from the office, sounding like Ash had fallen back into his chair. "I never should've had them leave."

"It was the only way to cool things down."

"I know that," he snapped. "But it's just like when Jensen's parents left."

"It's not," Sage countered. "Alyssum's alive."

"Yeah." He sighed. "But for how long?"

My breath came so quickly that I thought I was going to pass out. Alyssum could be dead. It didn't matter that I'd known her weeks and not years. She meant something to me and I had very little that meant anything.

Just so I wouldn't out myself to her dad, giving him something else to worry about, I hurried up the stairs and hid away in Alyssum's room, pacing as I waited for Aric to call that night.

But he never did.

Of course not. He'd have been busy trying to rescue Alyssum.

I didn't sleep that night and early in the morning, I sent Alyssum a text just so she'd know that I was worried and thinking about her. I never expected her to text back.

When she called, I leaped out of the chair by the window.

"I'm all right," she told me before I could say *hello.* "I'm all right."

"What happened?"

"Aric's brother found me alone. It was stupid. I shouldn't have gone out anywhere on my own, but listen, Sloane, we can explain everything when we get back."

"'Get back'?" I tried so hard not to get my hopes up.

"Yeah. Coming here didn't do any good. Obviously. So we're coming back tomorrow."

I let out a sigh of relief. "I'm really glad to hear that."

"Well, Jensen and I are going to Lansing, but Aric and his brothers will be heading straight home."

My heart began racing. As much as I wanted to see Aric, I hadn't let myself think about him coming home and certainly not without her.

"He can tell you everything. I have to go." The call ended.

But Aric was coming home tomorrow and it would have been a week since he'd seen me.

My chest was suddenly light, like the boulder that had been there since I'd heard that Alyssum had been taken had lifted and my whole body was vibrating.

As much as I didn't want to sleep that night, due to the lack of sleep the night before, I had to.

Aric was coming home tomorrow.

Since I didn't know what time the brothers would show up, I threw myself into my work with Fern. We'd made a lot of headway this week and things were in pretty good shape. I even felt like in an emergency, I could be helpful... beyond throwing someone in my car and bringing them to this house.

It was hard to not watch the clock, but when we heard a commotion in the foyer, I was glad that I hadn't. It would've been the longest day.

I quietly hurried out to the foyer and Aric was a

sight for sore eyes, as one of my foster grandmas would've said.

He was still tall—maybe taller. His dark hair was more disheveled curls than anything resembling a style. And he was beautiful. It didn't matter that he was just wearing jeans and a T-shirt.

When he glanced around the room, he didn't stop until his gaze landed on me. Sage and Ash were talking to them, but the corner of Aric's mouth raised the moment he'd laid eyes on me. I gave him a small wave, which made that smile grow.

As the men dispersed, Aric came over to me. "I have to go tell them what happened," he said, looking me up and down then setting his hand on my arm near my elbow. "Come see you after?"

I nodded fervently.

"I'm really glad to be back," he said before walking away.

Hopefully, no one had seen the exchange and I hurried up to Alyssum's room to wait. I paced the entire time before he came in without knocking.

"Come here," he said, causing me to hurry over to him.

He pushed both of his hands into my hair and tilted my head at the same time his lips found mine. I clutched his waist as he kissed me. Feeling his mouth against mine was what I'd been yearning for the entire week. He'd kissed me once before and I immediately knew I wanted more.

His tongue licked at my lips so that I'd open for him and he took the kiss deeper. He was so much taller than I was that he had to lean down a little, but I didn't hear him complaining. I was content to stand here kissing him as long as he let me.

When he brought it to an end, he said, "I've been looking forward to that all week."

I giggled. "Me too."

He dropped another kiss to my lips, but this one was soft and didn't lead to more.

"I'm very glad to be back," he told me as he took my hand and led me over to the bed, where we could both sit. "But I'm also leaving again."

I furrowed my brows. "Already? Was the kiss that bad?"

He chuckled and ran a hand down the back of my head. "Not bad at all and I'd much rather stay right here, throw you down on this bed, and kiss you all night, but my brothers and I have to go talk to Finch."

I cocked my head to the side, deciding to be playful. "Just kiss?" He growled, which made me laugh. "Who's Finch?"

"He's the Ash of our people."

"Ah, the leader," I guessed. He nodded that I was right. "Is it dangerous?"

He shrugged, which meant I wouldn't like the answer if he answered me truthfully. "It could be, but I think it'll be fine. I don't think they're out to kill us."

"Yeah, but they took you once before for treason, right?"

"Yeah, but—"

"Why can't just your brothers go?"

"I'm not letting them do that." His brothers could go without him since they were not in as much trouble as he was, if my understanding was correct, but Aric wasn't going to let them do that.

It was admirable and frustrating all at the same time.

"But it will be fine?" I needed the assurance.

"I think so."

"'Think'? Aric, thinking isn't good enough for me."

He cupped my face with one hand and ran his thumb across my cheekbone, as if that were supposed to calm me. "It'll be fine." After another quick kiss, he jumped to his feet and headed to the door. "I'll be back soon."

"Aric." I stood before he could leave the room. He hadn't gotten the door open yet. "I don't get close to people. There're three I could name from my normal life. Yet for some reason, I feel very close to Alyssum. I did as soon as I saw her in the forest." I took a deep breath, trying to muster up the courage to keep talking. "And especially after this week of talking to you and... sharing, which is hard for... I'm starting to feel things." I held up a hand when his mouth opened like he was going to speak. "It doesn't matter if it's one-sided. I just needed to be clear. I just needed you to know."

His face softened as he let go of the doorknob and crossed the room again, taking my face in his hand as he had before. "It's not one-sided," he said before he claimed my mouth again.

It was as if this was how it was and there was no other way for it to be for him.

I knew there was no other way for me.

This kiss was different than the one before. That one had been impatient and hungry. This was slow, like we had all the time in the world, and it felt like he was trying to convey all of his feelings with a single kiss.

That kiss would leave me dissecting it for hours.

When he brought it to an end, he rested his forehead against mine, his eyes closed. "I have to go."

I nodded slowly as he released me and made his way back toward the door. Once again, I spoke, but this time, right after he got it open.

"I don't like worrying about you," I told him.

He smirked this sexy smirk. "Then don't."

As if it were just that easy.

Chapter Nine

Aric left to do something dangerous as if it were no big deal. For him, maybe it wasn't. For me… it was a big deal. I was worried about another person in a way I had never been before

I worried about Rhea, yes, of course. But it wasn't the same. I worried about normal danger, not… whatever he was going to do.

And how could his own people kill him, anyway? What kind of community was that? Not that I had any idea how communities worked.

Alyssum came into the room and I was still standing where Aric had left me looking even more concerned that I probably was. But my body was tense. Had been since the moment he'd walked out that door. Who was I kidding? It had started before that. I'd listened closely to his footfalls as they'd made their way down the hallway. All the way until I couldn't hear them anymore.

"What's wrong with you?" I asked as she paced like it was her job to wear a path in the carpet. Finally, she stopped in front of me, her gaze meeting mine.

"Feeling cagey," she said. "Aric and Sage are going to Phoenix and that bothers the hell out of me. What about you? You don't really look excited by what I just said."

"I don't want anything bad to happen to any of you." I could've told her that something was happening between Aric and me, but I didn't know how he felt about that. She was my friend, but their relationship was so messy that I didn't want to make it more so.

And I'd heard comments about her friend Dahlia, who was no longer living here. It sounded like Aric had spent some *time* with her.

Alyssum's eyes narrowed on me. She opened her mouth, but before any words came out, someone knocked at the door and Jensen stepped inside. My shoulders slumped in relief.

"Too much energy?" Jensen asked, as if he had felt it through the door. She nodded. Hence, the pacing. She'd been trying to disperse some energy. "I think there's something we could do to get rid of some of that."

I bit my lips together to keep from laughing and Alyssum cocked her head, to the side making him bark out a laugh. It had sounded the same to both of us.

He help up his hands and once he'd gotten himself together, he said, "I didn't mean *that*. I mean, it's been a while since we did any training. Want to try to kick my ass after I go to this meeting?"

"Always."

His smile grew wider, and he nodded before leaving us in the room together.

"Things seem... different," I told her. It was something I'd noticed since they'd come back from New York—not that I'd seen much of them.

"Yeah," she said absently as she pulled clothes from her drawer. "We're... together again."

"Really?" I clapped my hands together in excitement. "That's awesome. That's what you've wanted, right?"

"Of course. I love him."

"The big question is... will I be sleeping alone from now on?"

Alyssum laughed loudly. "I think I'll be in my bed. Wouldn't want to leave you alone."

Though I wasn't totally sure I would be alone if she stayed in with Jensen or why she hadn't moved me to a guest room. They had the space.

Once we'd both changed into workout clothes, we headed down to their training room. I guessed Alyssum thought if she needed to run out some energy that I needed to do it with her. Or at least keep her company.

In the room, she hopped on a treadmill and I climbed onto the one across from her so it would look like we were running toward each other. At least it'd be easy to keep talking. She might have been ready to run, but I was ready to slowly walk. After all, I hadn't been out much since I'd gotten here and this was good exercise.

To keep both of our minds off what was happening in a place we couldn't control, I told her some funny stories about when I'd been a kid. Foster care might have sucked sometimes, but not all of it had been awful. Funny things still happened.

I don't know how long we were there when I noticed Aric and Jensen lingering outside of the room. "Are you guys coming in or going to watch us like a couple of pervs?"

Alyssum hit the *stop* on her treadmill and spun around in surprise as Aric and Jensen came into the room.

After jumping off the treadmill, she hurried over to them, leaving me to do the same, only much slower. "What happened in the meeting?" she asked Jensen.

"Later," he said quietly, but I wanted to know too.

I couldn't take my eyes off Aric. He looked OK. Actually, he looked better than OK, but the most important part was that he didn't look hurt. The best part was his gaze was on me like a blanket.

Alyssum seemed to accept Jensen's answer of discussing it later, but I'd bet she wasn't happy about it. Instead, she asked, "Should we show Sloane how we started training Jensen?"

Curiosity rose. I wanted to see it.

Aric chuckled but shook his head. "He and I are in a good place right now. He just stopped wanting to kick my ass. I don't think that's a good idea."

Wait. It involved something with Aric? Now I didn't think I wanted to see it.

Jensen snorted as he shook his head slowly and Alyssum slapped Aric on the arm.

"I didn't mean that, idiot," she snapped. "That's how he got his power to come out."

What the hell were they talking about? The worst part of being in this group was that they had a history that I didn't know. Couldn't know because I hadn't been there. It was normal, but frustrating. The inside jokes were killing me.

"Oh, you're talking about fighting?" Aric asked with a smirk. "We could do that."

"I wouldn't exactly hate a shot at you, either," Jensen added.

This only made Aric's mouth turn into a cocky—though sexy—half-smile.

"Wait," I called out. "Are you telling me that you guys fight each other? Like fisticuffs?"

Aric shrugged. "How else would we learn?"

Nodding, Alyssum said, "And those two..."

Hating everything about this, I wouldn't let on. This was their normal and I wasn't about to put a damper on that. Mostly because if I did, I thought Aric wouldn't do it, but it looked like he wanted to. The worst part of being in this room right now wasn't even that I was about to watch him get punched. It was that the last time I'd talked to him, he'd told me that my feelings weren't one-sided and we hadn't discussed it since.

I shrugged and murmured, "Well, that's hot."

She snorted but couldn't argue my point. "So, why don't you two go first? Give the lady a show."

She meant me, but I didn't want a show.

Keeping my mouth shut, I followed her to go sit on the mat near the mirrors and watched as the guys got ready.

Aric reached behind him and yanked his shirt off in one move, causing me to pull my bottom lip between my teeth to keep from saying anything. Goosebumps broke out across my arms. He knew exactly what he was doing.

Aric wasn't built like most human men. Neither was Jensen, but Jensen wasn't where my attention was. It was suddenly like I couldn't see anyone in the room but Aric.

Then they started to fight. They'd battle back and forth, each getting in great, if not hard, shots. I was glad. I didn't want Jensen punching Aric. Didn't want Aric hitting Jensen. Jensen had been nothing but nice to me since I'd arrived, but apparently, this was just something that they did.

Alyssum told Aric that he was leaving himself open at the same time Jensen took advantage of that open face.

It was like I heard Jensen's fist land before I saw

it. Or before I registered it. The forced pushed Aric staggering backward.

There wasn't a sound in the room after. All I could do was stare at the scene. My heart raced as I waited to see if Aric was going to retaliate and this "training" turned into an all-out war. Alyssum jumped to her feet, so I did too.

But Aric just stood there, not moving, until his tongue slowly licked up the small drop of blood in the corner of his mouth. That had been a hard punch and would probably bruise his beautiful face. Then he put his hands on his hips as his chest rose and then fell rapidly.

"Feel better?" he asked, making me furrow my brow. Boy politics were weird.

Jensen had the same stance as Aric, but he slowly nodded. "Yeah."

Aric stretched his jaw. "Good." Then he turned and left the room without even glancing at me, leaving me with so many questions.

Then Jensen glanced at us before leaving the room as well.

"So, that wasn't normal, right?" I asked. Their training could've always been this way, but given Alyssum's reaction, I didn't think it was.

"No," she told me.

"They had some issues to work out?"

"You could say that."

"Looks like they worked it out the boy way."

"'The boy way'?" She turned toward me with her eyebrows pinched.

I shrugged. "Yeah, you know. Grunt, scratch, punch, and now they'll be BFFs again."

Or at least that was the way it had happened more than once that I'd seen in the human world. Alyssum giggled.

"I certainly hope so," she finally said.

They'd been equally matched and I began to wonder if Aric had left himself open on purpose to give Jensen a shot at him. Kind of a payback for what Aric had done with Alyssum. Jensen and she might've been back together, but that didn't mean that Jensen didn't still harbor feelings over what had happened.

Alyssum shut everything down before we headed out. As we walked through the house, her dad's voice boomed loudly.

"Alyssum," he called out, making us both stop. Alyssum slid into his office, which we were right in front of, while I hovered near the door.

Most of the time, the Gremalians didn't notice

me there and it was how I'd gotten so much of the information that I had.

"Did you need something?" she asked her dad.

"Yes. I need you to run an errand for me." He glanced up at her and her shoulders slumped.

"An errand?"

He nodded. "I'm going to need you to find me several spools of ten-gauge copper wiring."

"Ten-gauge copper wiring?"

"Yes. Flint is working on something and we need it."

Alyssum folded her arms over her chest. Her stance told me that this was a weird request.

"Then why doesn't Flint go get it himself? We're surrounded by copper."

"I can't spare him. He's in the middle of something and it'd take too long to form existing copper into the wiring we need."

"What?"

Ash sat back in his chair and pressed the palms of his hands together in front of his face. Alyssum was testing his nerves. That was clear, but when didn't she? He loved her, but she probably gave him some gray hairs.

"I do not answer to you, Alyssum," he said, his deep voice steady. This was the voice of their leader.

"I'm going by myself?" she asked.

"Of course not. Jensen already knows he's going with you and maybe take the human with you as well."

My ears perked up at the mention of my... Well, not name. The mention of me.

She let out a defeated sigh. "Yes, sir."

Her dad gave her a curt nod to dismiss her. Then she hurried out of the room, making me hurry to catch up. We were making our way up the stairs when I asked, "What was that about?"

"He wants me out of here for a while."

"Why?"

"With him, who knows?"

Chapter Ten

As we got closer to the room, Aric's and Jensen's voices echoed through the hall. They weren't necessarily being loud, but they certainly weren't quiet. When Alyssum turned their way, I followed her there too.

"Hey," she said without worrying about interrupting them. "Ash wants me to go on some errand that sounds like a bunch of bull. He said you already know about it and are going with me."

Jensen folded his arms over his chest. "Yup."

"He said I could also take 'the human.' Sloane's coming. It'll be good to get her out of here for a while."

"Did he say anything about Aric?" Jensen asked as he went to his closet to grab some shoes.

"He didn't say much about anything, other than how extremely important it is to find this ten-gauge copper wiring."

Aric gave Jensen a look before wiping it away. I raised an eyebrow, but he shook his head imperceptibly unless you were really watching him. His jaw had a shadow that would turn into a bruise except that the copper around us would help.

"I can go," Aric said, but he was looking directly at me. It was then I knew that no matter what her dad had said, if I was going, he was too.

I just wished that we could've had a moment alone.

Aric and Jensen were waiting for us by the door after we'd changed our clothes. Jensen was flipping a set of keys back and forth in his hands as they talked.

"What do you think you're doing?" Alyssum demanded when we stopped in front of them.

"Well... I was ready quicker and got the keys from Fern. We're taking the SUV."

"So hand them over," she told him, holding her hand out.

"Well... again, I was here first. I got the keys, so..."

She rolled her eyes and sighed. "Fine. Drive. But I'm sure you'll get us lost."

Those two marched toward the car, still sort of bickering about who was the better driver, while Aric gently took my hand in his.

"Don't worry," he said quietly. "They do this all the time."

"I'm not worried about them," I told him. "Are you all right? What happened with your people? What about your jaw?"

He stopped and turned to me with a grin. "Don't worry so much. I can tell you about what happened at home, but it isn't much and not all that interesting. As for my face, it'll be fine. Jensen needed that."

I furrowed my brows, but he kept moving until we were both in the middle seat of the SUV.

We rode in silence, with me desperate to ask him what he'd meant by Jensen needing to punch him the face, but I couldn't do it here.

Then Alyssum asked, "So what's going on?"

I was glad she had because I wanted to know too. She had a better chance of understanding given that this was her world, but it was time that I also start asking questions.

"What do you mean?" Jensen asked.

"Don't play dumb. You had a meeting with my dad and then all of a sudden, we're on the hunt for something made of copper, which we are literally surrounded by. I'm not stupid."

Jensen didn't respond, which I could feel irritated Alyssum because he sighed as she turned in her seat toward Aric, looking at him with daggers of death.

Aric held up his hands as if he needed to shield himself. "Hey, *I* didn't have a meeting with your dad."

"But I heard you talking to Jensen."

"Just FYI, Alyssum, Jensen doesn't tell me every thought in his head. Thank god."

That made me giggle, given the kinds of thoughts Jensen probably sometimes had.

"All right." She turned back to Jensen because there was clearly something going on here. Something more than Ash needing the four of us to go find something that Alyssum insisted they had at the house. More weird that he'd said *I* should go. I hadn't left the grounds since I'd brought Alyssum there. "So cough it up, dude. What's going on?"

Jensen was silent at first and since I could only see his profile, I saw the muscle in his jaw tense and release.

"Flint really does need the copper wiring,"

Jensen surprisingly confessed. "Ash said it would take too long to produce ourselves."

"And Flint couldn't run out for twenty minutes to get it himself?"

"He could've. Your dad wanted you away from Delaware for a little while."

"Why?" Her anger was bubbling to the top and I hoped it would wait until we weren't all trapped in this car.

Without thinking, I reached over and grabbed Aric's hand.

"There've been some things reported in the human news that they want to test out. You and me not being there is part of the testing."

"What things?"

"Yeah. What things?" Aric asked, but when I glanced over at him, he was biting his lips together so clearly he already knew.

"Some natural-phenomenon-type stuff," Jensen said. "There was a small earthquake reported not far from Traverse City."

That didn't make any sense. Not here.

"Huh?" Alyssum said. "Michigan doesn't have earthquakes."

Actually, we did. They were just small and most

of the time weren't able to be felt, but this wasn't the time or place to correct her.

"Exactly."

"What else?" she pushed.

"The weather center reported the sighting of ten-foot waves in Lake Rocha in Wisconsin."

"Waves in a lake?" Aric asked. "It isn't even that big."

"Yeah."

"What does that have to do with us?" she asked him, taking the words right out of my mouth.

I was sitting back and watching this unfold without inserting myself, though I was clearly involved.

Jensen went on to explain that the time of the natural phenomena lined up with when he and she had used their combined power. But when had that been? New York. Though I hadn't known they'd used that particular power there since I was under the impression that they only used it when absolutely necessary. They didn't know everything behind it. Their ability to use it could be finite.

Then there'd been a small earthquake in Traverse City when they'd been in Lansing. Again, no one had told me that things had been so bad they'd had to suck the energy out of *people*.

Alyssum huffed out a sigh as she fell back into her seat as Jensen pulled into a little electronics shop not far from Delaware.

No one tried to get out of the car.

We'd been sent on a boring errand so that they wouldn't have a reason to use their power-sucking thing while a hell of a lightning storm hit Delaware. I kind of wished I could see that.

The first place didn't have what they needed. The second only had brass. Not copper. Five more stops and most of the day later, they found exactly what they needed. Though why they needed it, I still didn't understand why we were medical supply shopping in hardware stores. Working with Fern hadn't taught me everything.

Since we'd been doing this so long, Alyssum suggested that we go out to eat. After all, we were close to an actual city where restaurants lived and I was starving, so I was the first to second that idea.

Once Jensen had driven us further into the city, we pulled into an Italian chain restaurant and I knew exactly what I was going to be getting. The building and parking lot was on the top of a small mountain—we didn't have large ones in Michigan— and the view was gorgeous. I'd always known that Michigan was beautiful, but this... was breathtaking.

In the distance, there was a tiny sliver of Lake Superior.

We were halfway through dinner when Alyssum sat straight up and dropped her fork.

"Do you feel that?" she whispered to Jensen, causing both Aric and me to look around. What the hell did I think I'd see?

At first, Jensen looked confused and then his eyes widened and he began looking around the restaurant like he was searching for the enemy. My stomach tightened and threatened to return everything I'd just eaten.

"What's going on?" I asked, glancing between the three of them.

"There are Gobel here," she whispered.

I pinched my eyebrows together. "Yeah. Him," I said, pointing at Aric.

"No. Others," Aric said back, placing his hand on my thigh as if to calm me. "I think we should finish up—quickly—and leave. Try not to draw attention. They wouldn't know it's us, only that Gremalians are nearby."

"I agree," Jensen said.

I'd already lost my appetite. This was what it was like for them. They couldn't even have a single night out without some kind of danger. Now I knew exactly why they wanted to stop all the fighting between them.

This was stressful.

After getting the check, Jensen paid and we were heading out the door.

Once outside, Aric took my hand in his to help pull me along as we hurried toward the car. Alyssum visibly shuttered and I knew that didn't mean anything good.

"You two get to the car," Jensen called out as he shoved the keys in Alyssum's hand.

She tried to protest, but Aric cut her off.

He let go of my hand and said to her, "You need to keep Sloane safe. She can't be in the middle of this."

Alyssum nodded then grabbed my hand as we hurried toward the car while the guys slowed their steps to make sure they were between us and whoever else was here.

There was yelling as we climbed into the car, though I wondered if that gave us much protection. After only a moment, Alyssum quietly told me, "Stay here."

"They want you in here, too."

"Yeah, because they're idiots. You're human and could get very hurt. I can handle myself."

I grabbed her before she opened the door. "Alyssum, if you get out of this car, I'm getting out too."

Maybe it was stupid. I was just a human, after all, but I knew for sure that if I went with her, she'd at least try to be careful. Which wasn't something I could guarantee if she went on her own.

She glanced at me then back at them and swallowed hard. "Stay right beside me at all times, OK?"

That was easy to agree to.

We slipped out the opposite door so that the car would still shield us. Then we crouched down so she could peek around.

I didn't know what she saw, but she led me to the front of the car and held her hands out. Something I'd come to know she did to pull in energy. Tiny electrical snaps hit my skin. They didn't hurt, exactly, but they weren't enjoyable, either.

"Move over a little," she whispered.

"You said to stay right beside you."

"Yes. But I need to grab some energy."

And I sure didn't want her taking mine, though that had never happened before. I did as she'd asked to give her room and she continued doing her thing.

Until she let it all go.

And the ground beneath our feet began to move.

Chapter Eleven

I'd never felt an earthquake before. In Michigan, the ground didn't move. Even with us knowing that weird things had been happening, I wasn't prepared for this.

"What's going on?" My voice shook as I asked.

Alyssum stood with her arms out to the side like she was trying to keep her balance. Then she looked at me, and while I'd seen concern in her eyes many times, I didn't think I'd ever seen fear. Until now. "I don't know. But we've got to get away from this ledge."

The parking lot continued to vibrate like the largest massage chair you'd ever seen. That was what it felt like to me. Then it rumbled.

As soon as we got to our feet, the earth below us

shifted hard. Neither of us could move very far without almost falling over. Then Alyssum called out to Jensen as he was about to release more energy.

It was too late. He let it rip, which made the ground groan.

We both grabbed the bumper of the car. This was like being put into a paint mixer and shaken until we were well blended. We couldn't get our hands on the metal. Aric and Jensen were trying to come to us, but the earth was not cooperating.

And then... we were falling.

Alyssum grabbed me and I grabbed her right back as we plummeted over the cliff. There was nothing to grab on to. Nothing to stop us and it felt like we were falling forever, like it was all in slow motion.

Then we hit the ground and pain bloomed like the worst kind of flower through my chest. Alyssum was half under me, taking even more of the impact before being thrown away from me.

Were we dead? Was this what it felt like to be dead?

I couldn't breathe. When you died you couldn't breathe. It was like a fucked-up checklist that I was going through. Then I finally took in some air. It wasn't a lot, but breathing meant I wasn't dead.

Even if the pain made me wish a little that I were.

Alyssum wasn't dead. She was supernatural and they'd wrap her in copper. Seeing her on death's door in the woods then fine the next day had taught me that. I was the fragile human and for me, it wouldn't be so easy.

With a lot of effort, I forced my eyes open to find the pink, dusky sky over me. It was still somewhat light out because without moving my head, I glanced around and feared that if it was night, we would be in complete darkness.

"Sloane?" Her voice was quiet, strained, sounding like she'd gargled with a glass of gravel. Actually, she sounded like she was trying to catch her breath and the wind had been knocked out of her the way it had me. "Sloane?"

"Alyssum." A deep voice called down at us. It took thirty seconds for me to realize it was Jensen. He sounded close enough, but his voice was strained and full of concern.

"I'm OK," she said, but there was no way he heard her.

"Alyssum," he called again. "Fuck."

"Sloane," she said again while the guys called our names.

Something scraped nearby, but I closed my eyes and focused on my breathing. If I was breathing, I wasn't dead. Then something touched my arm.

"Sloane."

"Stop," I told her, though it hurt like hell. She was touching me and needed to stop. "That freaking hurts."

Alyssum's head dropped to my chest and I could've sworn she laughed. It sounded more like relief than humor. Or at least, I hoped it was.

"This is funny?" I asked her. "Is this something you all do for fun?"

"All the time." There was still something in her voice, but she took a deep breath and blew it out, wincing at the pain I assumed she experienced. "Are you OK?"

"I think so. Let me see if I can get up." Lying here wasn't going to do me any favors.

First, I moved my joints and most of them seemed fine, though my shoulders screamed the moment I asked them to do anything. Then I tested out my arms and legs. Everything moved the way it was supposed to, so nothing was probably broken there and I wasn't paralyzed, which was a thought that had run through my head. When I moved my hand, I winced in pain.

"Do you think it's broken?" she asked.

"No. I can move it. Just hurts. Maybe sprained." I'd broken that wrist once before and it had hurt worse than this. So... fingers crossed.

"OK, let's try to get you up."

"Slowly," I told her immediately.

This was going to hurt like a son of a bitch.

Alyssum hadn't stood up herself, so we were both moving carefully. She might've healed quicker than a mere human, but she still felt the same pain. Slowly, I pushed myself to a sitting position. A move that made my head throb.

A headache, I could deal with.

Then with careful precision, I got myself to my feet. We both swayed slightly and reached out to grab on to the other.

Now, I finally got a chance to look around. My eyes widened. "Holy crap."

Alyssum looked in the same direction and found what I had.

We'd fallen close to another drop-off that led to the deep darkness down the side of this small mountain. We couldn't see the bottom. If we would've fallen several inches out farther, we wouldn't have plummeted to nowhere.

That wasn't something even a gremlin could live through.

"Yeah, let's not look over there."

I was with her. I'd much rather focus on getting us off this ledge.

"We're OK," Alyssum called up to the guy who had been saying our names the entire time. "But, uh, we need a ride up."

Or at least a rope. Though I didn't think I'd be able to climb much of anything right now.

The leaves on the trees at the edge of the parking lot rustled, I thought, from the wind that we didn't feel down here. Then a branch lowered with Jensen holding on to it.

Aric was lowering him down to us.

"Hop on." Jensen slapped his thigh while he looked directly at Alyssum.

I didn't take offense. This was the woman he loved. Of course he wanted to get her to safety first.

The tree branch was wrapped around his waist while others created kind of a basket seat for him. The only way to get up would be to climb onto him and hold on.

"Her first," Alyssum said immediately. Before Jensen could argue, she said again, "Her first."

Jensen sighed and shook his head then waved me

over. But she wasn't going to allow that, so there was no sense in arguing.

Alyssum helped lift me onto his lap. It hurt so fucking badly, but this was the way out. I wrapped my arms around his neck while he put his around my back and held tightly, causing me to catch my breath. We were uncomfortably close and I couldn't look him in the eye.

"Bring us up," Jensen called out.

The branch moved up like an elevator until we were at the top, where Aric could help me off. He gently guided me off his friend's lap. While I was grateful for Jensen's help, I really didn't want to have to get that close to him again.

He was a very good-looking guy, but also my friend's boyfriend. It was awkward.

Seeing Aric meant that I was safe again and I let a few tears free. Maybe it was pain. Maybe it was relief. He pulled me gently into one arm as he used the other hand to lower Jensen back down.

"Are you all right?" He pulled back to get a look at me. Then he ran a thumb over my forehead, which meant there was probably an injury there.

"I'm OK. I think. Hurt, but not too badly." Looking into her deep-brown eyes, I wanted to kiss him. I was alive and five minutes ago, that hadn't been a given.

So I did. I reached up, cupped his cheeks, and brought his mouth down to mine. Good thing he was a multi-tasker because when Jensen called to be brought up, I wasn't ready for this to end. He kept one arm around me, holding me steady and in place, while using the other to command the tree.

Aric kissed me gently, which I appreciated. Anything more might've been too much. Then he broke the kiss right before the other two got to the top.

After moving me to the bumper of the car so that I could lean against it, he reached out a hand to help Alyssum off Jensen's lap. The tree branch snapped right back into place.

Right away, the guys got us into the SUV, Alyssum handed Jensen the keys so he could slide behind the wheel and took off without wasting a second. There was copper in the car, which meant Alyssum would start to heal and no one else had been in the parking lot though I wondered what they had seen from inside.

"What was that?" I asked as Aric slid a little closer to me so I could rest my head if I needed to, but I was determined to sit there on my own. Still, he slid his hand down my arm and covered my hand with his.

"I think that is what Ash was talking about," he told me.

Jensen took a hard right, which made me fall into Aric's side. "But we've used our powers a hundred times, and that's never happened before."

"That's not true," Alyssum said, already sounding stronger. "The ground moved in Lansing. When we used our combined power against those guys."

"Why not in New York?" Aric asked. "We used a shit lot of energy then."

While I wanted to know what was going on, I hadn't been there for anything they were talking about, so I didn't have anything to add. Being on the outside of their group was sometimes tough.

Jensen turned the radio to a news station and I was glad he had. If that was an earthquake all the way up here, there would be reports. It couldn't have been something that only the four of us had experienced.

"It's the copper," Alyssum said suddenly.

"What is?" Jensen asked as he turned the radio back down.

"That's why it's happening here and not there."

Yeah. That did make sense.

I took a deep breath and steeled myself. Even talking was going to hurt. "You mean you think the use of the copper to bolster your powers is causing geological shifts or something?"

"Exactly."

"Alyssum, it's a great theory, but we weren't by any copper back there," Jensen said.

I jutted my thumb to the back of the car. "What do you call all those spools in the back?" When no one replied, I asked, "What about in Lansing?" A new stabbing pain fired in my left side.

"What about it?" Alyssum turned in her seat to face me.

"Were you near copper in Lansing?" Aric finished my thought for me. Thank god he had. I wasn't sure I had it in me and trailed his fingers up and then down my arm, as he likely wanted to calm me.

"No," Jensen replied.

"Uh, wrong." Alyssum turned back to the road. "There was that huge copper statue near the museum. The guy on the horse or something like that. I don't even remember noticing it until now."

"That probably wasn't solid copper."

"It was enough," she countered. "Besides, it was a rumble, not an entire earthquake, like we just had."

"Did you hear that?" Jensen asked as he turned the volume up again.

"Hear what?"

"The news said there was a tsunami-like wave on Lake Superior that crashed into the far shore. There weren't many people around; it got picked up on radar or something. No one was injured, but everyone is confused."

"Well, yeah. Lakes don't have tsunamis, even small ones."

"No, they don't."

But the one in Wisconsin had. Or at least it had been reported. Jensen slammed his foot into the gas pedal, sending me back against my seat. I closed my eyes to focus on my breathing and I'd either fallen asleep or passed out because when I opened my eyes again, we were in front of the house.

Aric got out first then came around to get me at the same time Jensen and Alyssum hopped out of the car. Oh, if only I could heal like she did. Getting out of that car was hard. It was like each thing I did was now the worst pain I'd ever had.

I needed time to get better.

Aric wrapped his arm around me as the two of them hurried into the house.

"You won't let me carry you, will you?" he asked as we moved slowly toward the door.

"Not yet," I said between gritted teeth. "I want to hold out as long as possible."

He grunted, which I took to mean he didn't like the answer. "This is killing me."

"Yeah." I blew out a breath. "It's not that much fun for me, either."

The stairs were the worst and I knew then and there, I wasn't climbing the ones up to Alyssum's bedroom. That would take forever and be excruciating. I wanted to show that they didn't have to worry about me so much, not show them that I was a masochist.

Once the door had shut behind us, Alyssum turned to Aric. "Why don't you help her up to my room while we go talk to my dad?"

Aric gave a quick nod and turned us toward the stairs.

Once the two of them were on their way to her dad's office, Aric looked down at me and asked, "How about now?"

I nodded because again, those stairs may as well have been a snow-covered mountain with me wearing flip-flopsfor how likely it was that I'd get up them on my own.

Carefully, Aric slid an arm under my knees and one across my back. "I'm sorry," he whispered, then he lifted me. The pain made me groan, but I kept my mouth shut to keep the noise from traveling. "I'm sorry. I knew that was going to hurt."

"That's OK," I told him through clenched teeth. "I knew it was too."

As gently as he could, he got me up to her bedroom, but he didn't set me on the bed. Instead, he took me to the bathroom and had me sit on the toilet.

"I'm going to get you cleaned up," he said, but the muscle in his jaw tightened.

Maybe seeing me like this was as hard for him as if felt for me. But I finally got a look at myself. My hair was wild and there was dirt on my face. The spot he'd touched on my forehead had a small cut. Aric got a washcloth wet then went to work. He was so careful in the way he touched me, in the way he lifted my shirt over my head. His eyes slid over me, taking in each spot and each injury seemed to cause him physical pain. Luckily, there weren't too many visible cuts. I thought the worst of it was on the outside.

"Do you want me to wash your hair?" he asked.

I shook my head. That wasn't something I thought I could stand. We settled on just brushing it. Something else he did while trying his best not to hurt me.

Then he brought me back out of the bedroom, grabbed my pajamas where I'd directed him to, then helped me get dressed. When he undid my bra and let it slide down my arms, it was like watching him battle with himself. Like he wanted to look but wasn't going to let himself. I was injured. Then he slid my panties down my legs and replaced them with clean ones. All the while, his jaw was tense.

Once he had me settled into the comfortable mattress, he said, "Not exactly how I thought I'd see you naked for the first time."

I snorted, already feeling a little better. "This isn't how I thought you'd see me naked for the first time, either. But thank you. For taking care of me."

He shrugged and ran his hand over my hair. "I don't have a choice, Sloane. I have to take care of you. I'm just pissed you were hurt in the first place."

"That's not your fault."

"Doesn't piss me off any less." He leaned in and kissed me softly. "I have to help figure out what happened."

"I know." Though I didn't necessarily want to be alone.

Luckily, there was a quiet knock on the door and then Fern came through. I wouldn't be alone, after all.

Once Aric was gone, Fern went to work cleaning out the scrape on my forehead. It wasn't bleeding, so air would be best for it. Then she checked me over and didn't think I'd broken anything, but probably everything was bruised. It was going to take time for me to heal.

For the first time, I wished I were a gremlin or a goblin or anything else that would've made me heal quicker.

I'd just finished swallowing the painkillers she'd given me before leaving when all three of my friends here came into the room.

"Are you all right?" Alyssum asked, sitting on the bed a little too roughly.

"Fern said it didn't feel like anything was broken. Just bruised." They all looked so severe that something must've happened downstairs with her dad. "What'd you find?"

"Nothing much," Jensen told me.

"We're still looking," Alyssum added and I noticed that Aric's gaze was on me and hard. I wasn't going to like what was coming next. "But it's been decided that you need to stay back from now on."

"No way," I said right away.

Alyssum cocked her head to the side. "Sloane, you have to. You could've been killed today."

A deep sound rumbled in Aric's chest. "This isn't a discussion," he said. "You're staying back."

Alyssum glanced at Jensen then raised off the bed and the two of them left Aric and me alone in the room.

"Aric—"

"No." He came closer. "You're not going with us in the future. If you stay here, you'll be safe. I need you to be safe."

"Just because this happened this time doesn't mean it'd happen again."

He had begun to shake his head almost immediately. "It will happen again," he all but yelled. "It will. I'd hoped it wouldn't happen this time and Ash needed you gone for a while but this is what we're dealing with and you need to stay here."

Logically, I knew he was right. If they were worried about their human getting hurt or killed, it could put them in danger. I was about to say that when he kept talking.

Aric sat on the bed near me and said, "I didn't

intend on falling for a human, Sloane, but reality is reality." My heart tripped over itself. He was admitting to falling for me. "I need you to be OK. I can't have something happen to you."

"It won't," I croaked out.

"It did today."

"No." I blew out a breath. "Nothing will happen to me because I'll be here. At least until there's a way I can protect myself if I do go. So unless something happens here..."

He groaned, but he swallowed hard. That was the best he was going to get. "Good." Then his gaze took me in and he wet his bottom lip. "You look tired."

"Fern gave me a bunch of pain medicine," I told him. "Upside, I'm not having a ton of pain. Downside, I'm a wimp when it comes to pain meds and I'm sleepy."

He snorted then stood to kick off his shoes. Once he'd done that, he gently climbed in beside me so that I could snuggle into his chest.

"After today, there's no one who could say you're a wimp at anything."

The last thing I remember was him kissing the top of my head.

Chapter Twelve

The pain was manageable, though still very present, and the idea of getting dressed wasn't a pleasant one. Aric was still asleep next to me when I decided to gingerly get out of the bed.

"What're you doing?" His deep, just-woke-up, sexy-as-hell voice asked.

"Getting up," I told him as I swung my legs carefully over the edge of the bed. "I can't stay in bed all day. That will just make things worse."

Before he said anything, his side of the bed moved and he was suddenly standing in front of me. "You can at least let me help."

I sighed. "I'm not used to relying on people. Rhea and Charlie sometimes, but you have to understand that the way I grew up, I took care of myself."

Aric slid down onto his knees and cupped my face. "I do understand that. But you don't have to do that anymore."

His words caused a fluttering in my chest. Not having someone to rely on made it hard for me to do it. Yet everything about him told me that he was serious.

The more I moved around—though Aric was never more than an arm's length away, as if he wanted to be able to reach out and catch me should I fall—the less prominent the pain became. I was more sore than anything else.

After I was dressed, I was about to ask if we should go find Alyssum and Jensen, but then the bedroom door opened and the two of them came in. She looked at Aric then back to me and raised her eyebrow. Since I didn't know what she was silently asking, I glanced over at him myself. Jensen stood just behind her with his arms over his chest.

Ah. Yes. Arc was still in the clothes he'd been in yesterday. He'd never changed into the pajamas that were sitting on the chest at the end of the bed.

"You look a lot better," she said as she came toward me.

"I feel a lot better. Not a hundred percent, but

better." I gave her a grin. "You look completely better."

She snickered. "I am. I wish the copper did this for you."

Me, too. That would be incredibly convenient.

When Alyssum went over to her dresser and started pulling out fresh clothes, Aric asked, "Alyssum, do you think Flint has an extra Taser lying around?"

She looked over her shoulder with her brows furrowed. "Probably. Knowing Flint, he has some at his house just for fun. Probably shoots himself with it in his downtime. Seems like he'd be a freak like that."

I giggled because Flint was the straightest arrow I'd ever seen. Always down to business. I didn't think I'd seen him smile. Hell, I wasn't sure the guy had teeth. *Freak* wasn't a word I would've used to describe him.

"Why?" she asked.

"I was thinking since this one"—he pointed his thumb my way—"doesn't want to stay here where it's safe, maybe she should get one. You know, in case."

My mouth dropped open. I would've thought Aric's only opinion was for me to stay here. But if he wanted me to have a way to defend myself, that meant he thought I'd be with them at least some of the time.

Never in my life had I wanted to be a supernatural creature, but since being here, I had. Now, maybe I didn't need to. I knew they'd keep me here for anything super dangerous, though that errand wasn't supposed to have been dangerous at all.

Alyssum thought for a second, then said, "Yeah, I'll find him after I get something to eat."

Aric had moved away from me as he'd talked to Alyssum, so he came back, closing the gap between us. "Don't fight on this one, OK?" he whispered.

I didn't want to smile and look too excited by this so I nodded so he knew that I wouldn't. Then he swept his thumb over my cheek before saying he had to go get changed. Jensen left with him, but I didn't think he'd be helping Aric dress.

That left me alone with Alyssum and we rarely got only girl time.

"So... what's going on between you two?" She yanked her pajama shirt off her body.

"Nothing." I sighed, but she didn't believe me. I really needed to ask Aric if he wanted others to know that we were... something. "Aric's great," I told her, hoping to keep her curiosity at bay. "He clearly doesn't want me hurt, but... There's nothing happening. Friends, I guess you'd say. He's stupid hot, but yeah. There's nothing serious going on." Even to my own ears, I sounded disappointed. It wasn't disappointment, totally. Sure, there was some because I wanted to share this with Alyssum, but I was annoyed that I hadn't thought to ask him so I could.

"He is hot," she said. While I'd been talking, she'd continued changing her clothes.

Then for some reason, I needed a little extra assurance. "He said there isn't anything between you aside from friendship. Is he right?"

"I'm with Jensen," she said right away. "I only want to be with Jensen "There's nothing but friendship between Aric and me."

"What about you?" I asked because I desperately wanted to change the subject. "How'd your night go?"

She cocked her head and gave me the smallest grin. The way her cheeks pinked up, I already knew.

"Never better."

And that was enough. They were together. They were happy. And my feelings for Aric weren't going to step on anyone's toes.

Once she'd finished getting dressed, we went down to the kitchen to eat a bagel and grab a drink. Then it was time to find Flint. He was outside with a bunch of other guys discussing something that looked serious with their stern faces and rushed words. Three of the guys he was talking to were Aric's brothers, who greeted us quickly.

"Flint," Alyssum called out before we reached them. "Aric wanted to know if you have an extra Taser for Sloane."

"Why?" he called back, but then we were close enough that no one had to yell anymore.

She put her arm gently around my shoulders. "He doesn't want the stubborn-as-hell woman to be defenseless."

Laken and Stone snickered, making me scowl. What had Aric told them?

His brother Kale pumped his hand in the air. "Maybe we'll get another human in the family after all. Fucking finally."

I took two steps back away from them. Where was Aric?

Alyssum laughed as well then glanced back at me and the humor slid off her face.

"Uh, not this human," I told them, though I wasn't sure why. I could've kept my mouth shut. But he'd said 'in the family.' That wasn't where we were. "He's just being thorough."

"Yeah, I've got one she can have down in the

range," Flint said, not falling in with their humor. "But she's going to need training."

All of Aric's brothers groaned, reminding me of the first day I'd met Aric and how Alyssum and Jensen had used his brother to train on.

"Yes!" Alyssum made the same move Kale had, pumping her fist in the air as if she were excited to torment Aric's brothers.

"What is he talking about?" I asked. I didn't want to actually Tase anyone in the name of training.

"That means we get to use Aric as a guinea pig."

"It's basically her favorite thing to do," Laken explained, which made my chest feel heavy and my fingers suddenly cold. I didn't want to do this.

I didn't want to do that to him.

Alyssum told Flint that we'd find the guys and meet him down there, but I didn't hear exactly what she said. My brain was flashing images of me hurting Aric while my arms and legs shook.

Maybe we wouldn't find them at all.

Even that hope was dashed when as soon as we got into the house, Jensen and Aric were in the kitchen with empty plates in front of them.

Now I just wanted to escape.

Alyssum explained that we'd found Flint outside with Aric's brothers. She was animated about it, like this was her version of going to the carnival.

"You look far too excited." Jensen had said what I was thinking. "I feel like we should be concerned."

"Well... *You* don't need to be concerned, but..."

Aric folded his arms over his chest, setting his jaw. It was like he knew what was coming. "What?"

With a huge grin, Alyssum said, "Flint has a Taser for Sloane."

"Good?" The way Jensen said it made it sound like he was still confused. I didn't think Aric was.

"*He* says she's going to need some training," Alyssum continued.

"Obviously," Jensen said again, not putting the pieces together, but then... he did. His loud laugh made me jump, the sound echoing through the kitchen.

"Sorry, buddy," she told Aric as she patted his shoulder.

Why did it seem like they knew something I didn't? Whatever it was, I'd just agree to stay back because I didn't want to hurt him.

"We don't have to do this," I told the group.

"Yeah," Aric said with a sigh as he stood. "We do."

Once the guys had put their dirty dishes in the

sink, the four of us headed down the stairs to the basement. I'd been in the training room, but we were going to the range. Whatever that meant. Flint was waiting in a room to the side of what looked like a shooting range.

The idea of using a gun scared me more than this Taser stuff.

Flint explained how the Taser worked, that I could shoot once at a distance with the cartridge, so I always needed to have more than one on me. Then he showed how to load it up and then said to pull the trigger like a gun.

Acid churned in my stomach.

It wouldn't be like a gun, though, because there was no recoil. Once the cartridge was spent, I could use it as a close-up weapon and he showed me how to do that.

Now I was even more certain that I didn't want to do this. Staying here in the house forever seemed like the better option.

"Ready to try it?" he asked.

My heart was beating so fast that I worried I'd get light-headed. "Not really."

"She's ready," Aric told him, then he moved so that he was in front of me with a slight distance between us. "You can do this, Sloane."

Glad he thought so.

Raising the Taser to shoulder level, Flint instructed me how to stand, the proper way to hold it, and how I just needed to pull the trigger, but I didn't have to be aggressive about it.

He stepped back, but I didn't move. I held it there, staring into Aric's eyes, but I couldn't make myself pull that trigger.

Alyssum stepped next to me and asked, "What's wrong?"

"I can't do it." My muscles relaxed as I spoke and my hand dropped so that I was no longer pointing it at him. "I can't shoot him. It'll hurt."

"Listen, I'd have you shoot me, but it wouldn't work." In the background Jensen growled, which told me he wouldn't let her even if that hadn't been the case. But that was what everyone else knew and I didn't. It must've been because they controlled electricity that the electricity of the Taser wouldn't affect them.

"I can take it," Aric told me as he made the *come here* motion with his finger. "Do it."

I raised the thing again and intended to do it, but... I dropped it almost right away and turned to Alyssum.

"Alyssum, I can't do it." I swallowed hard. "Maybe I'll have to stay back."

"No way." I started to back away. "No, listen. I'd prefer you stay here because you're my friend and I care about you, but you can't not shoot Aric because you're scared. And yes, I know that sounds psychotic. He won't die. I promise. Do you know how many hits of electricity I've shot him with? Out of my own hands?"

I glanced over at him then back to her and shook my head. It didn't matter how many times she'd shot him with electricity. What mattered now was that I had feelings for him and couldn't do it.

"What if you shoot Jensen first?"

"Hey." Jensen scoffed. The grin on his face told me that he was mostly joking. He'd do it.

"I'm serious here, Sloane."

Jensen marched over to where Aric had been standing. "Let's just do this, all right?"

"It'll barely sizzle," she promised. So I could do it without hurting anyone.

With Jensen where Aric had been, I got myself back into position and took aim. I still didn't want to hurt anyone, but it was different with Jensen. I didn't... like him in the same way and apparently, it wouldn't even hurt.

Then I pulled the trigger.

The cartridge hit Jensen. His muscles tightened, but instead of dropping to the ground, he stood unnaturally straight.

"Get down," Alyssum yelled, causing me to hit the ground.

There was a loud *whoosh*, causing me to cover my ears, then a bright-blue light shot out from Jensen. Alyssum screamed, then something hit the padded wall behind me before hitting the floor.

That had to have been Alyssum.

"Shit," Jensen called out, then he was running and I finally looked up. "Alyssum."

"I'm all right," she said, but she was out of breath. "What about Sloane? Is she OK?"

"I'm fine," I told her as I crawled over to her. "When someone says *get down*, I get down."

"No one else was hit, Alyssum," Aric said, suddenly standing near me.

I got to my feet while the guys helped her up. The irony was that I was still hurt from yesterday, but during this, I hadn't felt a thing. "OK, that was really stupid." Yet it had been her idea. "I really didn't think you'd feel it. I didn't think it'd work."

"OK, now you can do me," Aric said as he went back over to where he'd originally been standing.

Pressing my lips tightly together, I turned to Alyssum. It would be so inappropriate to laugh right now, given that Aric had just told me I could do him. My brain was twelve years old sometimes. Alyssum didn't try to cover her own laughter.

"Uh, no way," I told him once they'd calmed down. "Did you see what just happened?"

Aric shook his head. "I don't control electricity. Now go."

Flint showed me how to change the cartridge and I knew that if I was going to do this, I had to just do it. Not think about it. So once I was ready, I raised the Taser and pulled the trigger.

Aric fell to his knees as the electricity went through his body. He clenched his jaw like he was trying not to make any noise. Then he fell to the mat.

My heart raced as I hurried over to him, but I wasn't sure I could touch him. Would I get zapped?

I'd done it. And I didn't want to do it again. Not to him. He lay there while Flint gave me a belt full of cartridges. I'd look like Lara Croft or something, but if it meant they could worry less about me, then I was all for it.

Jensen and Alyssum left the training room, as did Flint because Aric had told them to, while I sat beside him, waiting for him to recover.

I pulled my knees up and rested my head on them. "I feel so bad."

"Don't." He pushed himself up so that he could sit. His long legs went on either side of me, then he reached out and, with his hands on my hips, pulled me toward him, wrapping his arms around me. "I told you to do it. This way, I know you have some kind of defense."

His head rested on top of mine and it was like I was in this little Aric cocoon.

"Listen, Ash is going to send us to do something today. I don't think it'll be dangerous, but I know he wants to check out some of these phenomena. Today should go off without too much trouble." He gave me a grin, then added, "And now you have a Taser."

I groaned and rolled my eyes. "I didn't want to do that to you. I hated it."

"I know," he said quietly while his cheek rested against the top of my head. "But it had to be done. And hey." He pulled back and tipped my head up so that we could see each other. "Keep that instinct of when someone says *get down,* you get down."

I snickered. I'd say my mama didn't raise a fool, but I hadn't been raised by my mother. "I will."

Aric's thumbs rubbed gently across my cheeks as he lowered his lips to mine. His mouth was firm, but not demanding. This was a slow kiss. One that wasn't meant to go anywhere, but we were supposed to just sit back and enjoy it. The way his tongue slowly stroked over my lips had me inching closer to him. But we didn't have time for this to go any further, so he brought it to an end. It was always him bringing it to an end.

"I need to know what you want me to say to Alyssum," I said quietly. Right here, it was just the two of us.

His eyebrows pinched together in confusion. "What do you mean? About what?"

"Us."

"Oh." He shrugged. "Tell her whatever you want. I don't care if she knows there's something going on. My brothers already do."

Heat flashed across my face. "You told your brothers about us?" I asked. He nodded. "What did you tell them?"

"That we're together."

"We're together?"

"Aren't we?"

A nervous energy pulsed through me and I at least knew it wasn't coming from him. "*I* thought we were, but I didn't know what you thought."

"I told you it wasn't one-sided." He brushed

some of my hair away from my face. "My brother Kale was pretty excited at the idea of having another human in the family."

"He said." I slapped a hand over my face. "I told him *not this human.*"

Aric laughed out loud. "His wife is human."

"I figured."

Aric's dark eyes were on fire as he looked at me. "We should get up there."

"Yeah."

It was the right thing to do but I would rather spend time with just him. Still in the back of my mind, I was itching to call Rhea to tell her about him.

It was dumb but he was my first boyfriend and she was my best friend.

I wanted her to know.

Chapter Thirteen

Alyssum, Jensen, Aric, and I, along with Aric's brothers were in the entryway waiting for Ash to tell us what he wanted us to do. Though it was surprising he wanted us to go anywhere, given how the simplest errand had ended up, but I guess danger was just part of their day.

I'd garnered that what had happened at the restaurant wouldn't have been a big deal if I hadn't been there to get hurt. At least now Aric had put the Taser belt on me, so I'd have some kind of defense if necessary. I'd thought we could do it later, but he'd said *no way*. It was to be on me if I left this house.

Ash came around the corner with Flint and a couple of other people I didn't recognize. He told the four of us that we were going to go to the lake where the tsunami had been reported to see if we could find anything unusual.

There were some weird reporting he wanted us to check out, but then everyone else was going to Phoenix because Ash was going to meet with the Gobel leader, Moss. It could be an opportunity to attack.

Alyssum took a step forward before saying, "Then we should be there."

"You will be," he countered. "Since you'll be at the shore, you'll probably know when things really get going before we will. This isn't a joke, Alyssum. The Earth is angry. You'll feel the shift first then come help us. But I want you to check the other thing out first."

She didn't like it but agreed to it, anyway.

Once we had all the instructions we needed, we piled into the SUV and headed to the shore.

Alyssum pulled the car to the edge of the parking lot, then we all got out and began walking down the path to the beach. Aric walked behind me, as the path wasn't wide enough for him to be beside me.

"What the hell?" Alyssum whispered.

Once I got to the clearing, I could see what she did. The beach was overwhelmed with dead white birds and a huge pile of splintered wood. It looked like a scene out of a movie.

I knew exactly what we were looking at. "Is that a shipwreck?"

Without taking her eyes off it, Alyssum nodded. After a few more moments had passed, she said, "We did this." Not me, but them. "We did this."

The guys remained quiet, but Aric folded my hand into his as we stood there.

There was the soft sound of the lake lapping at the shore as if nothing out of the ordinary had happened here. We were just taking in the scene when Alyssum yelled, "Run!"

We moved as quickly as we could, though they could move so much faster. Aric didn't leave me as I hurried back up the path we'd just come through. If I tripped, he yanked me back to my feet. I thought it'd almost be quicker if he just picked me up. We got back to the SUV and just got the doors shut behind us when a squall of water pushed against the metal, surrounding us for a brief moment.

That would've washed us away if we had been outside.

As soon as it had stopped, Alyssum started up the car and jammed it into drive, sending all of us back against our seats.

"We have to get to Phoenix," Aric told her.

"That's where I'm headed."

This must've been the sign that Ash said we'd see before they'd know things were going wrong. As she drove, Alyssum explained that she'd seen the huge wave coming. That was why she'd told us to run.

We arrived at our destination minutes later. This was my first visit to Aric's town, but I wouldn't have the chance to play tourist. Alyssum skidded us to a stop then jumped out of the car, the guys following her, so I did, too.

"Dad," she called out as we ran toward the group meeting.

We didn't stop until Alyssum and Jensen were beside Ash, their hands clasped together tightly, clearly ready to suck all the energy out of the place. But if they did that, they'd get Aric's too.

"The beach is littered with dead birds and ship-wrecks," she explained.

"What?" the guy I assumed was Moss asked.

"Someone here used power, didn't they?" she asked. "While we were there, a fifty-foot wave almost washed us into the lake. It's bad and getting worse."

Holy shit. I didn't know it had been that big. We would've been swept out into the unforgiving cold water of Lake Superior for sure. It was possible that the other three would've been fine, given that they were supernatural, but *I* wouldn't have been.

"What is your offspring babbling about?" This Gobel sounded bored with this discussion.

"It's what I've been telling you, Elliot," her dad tried to explain. "The use of the copper has had some consequences. We need to form an alliance and find a way to make things right."

"An alliance." Moss snorted. "Let me guess. You keep the copper your people stole from us in the first place and we're out of luck?"

"No," his big voice commanded everyone's attention. "We need to share the copper responsibly."

Moss waved his hand in the air like he was brushing Ash off. "I don't buy it. There's no way you're going to share anything. And I don't believe anything you say including whatever you think's happening because of the use of copper."

Alyssum raised a hand, brave if you asked me given what she was surrounded by. "I'd like to prove it."

Aric stood beside me nodded his head slowly. Him being on board scared me.

Then he tugged my hand and asked, "Think you can shoot Jensen again?"

My stomach dropped. That wasn't something I

was interested in doing again and the dirty look Jensen shot Aric said he wasn't exactly happy about it, either. Still, I nodded. If they needed to do this, I'd do it.

"No. Shoot me," Alyssum said, stepping out from next to her boyfriend.

Jensen matched her and said, "Alyssum, no. It's fine."

"No." She turned to him. "This is on me. I started this in the first place. Bloodthirsty, remember?"

The way Jensen bit his lips together made it look like he was trying not to laugh. This was another inside joke I wasn't totally sure about, but it worked.

The blood was pumping so loudly in my ears that I didn't hear what she was saying to her dad. Then she twirled her finger in the air to tell me that it was time for me to shoot one of my best friends.

That triggered something in Aric's people because a branch shot out at Alyssum, but before it hit her, I pulled the trigger and her body began to shake the way Jensen's had.

A blue light beamed from her hands with a force that we could all feel. She flew back and hit the ground, but the light rained up from her. She screamed right before Aric's body hit me like a brick wall and took me to the ground. He lay on top of me, covering my head with his hands.

When it was over, Aric slowly rolled off me. "Are you all right?" he asked. I nodded. "No, really. Are you? I know you're still hurt."

"It's not bad. Just a little achy. I'm OK," I assured him. He moved to let me sit up. "I should've gotten down right away and I knew that."

As Aric helped me to my feet, the ground began to shake. Alyssum screamed for me to get back, but back to where? Alyssum rushed over to me and grabbed my arms as Aric pushed my behind him with a hard shove before he took off in a run.

A loud crack of thunder made me jump and the sounds of fighting filled the air as the ground broke apart, putting Aric and Jensen on one side, Alyssum and me on the other.

"Sloane!" Aric called, but the gap grew bigger and louder.

I grabbed on to Alyssum because this reminded me too much of the parking lot when we'd almost plummeted to our deaths. Without warning, and even though we were backing up, the earth beneath us crumbled and we fell. Not as far this time, but too far for us to climb out.

"What's happening?" I called over the loudest train I'd ever heard.

"Mother Earth is pissed."

Then the sound stopped, but I thought I'd gone deaf. My ears were cloudy, but the look of relief on Alyssum's face said that it had in fact stopped.

There was yelling in the distance and once again, Alyssum and I needed to be rescued.

When Alyssum snorted, I couldn't imagine what she found funny, but she'd laughed when we'd fallen before, too. There was no humor in this situation for me. My aches were going to have aches.

"What's funny?" I finally asked, though my voice sounded hoarse from all the yelling I'd done.

"Just thinking we could call this 'the Alyssum-Sloane Ravine.'"

OK, that was a little funny and made me laugh. At least neither of us had been seriously hurt.

We didn't have to call anyone this time because the yelling voices had gotten closer and when I looked up, there were so many faces looking down at us.

"Moss." Ash sounded so official. "Can't you see what we're doing? Gremalians... stand down. Protect yourselves, but do not use any power."

"What are you playing at, Bracken?"

"Hit me with another tree and you'll regret it, Dune," Aric spat.

My boyfriend had just been hit with a tree. Totally normal thing to happen.

"Stop," the other guy called out. "How do I know you aren't playing us?"

"Because of what we have to offer." There was an intensity in the air as Alyssum's dad and Moss stood close to one another. It was like something was about to pop off at any minute. "Copper. That's what we've been fighting over. We'll give you some and we'll keep some. "First, we need to get them out of this hole."

"We could use some help down here," Alyssum called up once they were done.

Aric and Jensen peeked over the edge. "Are you sure you don't want to stay down there?" Aric asked, smiling at us.

"Pretty damn sure." She held on to me even tighter. If I didn't know better, I'd say that Alyssum was scared of deep, dark holes. But she wasn't scared of anything.

We had to wait because no one wanted to use their power to get us out. They couldn't be sure it wouldn't trigger something. Then finally both Aric and Jensen were lowered into the hole with ropes and we had to climb onto them like I had Jensen at the restaurant.

"This is a better ride than last time, right?" Aric asked, making me chuckle.

"Yeah. It is."

But his face grew more serious. "Are you all right?"

Nodding, I told him, "Just bumps and bruises." He didn't believe me. It was written all over his face.

Aric kissed me gently, taking a moment to hold me there, then wrapped his arms around my waist as Jensen called to bring us up.

It was a much slower process, but I didn't mind being in Aric's arms the entire time. At the top, someone helped me off his lap and pulled me away so they could untie him. He didn't break my gaze once.

Alyssum and I sat in the back of the SUV on the way back to her house, clinging to one another like each of us was the other's safety blanket. The ride back was quiet. There wasn't much to say, I supposed. Then we climbed those stairs and went directly to her room, once again needing to get ourselves cleaned up.

Jensen took Alyssum toward her room, where I'd also been staying, but Aric set his hand on my back and led me toward his own room, where I thought his brothers would also eventually be.

"What are you doing?" Damn, I sounded tired. Felt it, too.

"You're staying with me tonight."

I furrowed my brows. "I am?"

He nodded. "Jensen needs to be with Alyssum tonight and I need to be with you."

I stopped walking when we were right in front of the door to his room, which I'd never been in. "Your brothers stay in here."

He shook his head. "Not tonight. They know to find other arrangements."

"Aric. I don't—"

"This isn't up for debate. Today scared the shit out of me." Could've fooled me. He was smiling and trying to make us laugh. "I might not show it, but that was terrifying. Watching you fall—again..." He closed his eyes and took a breath. "I need to be with you tonight."

Did that mean to sleep? Sex? We hadn't been there yet and I really didn't think tonight was the night. I hadn't even told him that I hadn't had sex yet. Sure, I was twenty. Some would say that was odd, given my age, but I'd been so focused on not being a teenage parent in foster care.

I'd done other things, just not that.

"I just need to know you're all right, so we'll go in, get you cleaned up, and you'll sleep in my bed."

"OK." That sounded reasonable though disappointing that it probably meant he'd be treating me like a porcelain doll that could break. So it would be hands off.

Inside, he started a shower for me and offered to help clean me up, but that was something I could do myself. He'd seen me naked already when he had to take care of me last time. Then the next time he saw me, I wanted it to be for a reason other than I was injured.

The only problem was, when I got out, I wasn't putting those dirty clothes back on. So I brushed out my hair so it didn't look slicked-back like a 1920s mobster with long hair, and wrapped a towel around myself.

"Hey," I said when I came into the room, causing him to turn. His lips parted as he stepped back like he was admiring a work of art in a museum. I shook my head. "I don't have any clothes in here."

"Right." He snapped his fingers but didn't take his eyes off me. "I can go get some from your room or you can just wear one of my T-shirts to bed. I know which I'd rather."

Fighting a smile, I said, "Then hand me a shirt. But I won't have any panties on."

He snorted. "Don't threaten me with a good time." And that... I couldn't help but laugh.

After giving me a shirt, he said he was going to clean up really quickly and that I should get comfortable in bed. He'd get me anything I needed when he came out. So I did as instructed.

But then he came out with just a towel wrapped around his waist and suddenly, *I* was the one admiring a work of art. Aric's stomach was hard with ridges tracing down. Men didn't really look like this. Scratch that. Human men didn't look like this. His arms were strong and his skin almost golden.

The man was beautiful.

"See? Now you know what I felt like."

His words made me realize that I was staring and quickly, I looked away.

"It doesn't bother me," he said as the sound of the towel hitting the ground goaded me to look again. "I don't mind you looking." A moment later, he continued. "All right, are you hungry?" He'd put on a pair of pajama pants, but no shirt.

"Not really. Just tired."

"Then a drink?"

I nodded. That, I could use.

He grabbed a bottle from the minifridge in his room, opened it, then set it beside me before doing the same for himself and climbing carefully into bed.

"If anything hurts, tell me to stop," he said, but all he did was cup my cheek so that he could kiss me long and slow.

His mouth moved against mine as he lowered us to the bed. His tongue poked at the seam and I opened for him. That was all he did. Kiss me.

When it was over, he tucked me under his arm and against his chest.

"It's really early," I told him right before yawning.

"It is. But you need rest."

And that was the last that was said about it.

In the morning, Aric was still there with his arm around me and for the first time in my life, I was waking up next to a man.

Chapter Fourteen

Once it was clear that I was up for the day, Aric went to Alyssum's room to get me some clean clothes and then was back so we could both get dressed.

"You need food," he said out of nowhere.

"I guess I could eat."

He narrowed his eyes on me, like he didn't believe what I'd just said. "You could eat? Girl, you haven't eaten in a while and you barely eat anything, anyway."

I shrugged. "I guess I don't have the goblin or gremlin metabolism."

He snorted like he did every time I called him a "goblin" or them "gremlins". "Well, it's my job to make sure you're satisfied in all ways, so I'm making you breakfast."

Heat licked at my skin, but there was no way he'd notice that his words had that effect on me. Instead, he led me down to the kitchen, where he made scrambled eggs and bacon while I toasted some bread. It was all he'd let me do.

We were halfway through our breakfast when Alyssum joined us. Without saying a word, Aric hopped up and made her a plate. She ate and none of us spoke. The woman looked tired. Her eyes were sagging and her mouth was a little droopy. How someone might look after a night of drinking, but she hadn't been drinking.

When her plate was empty, Aric hopped up and refilled it.

"How much do you think I'm going to eat?" she asked, making me giggle.

He grinned at her. "Probably two more. Jensen ate an entire bag of potato chips, six cookies, and three sandwiches after he got shot with that thing. And I think you'll be worse because you're smaller."

She nodded but asked me, "You OK?"

"Yeah. Actually, I slept really well and feel pretty good. You looked a lot worse than I did."

"It was the electricity." Which was what I'd been thinking. "But you probably won't see it again. Where's Jensen?"

"Council already started," Aric told her. "Moss and the guys got here about an hour ago. He said not to wake you."

"We should be in there," she said.

Aric agreed but didn't look happy about it. "Want to hang out with my brothers for a while? They're idiots, but they're harmless. Stay away from Laken." It took a second for me to realize he was talking to me.

Clearly, I wasn't going into the council room.

"Sure," I told him.

Before he went to do whatever they did in the council room, he walked me up to his room. He couldn't stay.

"So, we're babysitting?" Laken asked. He was lying on his stomach on Aric's bed—where I'd slept last night—his feet pumping in the air at an opposite beat.

"I don't need a babysitter," I told him. "I have a Taser now." His older brothers laughed. "But he did want me to hang out in here with you all while they went to the council room." A collective groan went over the room. "What?"

"I just want to head home," Kale started. "Back to my wife. If they don't drop the charges, then I won't be able to do that."

"Does Alyssum know how to get a hold of her?" I asked and he nodded. "I'm sure you won't need it. Aric isn't going to let you not go home to her."

Stone wet his lips before saying, "You have an awful lot of faith in him."

"Shouldn't I?"

"You should," he said. "All the faith. If something happens to you, it'll be because he's already dead."

I scowled. "Well, let's hope it doesn't come to that."

Kale reached out and patted my knee. "I am kind of excited to have another human in the family."

I threw my hands up in the air in exasperation. "I'm not in your family."

"Yet." He said it with so much conviction that I almost believed him.

"OK. Change of topic. Aric's not here, so give me all the brother stories."

"All of them?" Kale asked. I nodded. "I'm not sure you want all of them. There are a lot of us and we did a lot of shit."

"Can't wait to hear them. Do I need popcorn?"

The guys laughed, but at least we were all at ease, so they could start telling me stories about Aric when he'd been a kid. All the trouble they used to get in. The fact that their mother had had her hands full.

Stone told me about how their mother had reacted when Aric had moved out. Apparently, her response meant that he was her favorite, though Laken insisted it was him.

This was also where I learned that he had a lot more siblings than I thought. I'd been under the impression that it was just these men, but no. There were other brothers and a slew of sisters. They said names, but I couldn't make them out.

In the middle of a story about Aric getting into trouble, the door opened and he was there, bringing a giant smile to my face.

"Are you all lying to her?" he asked.

"Abso-fucking-lutely not," Stone countered. "Just telling her the truth so she knows what she's getting into."

Aric shook his head then came over to me, using a finger and thumb to raise my chin so that he could kiss me quickly. Apparently, everyone was going to know and I was fine with that.

"It's all lies," he murmured against my lips.

I gave him a grin and said, "I believe them." Which caused the whole group to break out in to loud laughter. Once they'd calmed, I asked, "So what happened?"

He took a step back then grabbed a chair to move

it so that he could sit next to me. "They're going to share the copper. I think there's more details, but Moss told Ash how they were sucking the power. Zinc. I guess zinc can block the copper or something like that."

"What about us?" Kale was the one to ask. He was the one who wanted to get home.

"They're dropping all of the charges. Kale can go home. By the way, they know where you live. Always have."

Kale groaned. "Well, fuck."

Aric snorted. "They left you alone, man. It'll be fine and there didn't seem to be any human hate toward your wife, so you're good. Probably should visit Mom, though."

"'Human hate'?" I asked.

Kale leaned forward. "Not everyone was excited that I fell in love with a human."

"Well... That's good to know, I guess."

The brothers went back to their stories. Each one, Aric tried to protest against, but he was just having fun. I had no doubt that he'd done every one of the things that they were saying.

In the middle of the loud laughter, Alyssum burst through the door with Jensen right behind her.

"You guys are all dorks," she called out, to which

I scowled. But she winked to tell me that she didn't mean me.

"How do you even know what we were doing?" Kale asked.

"I don't. I'm playing the odds," she said. Laken threw a pillow, hitting her in the stomach, but all she did was laugh. "So, Aric filled you guys in on everything?"

"Yep," Stone answered for him. "Laken and I are headed home in a little while."

Though that looked like news to Laken, he didn't contradict him.

"Yeah, I'm not going to miss not sleeping in a bed," Laken agreed.

"You're not leaving any little Lakens to wreak havoc on Delaware, are you?" Aric asked him. I had to cover my mouth to keep from laughing out loud.

When he'd told me to stay clear of Laken, he hadn't been kidding.

The kid grinned up at him. "Not a one."

"Aric's going to drive me home tomorrow," Kale said and Aric raised his hand to say *I am*. "It's not like I don't love being around you guys, but I love being around my wife even more. Then again, now that everyone's got their heads out of their asses and there's another human around us, maybe we can consider a move."

"Humans taking over." I pumped my fist in the air like this was a victory. At least they all laughed.

We were in that room for a couple more hours, talking and laughing before Aric and his brothers decided to go home. They wanted to visit their parents, given that death had been hanging over Aric's head and all.

There were just some things he had to handle first.

Once the room was vacant other that Alyssum and me, she came onto the bed to lie on a pillow, so I slid down to do the same.

"So, what's the plan now that everything is over?" she asked.

"What do you mean?"

"I mean, what are you going to do? Are you staying?"

"*Can* I stay?" That was a question I'd been asking. I didn't have anything to rush back to. There was Rhea, whom I'd text after this conversation, but she had her own little family. I could still be friends with her no matter where I lived.

There was the matter of moving all of my things

here, ending my lease, figuring out what I was going to do for work, but deep down, I wanted to stay.

"Oh, I'll insist that you do."

"I feel like I'm more in the way, though. All of you are these badass supernatural creatures and I'm... human." Which was such a disappointment.

"You're human, but you're badass," she countered. "Probably to your detriment. You shouldn't have been involved in any of this, anyway, yet you almost died with me twice."

"I like it here." I shrugged. "I feel like part of your family and I've never had that before."

"You *are* part of the family." She pulled me into her arms, wrapping one around my shoulders. "Jensen's moving in here right now. You can have his room. Plus, you're smart. I need you to help with whatever mystery comes up next."

"I'm going to need to go shopping," I told her, but she groaned. "I hate it too, but I brought, like, three outfits with me."

"Fine." She let out a long, dramatic sigh. "We'll go shopping, but know that I'm only doing it for you. Until then, we're basically the same size; take whatever you need from my room. I don't care."

Jensen came back in to find us lying on the bed. "Done."

That moving hadn't taken long. Probably due to excitement.

Once Aric came back, Jensen and Alyssum left his room.

I pushed myself up. "I have to go get my bags from Alyssum's room."

"Why?" His face pinched together in confusion.

"I don't really feel like sharing it with her and Jensen. It could be awkward."

He chuckled. "Why don't you just move in here?"

As tempting as that was... "I think I should move into Jensen's room, at least for now."

"I'd rather have you in here."

I swung my legs over the edge of the bed and stood. "I'd kind of rather be in here and this doesn't mean I won't be. I think I should have an official room of my own, though. I know it doesn't make sense... but I'm new here. I don't know how her dad would feel. I just... think it's the right thing."

"Fine." He sighed as dramatically as Alyssum had. "As for Ash, though, he gave his stamp of approval on Jensen moving in with his daughter. I think he'd be fine with us."

"I know. But again... I just think it's right."

He went with me to carry my bags, always

concerned with how sore I was, given the last several days. When we got to Jensen's room, he and Alyssum were just about finished getting all of his stuff in boxes to move to her room.

This made me think of my own loose ends to tie up. I had a conversation with Rhea to let her know I was staying here for at least a while, not yet ready, I guess, to telling her I was here permanently, but I did ask if Charlie and his friends would move all of my things to a storage unit. I could break my lease over the phone. Come to some sort of agreement with my landlord, but my things were harder to manage. I might not have had a lot but I wanted to keep what I did. She'd said it'd be no problem but wanted more information that I was ready to give.

I wasn't committed to living up here permanently, not totally, and could always find a new apartment if I went back.

With that settled, there was nothing left to do but heal.

A month later, we were in New York packing up Jensen's and Aric's apartments. It'd been a nice month of nothing happening, other than Aric and me getting closer and me finally feeling totally normal again.

New York was nice but I preferred the upper

peninsula of Michigan. Maybe that was because Aric was going to be living there. I wasn't sure.

We were on the road heading back home when Jensen's phone sounded in the quiet air.

"It's your dad," he said to Alyssum before answering. "What?" he asked. "What does that mean?" There was a long pause before he said, "We won't stop. We'll be there as soon as we can."

Good thing I didn't want to stop back home on the way back because it sounded like that wouldn't be an option.

"What's going on?" Alyssum asked as I drew closer to Aric. "What's wrong?"

"I'm not really sure." He glanced at her then back at the road. "But they found something and he says it has something to do with Sloane."

"Me?" I asked with all of the surprise that I had in me. "What?"

"Yeah. He doesn't want to explain on the phone. Just wants us home as soon as possible."

"What's that about?" Aric's worried gaze was on me. We'd been taking things slow, but clearly, we already loved each other.

"I have no idea."

I watched out the window as the world flew by, wondering what this could mean.

There was nothing of note about me and why would Ash Bracken know, anyway? Even *I* didn't know who my parents were. There were no record, so this felt weird.

Aric pulled my into his arms and ran a hand up and down my back to soothe me.

It would just have been better if Ash would've told Jensen over the phone.

Now we were racing back to Delaware, Michigan to figure out what was going on.

Chapter Fifteen

THE DRIVE WAS GRUELING, considering that we only stopped when we had to. The guys took turns behind the wheel and neither Alyssum nor I complained about that. I was too distracted to want to drive. We slept and drove in pairs so that the driver had someone to talk to. Alyssum and Jensen would sleep while Aric drove and I kept him company.

When I was supposed to be resting, I was actually watching the world pass us by. This whole trip was supposed to have been fun and completely relaxed, as much as moving the guys fully to Delaware, Michigan could be.

It was supposed to have been time for Aric and

me to know each other when we weren't in a high-stress dangerous situation.

As I stared out the window, Aric tapped my shoulder then spun his finger, telling me to turn. When I did, he wrapped his arms around me and rested his head on my chest. I supposed this was how he wanted to sleep. I leaned back against my door and pulled him closer, absently running my fingers through his hair.

Aric hadn't made a move to take things further—as in have sex—since everything between his people and Alyssum's had come to an end. Not even when I'd stayed at his apartment in New York with him to pack.

Oh, he'd spend a long time each night kissing me, which left me ready to beg him for more, but his hands didn't roam. I assumed that he was letting me heal, but I *was* healed.

"Hey," Alyssum said quietly as she gently shook my shoulder. "It's your turn."

Which meant that Jensen had taken his four-hour shift and that I'd fallen asleep at some point. I ran my hand over Aric's cheek. "Time to wake up."

The only way that I knew he'd heard me was because he squeezed me harder, making me snicker. "It's your turn to drive." I yanked his arm quickly.

"Or I can and you can keep sleeping, but Jensen's done."

He pushed up so that he could look at me. "I'm awake." Then he leaned in and kissed my lips quickly. It was gentle and over too soon.

At each stop, we'd use the restroom so that hopefully, no one would need to until we stopped in four hours. Though it didn't always work. Four hours was a long time to hold it.

"I have to go." Alyssum threaded her arm through mine then pulled me away from Aric.

"I was already coming." I snickered.

"The way he was holding on to you, how was I to know?" But she was laughing too.

Once we'd taken care of our business, we came out, but she came to a stop to stretch. The guys were by the car.

"I like you with him," she told me.

"I'm glad?"

She snorted. "No. I thought something was starting right after he met you, but you kept saying you were just friends. Now, you're clearly more than friends, but you've never actually said."

"Yes, Alyssum," I said, sounding like a chastised child. "We're more than friends. I didn't tell you because I wasn't sure he wanted me to, then he said he didn't care, yet we were constantly in danger."

"That's OK." She nudged my arm with her elbow when we started walking again. "I put the pieces together and just wanted to hear you say it."

"We haven't had sex, though." The moment the words were out of my mouth, I wanted to shove them back in. Why had I just told her that?

She stopped and turned to me. "Why not? You know how it works, right?"

I rolled my eyes and started walking again. "Yes, Mom. I do. I don't know why not."

"Well, I'd assume that it's because we were in one dangerous moment after another. You got really hurt. He's a good guy."

"Yeah." I sighed. That was what I thought too.

With all of us back in the car, Aric pulled out so that we could get home. Or to their home, I guess. It wasn't really my home, was it?

Aric and I talked about random things all the way home. Movies we'd seen. Books we'd read. Our favorite places to visit. For me, that last one was easy. I'd never been anywhere until I'd met them, so I chose Mackinac Island. The water was beautiful up there.

Though he teased me about liking my books with

romance then told me I should read one to him. My face burned and I said that I didn't think I could read that out loud, which made him want me to even more.

Then we rinsed and repeated the process until we were back in Delaware.

Alyssum thought we'd get some real sleep before seeing her dad, but that wasn't in the cards for us.

As soon as we stepped back into her house, Flint was there waiting for us with a stern eye on me that Aric scoffed at.

"I don't know what's going on here," he said to the big, military-looking man. "But I'd choose another way to look at her."

"It's fine," I told him right away.

Aric scowled at me, making me sigh. The last thing I wanted was for him to pick a fight with this guy. "It really isn't."

Flint gave a gruff snort. "Come with me."

I wasn't sure if he just meant me, but the way the other three moved too, I supposed it didn't matter. We were all going.

Aric placed his hand on my lower back as we walked behind Flint and it looked like we were headed to Ash's office.

"What do you think this is about?" I whispered, but we were all so quiet that everyone could hear me.

"I don't know." He didn't bother trying to be quiet.

So I swung my gaze over to Alyssum. "I don't want the memory-wiping thing. I like my brain the way it is. And I thought it was fine that I stay here."

She reached out to take my hand in her firm grasp. "You did. I wouldn't let them do that to you, Sloane."

"Neither would I." Aric kissed the side of my head.

They were trying to be supportive, but this felt an awful lot like the time I'd been called to the principal's office in high school, where my case manager had been waiting to tell me that after school, I wasn't going home to the place I'd left that morning.

Whatever was happening here, I didn't think I'd like it.

Ash's office was all dark wood and absolutely intimidating. I had been to the door but never inside for that very reason. It made sense. An intimidating office for an intimidating guy. Alyssum said he was a big teddy bear, but I felt fairly certain that that was reserved for her. He was perched on his chair behind the desk with his hands resting on top. His dark eyes followed me and were filled with curiosity. His brows pinched together in concern the moment I entered the room.

"I need that Taser back," Flint said while holding his hand out.

Without a thought, I undid the buckle holding it on my hip. I'd promised to always have it with me.

"Why, Flint?" Aric moved a bit closer to me. Any closer and he'd have to pick me up. "What's going on?"

"It's for safety." Flint took the Taser belt but didn't set it down anywhere and didn't elaborate. Suddenly, I was a security concern?

"'Safety'?" Aric asked with outrage, then he turned to Ash. "This woman—who's vulnerable simply because she's human—could've been killed multiple times helping us. She saved Alyssum's life more than once. What the fuck is going on here, Ash?"

Alyssum's dad raised an eyebrow. "Watch your words," he said, making that the first thing he'd spoken since we'd walked in.

Aric shook his head. "I'm not watching shit."

I reached out to place my hand on his arm. "Aric," I said quietly. "Let him explain."

He glanced over at me. His face softened and he took a deep breath.

"Dad." Alyssum took a giant step forward, but Jensen followed her, anyway. It was like Aric and Jensen were trying to be prepared for anything, but it wasn't like her dad was going to hurt us. Or not her, anyway.

In the month since they'd resolved things with the Gobel, I'd done everything I could to make myself useful. I'd worked with Fern some more, had taken care of Gremalians who had gotten injured in their daily life. It had been deemed a good fit for me because I was good at it and Fern could use the help.

Alyssum made sure that the council—their form of government—was paying me for my time so I'd have some money of my own.

Now... I had no idea what I might've done or what secret they could've found out about me that would cause this behavior.

Not to mention, what secret could they know that I didn't?

"We'll get to it," he told her. "Come here." He twirled his fingers the way I'd seen Alyssum do when she was pulling in power and all of my muscles hardened. I hadn't been hit with electricity before, but I had seen it and it didn't look fun.

So I stepped forward but could still feel Aric at my back.

Standing next to Alyssum really did feel like we were about to be chastised. As if we'd played some prank on the school that now had to be dealt with. I'd been out of school for a couple of years now, yet this put me right back there.

"Dad, come on. Tell us what's going on." Alyssum folded her arms under her chest, looking like a stubborn kid. This woman wasn't afraid to push her dad, that was for sure. I'd seen it several times. "You called us and said we had to get right here, which we did. Now you're procrastinating on telling us why? You said it was about Sloane. If you think you're going to wipe her memory—"

"Enough, Alyssum," he said, but he kept his eyes on me. It was like I was the only thing in the room he cared about in this moment. "What do you know about your parents?"

"Which ones?" That wasn't meant to be funny. I'd had more than one set of foster parents. It could've been any of them.

He scowled, anyway. "I'm talking about your birth parents."

"Oh." A sense of relief ran through me. "Nothing. Less than nothing. They dumped me then fucked off to wherever they ended up, but no one ever knew who they were." If they'd done something, I hadn't been a part of it.

"Nothing?" Flint asked again, making me look from one to the other.

"No. Like I said. They dumped me in a box then *nope*d the fuck out."

Aric leaned toward me. "A 'box'?"

"You know those boxes at fire stations?" That was where I'd been told that I'd been dropped, but he shook his head. Did they even have fire stations up here? I didn't think so.

"Tell us what you do know," Ash urged.

"Nothing." I put my hands in the air then let them drop. "I know less than nothing, like I said. I was raised in foster care. Had several different sets of foster parents but didn't stay with any of them super long. Nobody wanted me. Not enough to adopt me."

Aric's big hand settled on my shoulder and squeezed reassuringly.

"It's not like people are in a rush to make sure you know where you come from when you're a foster kid, so unless you have parents who are trying to get you back, you're left to guess and make up stories that you can live with."

There weren't any lingering feelings about how

I'd grown up. I didn't miss my "real" parents because I'd never had them. Parental love wasn't something I could relate to. It was just how it was.

"Can you just tell us?" Aric sounded like he was about to come out of his skin. He and I hadn't known each other two months. This last month I'd still been healing because my injuries had been worse than I'd let anyone know. Hell, they were worse than what I'd known. I had no idea how I'd done all of that with Alyssum—falling down a second ravine—given that I hadn't healed from the first time.

"I had Flint send one of his men on a fact-finding mission," Ash finally said.

"About Sloane?" Alyssum glanced at me but then focused back on him.

"*What?*" That didn't make sense. There were no facts to find when it came to me. Trust me, I'd tried. There was no birth certificate on record for me, which was a huge deal. They ended up having to create one and honestly, I didn't even know if my birthday was actually mine. They'd made a guess.

I'd been a very new newborn when I'd shown up in that drop box and there were no records in the area hospitals that matched my birth. Either the woman who'd pushed me out of her body had done it at home or on the street or I'd come from somewhere else.

The placenta had still been attached, so it was safe to assume that I hadn't been that old. But had I been born that day or the one before it? Given that I'd been put in the box in the very early morning, it could've gone either way.

"What?" I asked with surprise. Maybe Ash could get information that I couldn't. There was always a possibility, but I'd exhausted everything when I'd aged out.

"I thought it was odd that you came up here and stayed," he said.

"Alyssum wanted me to stay."

"That's right I did." She folded our hands together.

"Yes. I know that." He sat back in his seat and took a breath. Ash really wasn't in a hurry to tell us everything now, was he? "But most humans turn away. Most can't stand it up here. They experience creepy feelings because of the electricity. It's how we like it."

"I did get weird feelings up here," I told him. "I did. Just before I saw Alyssum in the woods, I was going to turn back, but she needed my help."

"And I'm grateful for that," he said. Because

without me in the woods, she might've bled to death before she could heal. I'd already been told that more than once. "But I wouldn't be doing my job as the leader of my people if I let you show up here and didn't at least look into it."

That made sense, but with me... there was nothing to find.

"Did they find anything?" Alyssum asked because something told me that I wasn't going to like the answer.

No matter what that answer was.

It wasn't exactly easy knowing that there was no history on you. Even medical information was a shot in the dark. I couldn't give a history, which meant doctors were going to be working blind if anything ever went wrong with me.

Ash reached out and pulled a file from the top of a stack. Most people would've just done this digitally, but apparently, Ash was old-school.

"We found the records of when you went into the system."

"Yeah. I found those too when I looked," I told him. "There wasn't much there. No record of me being born at hospitals. No idea who gave birth to me."

"Well, we were able to go a little deeper than that."

My heart pounded against my chest so hard that it took my breath away. Deeper? What did that mean?

"Some of what you were told when you looked into it wasn't accurate." He flipped open the folder. "We were told the same thing you were at first. That you were put into one of those safe haven type boxes where unwanted babies can go."

Well, that was like spitting directly in my face. I'd been abandoned, so yeah, I hadn't been wanted. I'd already known that, but hearing someone say it... It didn't feel good.

"*Dad*," Alyssum snapped, making him hold up his hand.

"I'm sorry," he said to me and at least he sounded sincere. "That was really bad wording."

"It's fine," I said, even though it wasn't. "I know I wasn't wanted."

"You're wanted now," Aric murmured from behind me, but I could feel the anger rolling off him.

"Flint's man was able to track down the fireman who took you in that night."

I furrowed my brows. "I wasn't told anyone was there."

"We know." He cleared his throat. "But he was there and your mother didn't put you in the box—she gave you directly to him. He lied and said you were put in the box so that no one could track her down."

"Why would he do that?" It didn't make sense to me. If a fireman had talked to her, then he would've had information about me. Apparently, that might have been the case.

Ash took a moment, like he was contemplating how much to tell me. I held his gaze, even though I felt like I was about to jump out of my skin. This was surreal.

"The fireman told us that your mother was young, but not a teenager, and she had to give you up, though he says it didn't seem like she really wanted to."

I took a step back as if something had slammed into me. The only reason that I didn't fall was because Aric was right there. "You know who my mother is?"

"No." He slid the folder across the desk. It would've fallen off if Alyssum hadn't slammed her hand down on it to stop the momentum. "I don't know who she is. But what's in that file should help and Aric should be able to get even more information."

"How in the hell would *I* be able to get more information?" Aric demanded.

"Because your people have been known to consort with witches. Gremalians have steered clear for centuries."

"*What?*" Aric asked. "Are you saying her mom was a witch?"

Ash's gaze fell onto me again. "Go ask your parents."

My parents?

A large boulder crushed my stomach making me want to throw up. In all of my years of foster care, I hadn't thought much about finding my parents except when I was very young. Anyone would be curious.

But if he was telling me to go ask them that had to mean they were alive.

How did I feel about that?

Without realizing it I'd started to pinch the skin on my wrist between my thumb and finger as I chewed on the inside of my cheek.

Find the people who gave me...

I wasn't sure I wanted to.

Chapter Sixteen

"We're going to Phoenix, right?" Alyssum asked as we left her dad's office.

I was walking in stunned silence. My mother might have wanted to keep me? Why hadn't she, then? I'd come to terms with my unwanted status a long time ago and now... Maybe I hadn't been so unwanted.

My body turned cold and there was a vibration running over my skin. That could've been the energy but I didn't think it was.

If only I could call her up and ask, but even Ash didn't have her name. At least as far as we knew. He had given Aric the folder, so I supposed there could've been something there, but there wasn't a doubt in my mind that whatever was in there, it wouldn't include who my mother was.

"Yeah," Aric told her as he held me tightly to his side. "We're going to Phoenix, but not tonight. We need to rest."

"I didn't mean tonight," Alyssum muttered. "How about we all get changed and meet in my room? We can go over the folder, have a snack. Just decompress a little before we try to sleep."

"Sleep would be better," he countered.

Alyssum sighed, but I was watching my feet to make sure they kept moving. For some reason, this information about myself had me reeling.

"Then Sloane and I can stay in our room tonight so we can have some girl time. You two can stay in yours."

Jensen snorted as Aric's body moved because he shook his head. "She's staying in with me."

Alyssum growled. "Are you really telling me that you're not going to open that folder until tomorrow? You're not going to sneak out of bed as soon as she falls asleep and read it yourself? Then give it to me and I'll go over it."

Aric stopped and dropped his arm from around my shoulder to face her in an almost challenging way.

"Listen, I get that you're like the Energizer Bunny. Never out of energy, which probably helps because you can take in electricity to keep your fucking body going. But she can't do that. Think of someone else for a change, Alyssum."

Now, *that* made me look up. I'd never heard Aric talk to her that way. They were basically best friends and had always treated each other as such. Alyssum snapped back.

"How dare you?" she countered. "I *am* thinking of her. Not knowing what's in there has to be killing her."

Jensen came forward and cleared his throat. "Has anyone thought to ask Sloane what she wants to do?"

Both Alyssum's and Aric's tense faces turned to me.

What did I want to do? Sleep, for sure, but knowing there was information in that folder meant that I wouldn't rest until I knew what it was.

After wetting my lips quickly, I said, "I won't be able to sleep knowing that folder is there, but not knowing what's inside." I took a breath because that wouldn't be what Aric wanted to hear.

"See?" Alyssum said, but I gave her a scowl. Not

really the time. "We can do that, then she and I can have girl time."

Aric opened his mouth to protest, but I cut him off, speaking to Alyssum. "I'll come to your room so we can go over what's in the folder, mostly because I doubt I'll understand most of it if it has to do with your world, but I'm not staying in your room tonight. I'm staying in Aric's."

He looked at her with narrowed eyes. "See?"

Rolling my eyes, I turned away from them. If they wanted to continue to fight, fine. But we'd left Putnam Valley yesterday and it'd taken almost nineteen hours to get here. I wanted comfortable clothes, something to eat, and a soft surface to sit on.

I would've suggest the library would be a better place to do this, but hunkering down on a bed was more my speed right now.

We all went whatever direction we needed to go to take a quick shower and put on whatever comfortable clothes we wanted to wear.

I went to my bedroom, the one that used to be Jensen's, and did just that. The hot water felt good—refreshing. Then I put on a pair of pajama shorts and one of Aric's shirts that I'd stolen from him in New York.

This was so much to take in all at once and it was

crushing me. Yet I couldn't not know. Inside, I was a bundle of live wire. Full of dread because what if the contents said something bad? Curiosity because I needed to know. It was all just piling on.

When I got to Alyssum's room, she was already there and had gotten us more food than we'd probably eat. There was a tray on the table by her window with sandwiches, chips, fruit, and yogurt, along with the drinks I knew were in the little refrigerator next to it.

A couple of minutes after I'd gotten there, Aric came through the door wearing pajama pants and a fresh T-shirt—which I could attest that he didn't actually sleep in. We were quiet as we grabbed something to eat and after my second bite, Jensen came out of the bathroom in the same kind of pajamas Aric was wearing. I would've bet he didn't sleep in them, either.

"Does this mean we're right back in it?" I asked as we ate.

Alyssum shrugged. "Probably not. I mean the war between the Gobel and Gremalians raged for centuries. I wouldn't think finding your parents would be as dangerous."

"I hope," Jensen added, which somehow reminded me that he was kind of new to this world too. Alyssum had told me that he hadn't known what he was until she'd shown up. He'd had to learn his powers and that had only been a few months ago.

Weird. He seemed so natural at it.

"It'll be all right," Aric assured me. "You have two gremlins and a goblin on your side. What more could you need?"

That gave us all a much-needed laugh.

"Why does it matter, though?" I set the half-eaten sandwich back on my plate. "So what if my mother didn't want to give me up? She still did. What does her being at least involved in witches change any of that?"

Alyssum held up a finger telling me to wait while she continued chewing the last bite she'd taken. It was like she was trying to rush, which we all knew meant it was even harder to get it down.

"I'm new to all this too, Sloane," Jensen assured me. "Most of it still doesn't make any sense. Honestly, it would've been much easier to let these two kill each other when they came to New York the first time."

I snickered. That was absolutely true the more I saw them interact. "I'll just be happy if I don't fall down any deep, dark holes."

Alyssum swallowed then laughed with me. "No kidding. I think I've had my fill."

"I'm sure that will turn into a trauma trigger. Maybe a therapist will make me jump off a ledge to overcome it."

"Over my dead body," Aric offered with more seriousness than the rest of us displayed, though he was still having fun with it. "We'll still need to be careful," he added once the laughter had calmed.

"Yeah," Jensen agreed. "What do you know about witches?"

Aric shook his head. "Not a lot, personally. I mean, I know they're around, but I didn't think we had anything to do with them."

"I know a little bit." Alyssum held up her hands when the guys narrowed their eyes. "Just from reading the books in the library. I know that most of the covens around here believe in the three goddess-es." Before we could ask, she continued. "That's the Maiden, the Mother, and the Crone. It's a flow that cannot be interrupted. They represent the three stages of life, I guess, and they don't actually have to be from the equivalent generation. But that's all that was in there."

We each took a moment with that. On the surface, I didn't understand what it might mean outside of the fact that maybe I wasn't so human after all, but hopefully, the Gobel would tell us more tomorrow.

For a time, I didn't want to be human. Now I wasn't sure I wanted to be whatever this was.

"All right." I swung my legs off the bed and hurried over to the table, where I set my half-eaten sandwich and grabbed the folder. "Let's find out about me now."

When I opened the folder, which was thicker than I'd expected, a piece of paper slid toward Aric.

"This looks like a birth certificate," he said as he handed it to me.

"It is. The one they created for me. Because they didn't know when I was born."

Alyssum furrowed her brows. "You don't know your birthdate?"

I shook my head. "Not officially. It's either this date on here or the day before. Since I was found early in the morning with everything..." I waved my hands over me. "Attached, I could've been an hour old or six hours old, which would put my birthdate the day before."

"Who decided?"

"The case worker assigned to me. She was new, which is why I had the same one the entire time I was in the system. She said she went with when I was found because she figured that was when my life really began. Then she named me Sloane because she said it was her favorite name, but she couldn't have kids, so..."

"There's no mother or father," Jensen observed once it had gotten handed around to him.

I shrugged. "No one knew who they were."

Next were some of my foster care intake, which included a note from my social worker saying someone had tried to intervene in her first place-ment, but that person hadn't had a legal standing. Weird.

Well, this was interesting. The next thing I found was an old, grainy photograph.

"Who's this?" Aric asked gently.

"I don't know." So I flipped it over. On the back was the name of the fire station that I had been left at and the date. *Wait...* "Oh, my god."

"What?" Aric sat up and moved closer.

"I think this picture could be of my mother."

"What?" Alyssum looked over my shoulder.

"Yeah. It has where and when I was found on it." The person in the picture wasn't very big. Probably about my size, actually, which made me think it was a woman. That and her features, like her shoulders weren't very broad, her steps weren't very long. She had a shawl-type thing wrapped around her head, so there was no chance I'd see her face.

Not that I would've been able to, given how low quality it was.

The next photograph was of a piece of fabric with odd markings. I assumed it was only part of something bigger, like a blanket that I'd been found with, though I hadn't had any blanket with me that I could remember.

"Oh, shit," Alyssum said under her breath. "Those on the ends... are a witch's mark." I glanced over to meet her eye. "I read that with certain spells, witches leave their mark so that other witches know who cast it."

With my face scrunched up in confusion, I asked, "What about the rest of the markings?"

"I think they're runes, but I've only seen draw-ings, so I can't be sure."

We hurried through the rest because the whole thing was so odd. I hadn't known about the supernat-ural world other than the fact that I believed in ghosts. Wait... if my mom was a witch, would that mean I could see ghosts? My brain spiraled from there.

There was the fireman's written account from

when he'd found me. He said he opened the box while the woman had still been there—which we knew he lied about—but he described that night and noted how desperate the young mother had seemed. She'd been scared, he'd said. Almost like she'd been running from something.

After that, I sat back because I needed a moment, but I told them they could go through the newspaper clippings that were in there. The headline of the first one indicated some local teens had been playing witch in the area by carving symbols into trees and leaving markings in the area that scared people. It reminded me of the documentary I'd watched about clowns showing up in different places and chasing people with knives.

But maybe it hadn't been teens playing.

Whatever had happened, this information was a start.

For tonight, I was done.

Aric pulled me toward him as he guided us back to his room. I held the large envelope Alyssum had given me to put everything into tightly against my chest. The envelope made more sense so that the papers didn't fall out since we were going to be traveling with it.

"Tired?" he asked once he'd shut the door behind

us, barring the world from our little alcove of the house.

"Bone tired. I never knew what that meant before." Climbing onto his bed, I snuggled down under the blanket before he even got to the other side. "Now I do."

"Yeah. It's been a long couple of days."

I nodded, too tired to answer. If I had any energy left inside of me, I'd have a completely different conversation, but tonight... sleep was going to have to be enough.

Aric threaded his hand into my hair to pull my mouth to his so he could kiss me. The feel of him there, so close, was almost enough to make me forget being tired, but in the end, biology won out.

I'd barely slept in the car on the way here and now, I needed it.

In the morning, we had a huge breakfast made for us by the cook—who normally only handled dinner when I'd been eating at off times and even then it was usually just a sandwich or something quick. But she made an entire breakfast bar that was hot and waiting for us when we got down there.

Pancakes had never tasted so good.

Then we headed out to Phoenix. Ash let Alyssum know that there would be people to unload the trailer of Aric's and Jensen's things from New York. We'd labeled the boxes so they'd make sure they got in the right place. And the motorcycle would be waiting for Jensen in the garage.

Phoenix was quite similar to Delaware. They weren't far apart, so that made sense. It was another abandoned mine town, Aric told me. One huge difference was the greenery and vegetation. It was lush and beautiful. Almost like stepping into a secret garden. When we got out of the car, that constant hum of electricity wasn't there.

"How do you keep the humans away if not electricity?" I asked once we were out of the SUV.

"The thick brush," he told me as he threaded my fingers through his. "We have areas that would be pretty inaccessible to humans. You probably wouldn't have made it through, yet you made it to Delaware." A smile played on his lips, which meant that he was messing with Alyssum. She knew it too because she grunted.

As we approached a house, he pointed to it and said, "This is my parents' house."

"Where you grew up?" I asked. He nodded. Looking up at it, I saw a large house that wasn't anything like Alyssum's. On the outside, hers looked less like a home and more like an institution, which made sense. His looked like a home. There were a lot of windows to indicate a lot of rooms and it was farther out than where I'd been in Phoenix before. "It's looks big."

He shrugged. "Lots of kids." Then he pushed through the door and headed toward the noise we heard coming from the back.

Aric had five brothers and five sisters and some of them were responsible for how I'd found Alyssum in the woods that day. To say that put me on edge was an understatement. I held on to his hand even tighter since we were now inside.

My mouth watered a little too much, either from the smell of whatever someone was cooking or from the fear welling up in my chest. Hopefully, it was the food, even though I wasn't hungry at all.

We walked into a large, white kitchen, where a tall woman with dark hair that had strands of white mixed in was taking a pan out of the oven. A large man with dark hair sat at the table.

"Hey," he said, causing them both to look up.

They were definitely Aric's parents. He was a mix of the two. Neither seemed to notice when we'd come in, but with so many kids, maybe they were used to people coming and going.

"Aric," his mom said with a smile not only on her

face, but in her voice. She hurried over to hug him, but he didn't let go of my hand, most likely from the death grip I had on it.

"It's good to see you." His father reached out and shook his hand.

"This is Sloane," he said, looking down at me.

They both said it was nice to meet me, but their gazes seemed more stuck on our hands. Once his mom had snapped out of that, she asked us to sit and greeted Alyssum and Jensen. I didn't know if they'd actually met already, but they for sure knew who everyone was.

"So what brings you all here?" his mom asked.

Aric held a hand out so that I could give him my envelope. One I had, he slid it on the table.

"This."

"What is this?" his dad asked.

"It's information about Sloane." After giving them a quick recap on the fact that I had always thought I was human and how I'd gotten up here, along with the way I'd helped save Alyssum, he added, "Ash Bracken thinks there's more to it and he told me to ask my people since we've been known to consort with witches." His parents quickly looked at each other then held a silent conversation. "Do we? Do we consort with witches?"

His dad gave his mom a severe warning look, but she shook her head. "I haven't heard anything about anything involving witches in twenty years."

"I'm twenty," I offered. Which, of course, Aric had already known.

"What did you hear?"

Mr. Bramble was still going through the information while Mrs. Bramble spoke to us. "Not much, honestly. Just that there was some kind of problem that the witches needed to fix, but we didn't participate in that. We just heard about it."

"How?" Alyssum asked. "How did you hear about it? My father said the Gobel *consort* with witches. What did he mean?"

Mrs. Bramble sighed. "We don't *consort* with witches, but one of us married a half-witch."

"One of *us*?" Aric practically yelped and I could see him going through all of his siblings trying to figure out who could be the one.

"A Gobel. Not one of our family." She wet her lips quickly then shifted. "You'd have to talk to Flora Dagney, but I don't know if she'll talk to you about this."

Aric looked over to the three of us. "Flora is Mom's best friend."

"I can ask her for you," his mom continued. "She won't be back until the morning, though."

"That's fine," he said. "We can stay here."

But tomorrow, I was likely going to meet a half-witch to figure out what the hell this all meant.

Until then... what?

I wasn't sure I knew how to act if we weren't fighting something anymore.

Chapter Seventeen

With almost the entire day to wait, Aric suggested that he show us all around Phoenix. It wasn't a big city by any means, but there were a lot of places and things to see. He thought it'd make us all more comfortable.

It was going to take a while before the Gobel and Gremalians were all friends the way Aric and Alyssum were and then there was me. A person we all thought was human, but maybe wasn't? Or was and was part of a witch's plot? No one knew what to make of me anymore, including myself and nothing strange had happened to make me think I had some kind of magical powers.

We walked around Phoenix since Aric said there was no reason to drive. It'd take more effort doing that, anyway. He showed us places that he'd played when he'd been little. Where his brother Dune had broken his nose the first time. Apparently, it had happened more than once. The way Jensen snorted, I didn't think that there was any love lost there and the fact that Dune wasn't one of the brothers that I'd actually met definitely said something.

"I'm hungry," Alyssum said, sounding slightly whiny, but I was glad that she had. My maybe-human stomach head been warning me for an hour.

"Let's go eat. We only have one restaurant that you can go to, but the food's good." Aric led up the way.

Once we were inside... every person in the place noticed. "Everyone's staring," I said, gripping his hand tighter.

Aric glanced around but didn't look bothered by what he found. "They're not staring at you. It's them." He pointed quickly at Alyssum and Jensen.

Yeah. Most of the people here grew up hating the Gremalians. Now, they were allies, if not friends. It was going to take time and I was seriously proud of Alyssum and Jensen for coming here as if it were no big deal. For Jensen, it probably wasn't. He hadn't grown up hating the Gobel the way Alyssum had.

Aric was right. The food was delicious and Aric insisted on paying for me. Then we were on our way.

Overall, it was a good day of waiting for a goblin who knew a witch to get back so that we could talk to her.

Life had taken such a weird turn.

As the sun set, we were all still dealing with what'd we'd recently been through and I wasn't sure about them, but a few hours of being a vegetable before bed sounded good. When I said as much, they agreed.

Aric got Alyssum and Jensen set up in the bedroom next to the one he told me had been his when he'd lived here. Then we went to his room.

There wasn't any sign that he'd lived in this room once. As I was sure many parents changed the room once their kid moved out. We'd each brought a bag of clothes with us and they were in the room—how, I wasn't sure—in case we needed them. At this point, we never knew what was next.

"Do you want a drink?" he asked as I stood there, taking in his space.

"That'd be great. We can just relax for a while, right? Before whatever happens tomorrow?"

Aric came close to me, cupping each side of my cheek as he brushed his thumbs across my skin in such a soothing manner. "Sounds perfect to me." Then he kissed me, lingering for longer than I'd thought he would before he said, "I'll be right back."

I planned to change into my pajamas. It was shorts and a T-shirt, but it was comfortable. When he didn't come back for too long, I went to look for him. Kind of freaked me out. It was clear that his mom and dad weren't exactly happy that two Gremalians and a maybe-human were whom he chose to spend time with, but I did it, anyway.

"I know you're grown." His mother's voice made me stop right where I was. Close enough to the kitchen to hear them, but not close enough for them to see me standing here.

"She's staying in my room with me, Mom."

"It's my house, Aric."

He sighed. "It is. And if you really want to stick to that, we can go back to Delaware and come here in the morning, but I'm not leaving that woman on her own here. Besides, I want her with me."

There was a moment of silence where I could feel the tension all the way out here.

"Do you love her?" she asked.

Aric snorted. "I can't tell you that, Mom when I haven't even told her that. So, what's it going to be?"

My heart thudded against my chest. Now *that*, they were going to hear.

Did he love me? Was that what he had just said to his mother?

"Fine." The sound of the word came out in a way that I knew she'd spoken through clenched teeth and wasn't that happy about it.

His heavy footfalls moved, so I ran on tiptoes back to his room and jumped onto the bed, sitting just as he opened the door.

After handing me the water, he changed into pajama pants and a T-shirt, though this wasn't how he'd sleep, then got comfortable on the bed beside me. I turned so that I was facing him.

"How are you handling all of this?" He took a long drink of his water.

I swallowed hard. That wasn't exactly what I had wanted to talk about, but we'd get to it. "I'm... OK?" Yeah. It had come out as a question. "I don't know. Physically, I'm fine. All the aches and pains are gone." There I went downplaying how hurt I had actually been. It'd taken me weeks to be able to move without some kind of pain, though I had faked it well enough.

There was only one small light on and we didn't need more. This made it feel like we were in our own little space and no one else was going to breach it.

His eyes darkened when I mentioned my aches and pains. "Are you worried? About what we're going to find?"

Was I? I wasn't sure. But right now... "No," I told him. "I'm not worried because there's not going to be anything to find. I don't think. I'm not anything special. I'm just..." I waved my hand over my body. "Human. Utterly human." After wetting my lips, I said, "I hope that's enough for you." Maybe this was denial but I felt the same as I always had. Maybe my mother was a witch or something but that didn't mean I was.

Aric pushed up so that he could reach out and cup my face. I couldn't help the way I leaned into his touch. "Of course it is. I've thought you were human until this point and it hasn't mattered at all."

"I overheard you talking to your mom." My eyes widened. That was not what I'd meant to say. "I'm sorry. I shouldn't have told you."

"I'm fine with you listening, but you could've come into the kitchen."

I shook my head. "No way was I doing that, but she asked you if you love me," I said quietly.

"Did you hear what I said?"

Taking a deep breath, I blew it out slowly, hoping to calm my racing heart and slow down how clammy my hands were getting. "I did. You said you couldn't tell her when you haven't told me. You don't have to tell me. This isn't me pressuring you. But..." I'd never told a man this in my life, but there was a first time for everything. "I love you, Aric. If that makes a difference."

"Sloane, I've loved you since... Fuck, since maybe that first day in the training room. I haven't told you because I didn't want to scare you off."

I snorted and acted like that was ridiculous, but it wasn't and I knew it. "It wouldn't scare me off," I told him. "I've created elixirs with copper that magically heal all of you. I've been thrown in a deep ravine, not once, but twice and I doubt Alyssum's best friend is going to like me much by just showing up here and suddenly being ingrained in everything you do. Groups of three girls rarely works out and Alyssum said she doesn't even want to meet me. If those things didn't scare me off, nothing will."

Again, his eyes darkened as he pulled me down to him. He lay out flat and tucked me into his side. "Well, I love you."

Snickering, I told him, "I love you."

We spent some time talking about what we

thought was going to happen if we got to talk to Flora tomorrow. With each turn we took, Aric assured me that he'd make sure I wasn't thrown into another ravine. At this rate, I'd probably need some exposure therapy because I hadn't been afraid of heights before, but now... that might not be the case.

"It's your fault that Dahlia doesn't want to meet me, isn't it?" I asked as I ran a hand over his chest.

"Yeah." He sighed. "Probably."

"Are you a manwhore?" I asked him, meaning for it to be playful.

"I'd like to say *no*, but I think others would disagree." He took a moment to trail his fingers up my arm then back down. "Does that bother you?"

I shook my head. "Not unless you continue to be one."

"Not a chance."

There were conversations that I'd never had with anyone before. "So if you're a manwhore, why haven't you wanted to be with me?"

The fingers that were trailing almost absently up my arm stopped. "I've wanted to," he said quietly with an edge of hunger. "Since I saw you walking behind me."

So the moment he'd seen me? A shiver ran through my body.

"Then why haven't—"

"Do I need to remind you that you've been hurt? A lot?"

"No."

"I didn't want to hurt you more."

Once I could gather all the nerve I had, I climbed up and straddled him. His erection pushed against my sensitive area. I had no idea how I'd made myself do that, but I had.

"I'm not hurt now."

His dark eyes burned a path over me. I thought he'd say he still wanted to wait, but he didn't. Instead, he sat up, roughly thrust his fingers into my hair, and rolled us over at the same time so that he was on top of me.

A little yelp of surprise came out and I hoped no one else in the house heard it.

Aric's mouth covered mine as his body pressed down on me.

His hands traveled down my sides as his tongue pushed into my mouth. He was kissing me in a way he hadn't yet. He'd kissed me hungrily before, and sweetly before, but all of those, I'd known were going to come to an end. This one... promised to go on forever.

When he lifted off me, I was going to protest

until he yanked my shirt over my head, then he reached back and did the same to himself. We were skin to skin and his touch left a burning mark on mine.

He cupped my breasts, then kissed down the side of my neck before taking a nipple into his mouth. There was an urgency to it, yet the way he handled me said he didn't care if this took forever.

Aric's touch was addictive. The moment his hand left any area, I wanted it right back. Warmth flooded my body as if someone had turned the hot water on and I could feel myself get wet.

He kissed down my stomach, leaving a scorching path like breadcrumbs that could easily be followed back up. As he moved, he pushed my shorts and panties off me, leaving me exposed to him, but this wasn't the first time. He'd seen me naked before under far worse circumstances.

Yet he was still here, handling me as if he'd never seen an ugly thing about me.

His strong hands pushed my legs apart, then he licked me. It was almost too much and not enough all at the same time. I groaned and willed myself not to leap right off that bed.

Aric and I hadn't talked about our pasts. Not this part of it, though I knew enough about his. He wouldn't know that no one had ever done this to me.

All of these new feelings and emotions washed over me, most of which I wouldn't be able to make sense of for a while.

Then he licked me again and I arched my back while pushing my fingers into his hair. I had no idea what I was doing, so I decided to just go with it. Go with what he was doing, as long as it felt good.

Aric wouldn't hurt me. In this case, he wouldn't hurt me any more than what was going to happen naturally—or so I'd been told.

Reaching his hands up, he cupped my breasts while his face was buried between my legs. I let every delicious feeling take me over. Soon, the pressure built. This, I was familiar with because I'd given myself this feeling. The pressure was frustrating, telling me there was an inevitable ending and if I just lay there letting it happen, it promised to be a good ending.

The pleasure plateaued, making me want to pull his hair in frustration, but then pleasure crashed into me like a dense wave trying to push me out to sea.

Forget what I'd thought earlier. I wasn't familiar with this at all.

The waves kept crashing, one after another, until

the next was weaker than the last and I was let on the metaphorical beach boneless, heart racing, and breath coming so quickly that I should've been embarrassed.

There wasn't a chance in hell that I would be.

Aric moved back and wiped a hand across his face before slowly climbing back up. He kissed my collarbone, my neck, and then my lips. It took everything I had to even lift an arm to cup his cheek as he did.

Then he reached over to pull a condom out of the drawer on the bedside table. Leaning back on his heels, he ripped the thing open and this was my first chance to actually see him. When had he taken his bottoms off? No idea. Probably while I'd been lost in the euphoria of what he'd done to me.

But Aric was... something to see. His cock was longer than I'd expected—though I hadn't seen an erect one in person—but not so long that I worried it wouldn't fit, the way you sometimes read in romance novels. It would fit because it was supposed to.

He was thick but did not handle himself with care as he rolled the condom down his length. I supposed those things were sturdier than was normally suggested.

Then he was back over me, kissing me, touching

me, working me up again before he pushed inside me with one hard move that took my breath away. His brows were furrowed when I caught my breath and opened my eyes.

But he didn't say anything. Instead, he worked himself in and out of my body, making sounds come from me that I wouldn't have been able to stop if I'd wanted to, but I didn't want to.

I dug my short nails into his back to hold on for the ride of my life.

He'd been right to wait until I was fully healed because if we had done this while a single muscle had still been aching, I didn't know that I would've recovered.

Aric was everything that I'd wished for and he loved me.

Again, his mouth covered mine as he made a noise in the back of his throat, slammed into me harder, then came to a stop. He dropped his forehead against mine, his breath feathering against my skin.

"Wow," he said, sounding like he'd just run a marathon. "I love you so much, Sloane."

I cupped both sides of his face and kissed him softly. "I love you." And I didn't care how breathy it came out due to his entire weight lying against me. I didn't want him to move.

But then he did. He rolled off and laid a hand against his stomach.

For a first time, that was better than I'd hoped for. Better than I would've gotten had I not waited. And there was so much more we could do, so much I could learn to make him feel good, but this... had been perfect.

Aric asked if I wanted to use the bathroom to clean up first, but I told him to go ahead. At that moment, I wanted to savor the feeling of what we'd just done and not return to normal things right away. Oh, and my legs were vibrating, so I wasn't totally sure I could walk.

Once he was done, I went into the bathroom myself. Turned out, my legs did work. After cleaning up, I looked at myself in the mirror, not expecting to see anything different. I was still me, but my skin was flushed and there was absolute satisfaction on my face.

Shaking my head at myself for thinking it, I washed my hands then opened the door and turned off the light.

In the bedroom, Aric was on the bed with his boxer briefs on, waiting for me. I was still naked, so I grabbed my pajama shirt and pulled it over me then did the same with my panties. I didn't need the shorts if I wasn't leaving the room. Then I crawled up on the bed and snuggled down against his side as he wrapped an arm around me.

After getting himself under the blanket, he pulled me closer.

"That was your first time." It wasn't a question that he was asking. It was more of an observation. I nodded slowly. "Why didn't you tell me that, Sloane?"

I shrugged, but he waited me out, clearly wanting me to verbalize it. "Because it didn't matter."

"'Didn't matter'?" He chuckled. "I could've hurt you. I would've gone slower."

"It was going to hurt, anyway, and I'm incredibly happy with how you did it. Like ripping off a Band-Aid. Get it over with."

He sighed and kissed the top of my head. "Next time, tell me important things."

Again, I nodded, but there wasn't anything else I wanted to say, so I let the night take me.

In the morning, we dressed and headed to the kitchen, as that seemed to be where everything happened. There were other rooms, but Aric knew his parents would be in there.

"So?" he asked as soon as we got in there without bothering to sit down.

"Sit down and eat something." His mom waved her hand to the table that was covered with breakfast options. I was starving and Alyssum must've read my mind because we both hurried to the table at the same time.

Aric and Jensen followed us slowly.

Once we'd gotten started, he asked again. We should've heard from Flora by now, right? Everyone wanted to get this started.

"I've heard from her." Mrs. Bramble sat at the table with us, but she only sipped at her coffee. "She wants me to explain first."

"Explain what?"

Jesus, Mrs. Bramble could bake a cinnamon roll. It melted in my mouth and took over. Alyssum nudged my foot to make sure I was still paying atten-tion then grinned.

"Flora is half-witch and most people don't know. Most around here, Gremalians included, don't really take kindly to witches."

"Why not?" Alyssum asked. "Seems like it'd be helpful to have them on your side."

"That's why." She took another drink. "Witches are

on the side of witches. Sure, you can get them to help, but it costs you and they will always be the ones to come out on top. Flora isn't like that because she's committed to the Gobel, but it's why she keeps it secret."

"But she'll see us?"

Mrs. Bramble nodded. "She'll see you. Doesn't think she can help, but she'll see you."

My mind immediately went to the cloth that had had the runes on it. If there was a mark saying which witch or coven had cast the spell, maybe she'd know. Or know someone else who would.

It was all we could hope for.

"I told her that you have some questions and she's happy to do what she can."

Now we were off to meet a part witch, part goblin who might have information on my mother.

Chapter Eighteen

Flora Dagny was the key. Or the path to finding the key. I didn't freaking know.

All of this was new to me, so I was going along with whatever Alyssum, Jensen, and Aric said because what else could I do?

Having to face his parents after what we'd done last night was so weird for me, but only because I'd never had to do it before. But I was glad when we left their house to go to Flora's. Again, we walked because Aric said driving in Phoenix was usually more trouble than it was worth.

Fine by me. It wouldn't be long before summer wasn't in Michigan anymore and I would be wishing I'd spent more time outside.

We approached a white house similar to Aric's.

When the door opened, a tall, thin woman with short, brown hair stood before us.

"Aric," she said with a smile. "Haven't seen you in a while."

"How are you, Mrs. Dagny?"

"As good as anyone. Come in." She waved her hand at us as she walked away. Aric led the way. "You know if someone had told any of us that we'd have Gremalians in our houses even a few months ago, we would've called them crazy."

Aric chuckled. "I know." Then he introduced each of us as she motioned for us to take a seat at the table. Alyssum and Jensen sat on one side while Aric and I were on the other. Both Aric and Jensen put themselves in the seat closest to her. "My mom told you what we're looking for?"

"She did." Flora asked if any of us wanted a drink, but we declined. We just wanted what she knew. "She called me. Not many people know that my mother was a witch. My father liked to keep that information quiet."

"So do you have witch powers?" Alyssum asked.

Flora shook her head. "I don't. Once the witch blood got diluted, the natural powers went with it. I supposed I could learn spells and everything, but my mother never wanted that for me and they wouldn't be very powerful, given my father."

She meant since her father was a Gobel.

"How do you feel about that?" Aric asked her.

Flora sighed but was quiet for a moment before saying, "I don't actually have a strong feeling one way or the other. My mother didn't want me involved in any of that. Which means that to me, it doesn't feel like I've lost something."

"Which means you don't miss it."

"Right."

"Well, this is what we have." Aric took the envelope from me and slid it toward her.

The room was quiet as she slowly went over the limited amount of information that we had with us. She took her time and hope bloomed inside me at the idea that there might be more there than we could see.

"This is definitely the mark of a witch," she said. "I can't tell you what witch or even which coven. I just remember seeing some things when I'd visit my grandma in the summer."

"Your grandma?" I asked. She'd said her mother hadn't wanted her to have anything to do with the witches, so that had made me assume that her mother hadn't as well. But her grandmother still having witch artifacts when she'd gone to see her was intriguing.

Flora nodded. "She lives on Mackinac Island. She was fully schooled in the craft and her powers, but..." She swallowed hard. "She's no longer part of any coven."

"Would your grandmother see us?" Aric asked.

"I don't know. But I can ask her."

There was nothing left for us to do but wait.

On the way back to Aric's house, Alyssum rushed forward and threaded her arm through mine. "We need some girl time," she declared. "Let's go for a walk."

Aric furrowed his brows. "You can't walk through Phoenix by yourselves."

"We can, but I was thinking we'd take a walk in the woods."

"Not without us," Jensen said, suddenly closer than he had been. "Alyssum, that's just not smart."

She scowled. "Fine. Then let's go back to Aric's, where Sloane and I can sit in the back yard and have some girl talk like proper Southern women."

I raised an eyebrow. "Drinking sweet tea."

She winced. "How about lemonade?"

Snickering, I agreed, so when we got to Aric's

house, that was where we headed. The guys just had to find something else to do.

Once we were settled in the back yard, in the shade, with our glasses of lemonade, she stretched and let out a sigh. The guys were out there, but across the yard, which was huge, so unless we started yelling, they wouldn't hear us.

"I love the guys, but sometimes, it's nice to be just us," Alyssum said before sipping her lemonade. "So." She set it on the table between us. "The last time we talked about you and Aric, you finally admitted you were together."

I snickered. She was right. "I think you knew that's not the case."

"Maybe by the fact that you stayed with him at his apartment in New York?" she asked. I nodded. "Or that you're staying with him here? But you didn't tell me and I think I have to be offended by that." A smile tugged at the corners of her mouth.

Alyssum was either messing with me or trying to distract me. Either way, she was being a friend. "Oh, please, Alyssum." I folded my hands and dropped to my knees like I was begging. "Please forgive me for not updating you on my relationship with your best friend sooner."

"OK, OK." She slapped at me until I got up off

the ground and sat back in my chair. "I'm just messing with you." She tapped my leg with her foot. "You don't *have* to tell me things, but I like you two together. He watches you so intensely."

I glanced over my shoulder to find Aric doing just that then turned back to her. "I think he's waiting for me to crack. Like all this stuff is going to make me crumble."

She snorted. "He obviously didn't see you in the woods the day we met."

"Hey," Aric said, suddenly closer. "Flora just called. Her grandmother will see us."

My heart felt like a stone ping-ponging its way through my chest. Each step closer to finding out what any of that evidence Ash had given us was a step closer to possibly finding out who my mother had been. Something I hadn't even thought I'd wanted until the possibility had presented itself.

"Her grandmother isn't sure she can help us but is willing to try," he added.

"So we're leaving?" I created a visor with my hand to block the sun so that I could see him.

"We're leaving. Want to go tonight so we can see her first thing?"

I nodded then pushed to my feet. "I'll go make sure everything is in my bag."

There was no reason to freak out. Not yet. Something a witch told us could change all of that. The weirdest thing to me was that even Alyssum and Aric, who'd grown up knowing about supernatural creatures, had very little knowledge about witches. Yet they didn't seem all that worried about going to see one.

I'd have to trust them.

It took six hours to get to Mackinaw City, where we debated whether we'd go to the island tonight or wait until the morning. I voted to go in the morning because it was expensive to stay on the island and if we went now, we'd only have a couple of hours before we had to get back on the ferry.

Since it was last minute, the four of us had to stay in the same room. Two beds at least, but it was a little crowded. Luckily, none of us cared. We sat out on the beach to enjoy the sunset and got a decent night's sleep.

Or they did. I'd been awake staring at the ceiling a lot of it, given that whatever this stranger told us the next day could change my entire life.

The lake was beautiful in the morning, but we didn't have time to enjoy it. We grabbed something to eat quickly and headed over to the ferry. The ride didn't take too long and then we were hit directly in the face with the smell of manure.

"You'll get used to it," Aric promised. "You won't even notice it in a few minutes."

I desperately wanted him to be right.

"And we'll get fudge before we leave," Alyssum assured me, as if that were a given I'd been thinking about.

I was from Michigan. Yes, I knew that Mackinac Island was famous for their fudge, but I hadn't given it a thought.

Mackinac Island was flat on Main Street and luckily, we were walking on the outside of the island, so we wouldn't have to climb the massive hill that would make my little maybe-human legs fall off. We just followed Aric to the address that Flora had given him.

Everything on this island was beautiful and when I looked out over the blue, sparkling water, it was almost easy to forget why we were here. Too soon, we'd arrived.

Aric knocked without hesitating, but I wanted to run and throw myself into the water. My skin was hot—*too* hot—and there was a stabbing in my shoulder. It all had to be anxiety over what this woman was going to say.

Flora's grandmother came to the door and took in each one of us. She was small, a waif of a woman, really. She had silver hair with glimpses of black peeking out and while her face was wrinkled by time, there was a youthful glow to her. As if time had marched over her skin, but not her eyes. I wasn't sure how to explain it.

"I've been expecting you. Why don't you all have a seat at the table out here while I get us some refreshments?"

Her porch was large and there was a table on one side with enough chairs for the five of us. But it made me wonder if she just didn't want us in her house.

She came out with a pitcher of water and some cookies, but I wasn't going to be able to eat. She sat in the chair across from me. "We're here for you." It wasn't a question. "You're the one my Flora told me about."

"I am," I told her quietly, then I introduced all of us.

"Well, I have to say that I'm quite uneasy sitting across from you." She leaned in a little. "That's a first."

"Uneasy about me? Why?"

"You carry a curse," she said matter-of-factly, like

I already had this information. "I can smell it on you."

I leaned my head over to take a whiff but didn't smell anything.

"What does that mean?" Aric demanded. "A curse?"

She nodded then held out her hand. "You have something for me to look at?" Right. The envelope.

After giving that to her, I sat back, draining half the glass of water to soothe my suddenly parched mouth.

"Are you the only witch on the island?" Alyssum asked, causing Flora's Grandmother—who had not given us her name—to look up.

"Yes," she said. "Only one keeper needs to be here. Only one keeper is *allowed* to be here."

Aric narrowed his eyes. "'Keeper'?"

Flora's grandmother sat back. "Yes, keeper. I assume you haven't been told anything about this place?" Aric shook his head. "I'm a keeper. I live here—on the island—to protect the drowning pool and the souls it contains."

"'Drowning pool'?" Jensen pushed.

"A long time ago, there were witch trials on this island, not unlike in Salem. However, here the souls lingered and it was decided that a witch would need to live close to protect the souls of the dead witches."

"I didn't think witch trials killed actual witches."

She shook her head. "That's what they want people to think, but I assure you, some witches died and it's my sworn duty to protect the souls at the drowning pool." She turned her attention back to me. "Where is your sigil?"

"My what?" I asked her.

"Witch's mark."

"I don't have one."

"You must have one. It's part of the curse." She came over to me and began pulling at my T-shirt. Aric grabbed her hand to stop her, but she said, "See? There." She was pointing at my shoulder.

When I looked down, there was a thin, golden line just under my right collarbone. Then she ran her hand over it and more lines appeared. "That's the sigil—the witch's mark. Left by the witch who cast the curse."

She leaned over the table to bring the evidence Ash had found back to us.

"A sigil will only appear when witches are near. Most think of it as a warning sign, but it's a GPS for witches, to put it into terms you kids are more likely understand."

"I'm confused," I told her. "Why would a witch put a curse on me? *When* did a witch put a curse on me?"

"Just after you were born. Within moments." She moved through the papers until she found the picture of the cloth with the runes on it. "These runes were what cast this curse on you. Unfortunately for them, when you cast a curse, your signature is on it. Easily identifiable. But finding the witch will do no good. With a curse, there's a built-in way to break it. You just have to figure out what that is."

I furrowed my brows in confusion. "Could it be anything? How would I know how to break it?"

She thought that over then snapped her fingers. "This makes sense. Years ago, I heard about a curse that had been cast. It was maybe twenty years ago. The curse was cast to keep sisters apart. The triad. Now, I didn't give it much thought because my job was to protect the pool."

"What's the triad?" I asked her.

"The three goddesses. The mother, the maiden, and the crone. Three sisters."

My hand vibrated as I wiped them down my legs. "I don't have any sisters."

"Of course you do. Your kind are always born in threes."

"My kind?" Adrenaline shot through my body and it felt like someone was holding a pillow over my face making it hard to breathe. I could have sisters? Siblings? Born in three. If I was one of them, then I'd have siblings. What the hell was my kind.

Before my panic could get too off the rails, Aric placed a hand on my back and rubbed in soothing circles.

"Gorgons. They are only born in three if they are the triad. Restore the triad, break the curse." She took a breath and nibbled on the corner of her mouth before adding, "Though I'd be concerned as to why the spell was cast in the first place and what you'd be undoing, but I can't tell you that."

"So you're saying I'm one of those goddesses?"

"You are the maiden. You represent youth, fertility, and curiosity. Together... the Gorgon Goddesses would be quite powerful."

Aric's eyebrows shot up. "The what now? Gorgon?"

"I'm a triplet?"

"You are," she answered. "And a Gorgon is a fierce creature. In modern tellings, she's represented with snakes for hair and the ability to turn others into stone."

"Medusa?" I yelled as I hopped to my feet. "You're telling me I'm Medusa?"

"I'm not telling you *that*," she snapped. "Much like modern tellings depicting them as gremlins and him as a goblin, they depict you as Medusa. That doesn't mean that's what you are."

She turned quickly and stared out at the water. "Now, You must go. I've told you what I can and the pool is calling."

Flora's grandmother went into the house so quickly, there wasn't time for a follow-up question.

My head buzzed with the information Flora's grandmother had given us.

A Gorgon? The triad? I didn't even fully understand what any of this was.

I was a human. None of this could be real. Every step we took on the worn cement leading away from her house felt heavier as all of this new information sat heavily on my mind.

Alyssum kept glancing at me out of the corner of her eye, clearly wanting to say something, but she didn't. She'd probably wait until we were in the car on the way back to Delaware. The silence from the three of them was unnerving. Usually, they said what they were thinking.

Aric walked beside me, his hand brushing mine

with every movement. He was giving me space. They were all giving me space, but I wasn't sure I wanted it.

"Are you OK?" Aric finally asked, his voice low.

I opened my mouth to answer, but there were no words.

How was I supposed to vocalize that I didn't know if I was OK? I didn't know if I even wanted any more information. Then I rubbed the spot where the sigil should've been, but it had disappeared.

"It's gone," I told the three of them as I pulled my shirt back as proof.

Alyssum touched my skin as if she thought it would appear. "Maybe it only shows itself when witches are near."

"That could be handy," Jensen said and I could see his point. If we knew that witches were nearby before we could see them, it would help us because I was fairly certain this wouldn't be the last witch we encountered.

In the span of a late morning, I had gone from knowing nothing about my birth family to being told that I was part of some ancient mystical sisterhood and that I was a Gorgon. What that was I was still unclear about.

I closed my eyes and pulled in a deep breath through my nose.

Alyssum broke the silence before I could even attempt to respond. "Hey. Maybe you're really a Gorgon princess. You'll rule over all the other Gorgons." She tried to keep her tone light to make me feel better, but I wasn't sure I felt bad.

Right now, I just kind of felt... nothing.

"Yeah, but why?" Alyssum asked, but I didn't think it was to any one person. "Why curse them in the first place? What could three newborns do?"

"Maybe it's not what the newborns could do," Jensen offered. "But what the newborns would *become*."

Aric stopped walking and turned to face me, placing his hands gently on my shoulders. His touch, usually so steadying, only made the turmoil in my stomach worse. "We'll find out. Together," he promised, his eyes locking on to mine. "We'll find your sisters. We'll break this curse."

We just had to find someone who would know what to do next.

Chapter Nineteen

We didn't wait until the next day to leave Mackinaw. There was plenty of day left, so we could still get back to Delaware before sundown to figure out what was going on. Technically, I thought we should go back to Phoenix, but Aric and Alyssum thought that the Gremalians would have more information buried in their library than the Gobel would.

Aric had never heard of Gorgons before, either. But if we didn't find anything in Alyssum's library, we'd go to the Gobel. Hell, maybe we'd do both.

Jensen drove as Alyssum did whatever research she could online, but she didn't find much.

It was both the longest and shortest six hours of my life.

Aric, Jensen, and I headed directly to the library

while Alyssum went to update her father on what we'd found. She wasn't gone long and then was right there with us.

"I have no idea what I'm looking for," I whined as I shut the second book.

"Anything about witches or Gorgon," Aric told me.

The door to the library opened and Fern stepped in. I was suddenly hit with missing the days she and I had spent together.

"I brought you all some food." She carried a tray that had to weigh half of her. The woman was small. She set it down on the only surface that didn't have books piled on it. This dinner wasn't sandwiches, which had been our normal go-to when we needed something quickly. "Your dad asked me to bring it up."

"Thank you," Alyssum told her before abandoning the book she was looking through. This was a hot meal and none of us were going to pass it up.

Aric cleared off the table he was working at since it was the only one with four chairs and big enough for all of us to eat. Fern stayed nearby while we got settled.

Then she said, "Your dad asked me to bring it

because I told him about something I heard your mother talking about long ago."

Alyssum stopped eating the roast beef and turned to her. I, however, kept eating because until I'd smelled this delicious meal, I hadn't realized how hungry I was.

"What'd you hear, Fern? Was it about the witches?"

She nodded, but the way she did it told me the real answer was sort of yes and sort of no. "I'll tell you as long as you keep eating. You can't do all of this and heal if necessary if you're malnourished."

Alyssum sighed but picked the fork back up.

"This was just after your father took over as leader," she began, which meant it was just after Jensen's biological parents had died. "Your mother was organizing, touching base with the elder parts of our generation to make sure there were records of everything that needed to be recorded."

Alyssum nodded. "She did love to have her accurate records." That might've been the first time that she'd talked about her mom around me without any sadness.

"She did. Well, there was one elder—long gone now," Fern added, my guess was because she saw hope flash in one of our eyes. "It was about twenty years ago now." Twenty years seemed to be the magical number to mean it was about me. I was twenty. Even if it had been twenty-one years ago, that would make sense, given gestation.

"What'd the elder hear?" Aric asked before dipping his roast into the mashed potatoes.

"She'd heard about a coven who had to dissipate a great power that was coming." She looked off to the side like she was running through her memories. "Or had just come. I can't remember that detail. It was the first time I'd heard of Gorgons."

My stomach tightened and the food on my plate was no longer appetizing. I swallowed hard.

"Your mother and I were there," Fern continued. "I used to always go with her, but anyway, we were told that Gorgons were deemed too powerful by this coven, especially because of the three goddesses. Now the elder didn't know what the three goddesses were."

"We do," I muttered. Apparently, I was the maiden. I guess that was better than being called a "crone."

"To dissipate that power, they had to use a curse."

Alyssum nodded, glanced to me, then said, "That's what Flora's grandmother told us."

"Why didn't she tell us her name?" I asked, hoping Fern would be able to answer that.

"The older witches are very careful with their names because it's a way to find them."

"But we already know where she lives."

Fern shrugged. "I can't make sense of witch logic."

"Do you know anything else about the Gorgons?" I asked. Other than supposedly, I'm super powerful, when in reality, a little rumbly ground had almost taken me out twice.

"I do. But it's all hearsay and rumor. Your mom wrote it all down, Alyssum. I'll get the book." Fern hurried over to the shelf then used the ladder to get high up enough. When she found what she was looking for, she brought it back to us.

As she dropped the book on the table, Alyssum and Jensen quickly moved their plates out of the way. Fern opened it and flipped until she found the page.

"Here it is." Alyssum leaned over to read as Fern kept speaking. "The elder didn't think it was that the Gorgon power was too much. The rumor that she'd heard was that the witches didn't want the blood of a Gorgon to heal something even more powerful. Something they saw as a threat."

This didn't make sense. "Are you saying that Gorgon blood can heal?"

Fern bit into her bottom lip nervously. "I don't know," she finally said. "But it would make sense."

"How?" I snapped as I fell back into the chair. "How does it make sense?"

"The falls you took, Sloane," Fern said, her brow severe. "You shouldn't have survived them. Any other human wouldn't have."

Acid threatened to burn a hole in my stomach. It was something I'd thought before—that I shouldn't have survived either fall. But I'd chalked it up to Alyssum doing what she could to protect me. Not me healing myself.

My knees started to bounce and I wasn't sure what I could do with this information. Medusa turned people into stone. Would I do that? Fern said the Gorgon could heal. Could I do that?

Yet there wasn't a single person around who actually knew anything beyond rumors or hearsay. Growing up the way I had, I tried not to rely on people, but with this... I had no idea what to do.

Alyssum turned the book toward her and kept reading. "Thank you, Fern."

"I'm sorry I snapped at you," I told her quietly. "I appreciate you telling us this."

She nodded and turned to walk away but then faced us again. "This isn't a bad thing, Sloane. If any of this is true, you could do so much good."

Oh, sure. The cursed Gorgon would be everything the world needed her to be.

Fern left the library as Alyssum kept reading.

"This makes sense," she said.

"Glad it does to you," I muttered, but she heard me.

"No. It lines up with what Flora's grandmother told us. Mom wrote that the elder was told that the curse had been placed on the three sisters to ensure that they never met." Her blue eyes glanced up at me. "Maybe that's why your mom gave you away."

"Why would she give me away? Or why would that make her give me away?"

"If she thought there was a danger to her three babies, that them being together would cause something bad to happen to them... what would you do? You'd give them away. Try to keep them as far away from one other as you could."

Aric was watching me, watching for my reaction, but right now... I couldn't process it all to have one. "She'd give you away," he said. "To protect you."

Which, if true, would mean that my mom had actually loved me and would be why the fireman she'd given me too would've said that she'd been reluctant.

"Unfortunately," Alyssum continued, "it does say that if anyone tries to break the curse, the coven who placed it will fight back."

The room was silent because that meant more danger and more killing and more possibility of losing those we loved.

Aric sat back and folded his arms over his chest. "Then we'll fight with her."

Which was the last thing I wanted. That only ensured the whole *losing someone you loved* part of this equation, but I couldn't do it without them.

We sat there for a few moments, letting everything sink in, but I couldn't just sit there. Instead, I started clearing the table to put everything on the tray that Fern had brought. Alyssum, Jensen, and Aric were talking about strategy, making plans, wondering what it all meant—out loud.

I just couldn't take it anymore, so I slammed a plate down onto the tray, where it cracked into five pieces. Well, I hadn't meant to do that.

"You all right?" Aric was suddenly closer to me, but I stepped away before he could touch me.

"Have any of you considered that the curse shouldn't even be broken?" I yelled. "It was put in place to stop something the witches felt was a threat. To whom? Them? Us? The world?"

"We don't know." Alyssum pushed to her feet. Now the three of them were watching me like they were waiting for me to completely lose it. I wasn't going to lose it—at least not any more than I already had.

"Exactly. So why not just stop here? Why not ignore the idea of trying to 'cure' me of the curse— and we don't even know how to do that, by the way— and go back to living our lives?"

Alyssum stepped forward so that she was closer to me than the guys. "We can't do that, Sloane. Something about you being here has caused the Earth to revolt. I'm pretty sure the natural things we're seeing aren't so natural and this is the only way to stop it."

"But why?" I cried, my eyes burning with tears, my hands shaking like a freaking paint can in the mixer. "Why would I have anything to do with it?"

"Because it didn't happen until you were here," Aric answered. "We thought it was just Alyssum's and Jensen's combined power, and maybe that was part of it, but the Gobel and Gremalians coming to a truce has sparked something as well. It's almost like we were supposed to be enemies and now that we're not… I just don't completely know, but I am one-hundred-percent sure that you're part of this. We can't figure it out without you."

"Your friend and her family could get hurt," Alyssum said gently. "If we don't fix this, it's not just us who are in danger."

"I know." A tear slipped from my eye, the dirty traitor. I wiped it away, thinking that if I did it quick enough, no one would notice.

Of course they did, though.

"Listen." Jensen moved past both of them, gently grabbed my arm, and pulled me way. They'd still hear us, but at least I didn't feel so caged in. "I know exactly what you're going through. Not that long ago, this short, blonde tornado came to my town and told me I was a gremlin." Alyssum snorted from her spot away from us. "I didn't believe her. She proved it. Told me I had to save our people. I thought she was insane. But we've worked hard and now, the war she wanted to prevent was prevented. We're all friends."

"I wouldn't go that far," Aric added, getting him a dirty look from Jensen.

"I'm just saying, I know how overwhelming this shit is. How absolutely batshit crazy it all seems. But we're here now and we can't let anyone we care about in the human world get hurt."

That's right. He did know what this was like. He hadn't grown up in this world. He'd grown up in the human one like me.

To think both of us could've lived our whole lives not even knowing this other world existed blew my mind.

"You're right," I told him. "I just freaked out a little."

He chuckled. "It won't be the last time, but when it's getting bad, come talk to me. I can relate to what you're going through in a way that they can't."

I swiped a hand under both eyes, just now realizing that I had started to cry. He was right. I had to take this in pieces and try not to get overwhelmed. And I needed to rely on him more than I had been because he'd been through this very thing recently.

"Thank you, Jensen." I reached up to hug him. He wrapped his arms around me and I felt safe. Like Aric wasn't the only one who was going to have my back. I'd known that was the case, but now, I felt it.

"We're going to turn in for the night," Aric said once I'd let Jensen go.

"Yeah. We'll clean up here," Jensen told him.

Aric led me to his bedroom and shut the door behind him. In here, the outside world was far, far away.

"Are you all right?" he asked as he leaned against the door.

"Yeah. I'm fine." I took a deep breath. "I just got overwhelmed for a minute and let the fear take over."

"You're sure?"

I gave him a reassuring smile. "I'm sure."

He pushed off the door and came over to me. When he reached out, I unconsciously stepped away, which made him pinch his eyebrows together. "What?" he asked.

"Do we know it's safe for you to touch me?"

He cocked his head to the side and gave me a devilish grin. "Felt pretty safe the other night."

"We didn't know I was a Gorgon then. What if I turn into a monster with snake for hair?"

He snorted. "That's not going to happen, but if it did, you'd be the most beautiful snake-haired monster who ever lived."

"I don't want to hurt you."

"You couldn't hurt me."

His mouth crashed into mine. It was hurried and hard. Like he needed to prove something to me, but all I needed was to know that I wouldn't hurt him.

If I did, I'd never be able to live with myself.

Aric pushed my shirt over my head and I let him. The way he worked his mouth over mine, it was like he washed away any doubt I had. It was still there, but in this moment, I couldn't find it. All that mattered was that he was touching me.

But I was still hesitant.

He didn't give me a moment to really think about it, which was probably for the best.

My clothes were taken from my body one piece after another. Then he stepped back to rid himself of his own. We were both there and naked and I was needy when he laid me back on the bed. His fingers worked me up but never let me go over the edge.

Quickly, he put the condom on and pushed inside of me. "If you don't want me to touch you," his said, breathless in my ear, "I won't. But it shouldn't be because you're afraid of hurting me."

My short fingernails dug into his back, begging him to move. "I want you to touch me."

Finally, he jerked his hips and I got the tiniest amount of relief. It wasn't enough, but this right here was what I needed. As he moved, I let myself fall into a state in which what I was didn't matter. Whatever we were going to face out there didn't matter. Everything around me was Aric.

Then he turned, putting me on top of him, and fear ripped through my chest. I'd never done this and had no idea what I was doing. He must've seen it because he sat up, pushed his hand into my hair and kissed me. "If it feels good, it's not wrong."

Yeah, but feels good to whom? Him? Me? Those could be different things, but this was where it was time to muster courage.

I pressed my hands against his chest and moved my hips, testing the waters, so to speak. He clenched my hips but didn't to make me do anything. They were just there, holding on. So I did it again and he groaned. His hands slid up to my breasts, squeezing the nipples, which sent a shot of excitement to my core. I dropped my head back and let instinct take over.

Wanting to try something different, I lifted straight up then dropped myself back down on him, which elicited a deeper moan and a tighter squeeze. Then I did it again and again until he said, "If you keep that up, I'm going to cum."

But that's what we wanted, right?

He shook his head, bringing his hand down so that his thumb brushed over that glorious bundle of nerves that were sitting there, waiting to be stroked. When he applied pressure, I moved quicker, chasing a release that we both needed.

"Aric." His name slipped through my lips sounding like a warning. A warning that I too was about to come undone. Two more swirls and movements because erratic, my legs started to vibrate and my entire world exploded into a magnificent display of colors and pleasure.

He made a deep sound and tightened beneath me. That was all I needed to know and once I knew he was done, I collapsed against his chest.

Aric clearly knew how to distract me and get me outside of my own head. He wrapped his arms around me and flipped us over again. Aric kissed me slowly so differently from how it had started. He nipped at my bottom lip then slowly pulled out of me.

"Fuck, Sloane," he said quietly, which made me smile.

If I affected him even a small percentage of the way he did me...

I loved this man and still had my reservations about what I might do to him, not that I knew for certain what I was. He just wasn't going to let me allow that to come between us.

Instead of cleaning up with a cloth, I turned on the shower and stepped in. Moments later, Aric was in there with me and this time, he took control and had me hoping that the sound wouldn't travel too far.

Chapter Twenty

WITHOUT KNOWING what was coming next, I had so much apprehension about meeting in the library. I didn't want to do any of it, honestly. I thought I just wanted to go back to my regular life, but was that really what I wanted?

No. My regular life didn't include Aric. As much as Rhea wanted me closer to her and thought I was out of my mind to stay here with people I barely knew, I didn't want to leave him. She was right, though. I was clearly out of my mind.

"What do I tell Rhea?" I asked Aric as I sat on a desk with my legs dangling off, waiting for Alyssum and Jensen to come back from talking to her dad.

"About what?" Aric glanced up from the book

he'd been skimming, always looking for more information.

I waved my hands around in the air to indicate everything.

"I never intended to tell her about you all because it wasn't my story to tell. But now... I'm involved. It's about me. So what the hell am I supposed to tell her?"

"Oh," he said with a sigh. Then came over closer to me. "Tell her what you want."

I snorted. "The truth."

"If you want to. I'd personally wait until we know more, just because she's going to want proof and right now, you can't really prove it." He pushed his fingers into my hair, a move I was starting to find comfort in. Feeling him there, knowing he was close —it brought me peace.

"So I can just tell her?" I asked. "That I'm... whatever I am and that you're a goblin?"

He scrunched his face up, like the thought of what I'd said disgusted him. "I'm not a goblin. If you tell her that, she's going to think you have a very particular type."

It was moments like this where I could laugh that were going to get me through whatever was ahead of us.

"If you only know the myth, goblins are small." He looked down himself. "I'm not small. They're also grotesque and I'm not trying to have a big head here, but I, at the very least, am not grotesque."

No. He wasn't grotesque at all. Aric was strong and beautiful with his dark curls and dark eyes. He looked like a dream.

"Hey, guys," Alyssum said as she came through the door, causing Aric to drop his hand, but he didn't move away.

There was no way he'd dropped it because she was there, but I had to believe it had been because now was the time to get serious.

"Ash had an idea," Jensen told us. "That Alyssum and I stay here to try to work things on this end. Find out what anyone knows, follow any leads, shit like that."

"Then you two," Alyssum said, taking over, "would go find your sisters."

"Why would we split up?" I asked. "And why do I need to find my... sisters?" It was a hard word to get out because I'd never had them before.

"Split up because there's too much to do," Jensen explained. "He also thinks having us there might cause some problems, given that the witches would likely sense the added power. It's a guess, but it's a logical one."

"'Sense the added power'?" I looked to Aric to explain this.

"Well, Gobel and Gremalians can sense each other, you know? It'd be like that. The more power in a specific area, the more likely someone is to sense it."

OK, yeah. That did make sense.

Alyssum took my hand in hers in that way someone did when they wanted to say something gently. "And Dad agrees that with everything we have, finding your sisters is the only way to break the curse. I asked if maybe there was another way, but this is it, as far as we know."

"The witch said it was the first step," Jensen reminded me. "You two start on that and we'll try to figure out what comes next so that we already know when you find them."

Alyssum nodded as he spoke. "Things can happen quickly, so it'd be best if we were ahead."

I dropped my gaze to the floor, avoiding looking at any of them, and pressed my lips together. My ribs tightened and my stomach quivered at the idea of doing this. Yet they were so nonchalant about it that it made me feel... weak... human.

"Hey, what's going on?" Aric asked as he slid an arm around my back. "We're going to be fine. I'll protect you."

But I shook my head because that was the exact problem.

"You don't think I can protect you?" he asked gently when that wasn't what I'd been thinking.

"It's not that," I said quietly. "It's what happens if you do."

He pulled me into his arms and held me tightly. "Nothing's going to happen to me, but..." He pulled away and leaned down so that we could see each other eye to eye. "You need to know that if it came to that, I'm absolutely putting myself between you and anything that can hurt you."

As I swallowed hard, I knew I had to voice this or I'd regret it.

"I still say we need to think about the fact that maybe the curse was cast for a reason?" I asked, but they all raised their eyebrows and looked at me as if I was talking crazy. "That maybe it shouldn't be broken?"

"I think all of us probably thought about that at first," Alyssum said as she took a step forward. "But the basic reality is that if we don't stop what's happening, there will be nothing left. None of us will be here. The unnatural shit going on is going to eat us all up. We have to stop it."

"She's right," Aric said quietly.

I threw my hands in the air in frustration. "Fine." Then I hopped off the table because I wasn't mad at them. They were doing what they thought was right.

But this whole thing was giving me anxiety.

Aric and I went and packed our bags because it was clear, we weren't going to be back for a while. After hugs and promises to keep them up-to-the-minute informed, we needed to get on the road.

Outside, there was a black car waiting for us. When I looked up at him, clearly, there was a question on my mind.

"Ash wants us to take this. It has a GPS on it for them to track us. In case anything happens."

Yeah. That made sense, I supposed.

Our first stop was back to Flora. Not long before we left, Aric got a text from his mother telling him that Flora had something she needed to give us. It was fine. We were going to pass Phoenix, anyway.

We rode in silence, though he held my hand. Having that connection to him did a lot to calm me. This would be fine. I was positive that he could handle whatever came our way. I just didn't want to be the reason that he got hurt.

It didn't take us long to get to Flora's house. She pulled the door open before we had a chance to knock, then she waved us in but didn't invite us to sit down. This was going to be a quick visit.

"My grandmother called my mother, who came to see me." Her words were rushed, as if she wanted us out of there as soon as possible. "My mother gave me this to give to you, along with the address of a seer whom she recommends you contact first."

Flora held out an obsidian pendant with a gold engraved spiral and inlaid stones. It was beautiful, but I wasn't sure why she was giving this to us. Then she gave Aric a slip of paper.

"A talisman?" Aric asked eyeing the pendant.

Flora nodded. "The pendant is polished obsidian, which symbolizes protection, clarity, and insight. These are things the seer possesses, as does my mother."

I asked, "Doesn't obsidian ward off negative energy?"

"It does," she told me. "It can also help pierce through illusions. Though it doesn't always work."

"What's this engraved in the stone?" Aric ran his thumb over the gold engraving.

"It's the unbroken connection between my mother and the seer. Though some say it represents a journey toward enlightenment, which you happen to be on."

"And the stones?" I asked her.

"Those are moonstone and amethyst. They're in a spiral to represent protection in the moonstone and intuition in the amethyst. It can help guide you." She took a breath and glanced out the window, like she was worried someone would see her talking to us. "If the seer lets you keep it, which she should, it would help you with what you're doing. You're going to need it, I'm told."

"And this will tell the seer to help us?"

Flora ran her finger over the stones. "It will tell her that we sent you and what kind of help you need. It will also provide guidance along the way." She took the pendant from Aric then slid the chain over my head. "Keep it there except when the seer needs it."

Aric took the location of the seer from me as we walked back to the car.

"Where are we headed?" I asked once he'd gotten the car moving.

He opened the paper he'd been given and said, "Pictured Rocks National Lakeshore."

Well, that didn't ring any bells. "Where is that?"

"About four hours from here along Lake Superior," he told me. "Here, put it in my GPS." He handed me his phone then rattled off the passcode to get into it. "Luckily, it's to the east of us, which means it's sort of on the way to everywhere else."

He was right. According to his phone, it was around a four-hour drive. Just enough time for me to obsess.

Aric did his best to distract me on the drive by asking me a ton of questions about growing up and telling me more of his childhood escapades. Even in this situation, he could make me laugh.

When he slowed, I realized that we were there. Not exactly pulling up to the seer's house, but we were at the lakeshore and it was beautiful. I'd heard of this place. People would kayak out to see the pictured rocks. We weren't going to do that specifically, but it was still gorgeous.

The beach he brought us to was serene. To the left and right of us, there were colorful cliffs that were breathtaking. An ethereal beauty that I couldn't believe I was seeing.

"We have to go this way," he said while gesturing toward the forest line. "It'll be a bit of a walk."

That was something I was growing used to.

It was slow-going as we stepped over tree limbs and brush. There were no paths here, just dense forest. If I hadn't had him with me, I would've turned and run the other way.

"This is warm," I said, folding my hand around the pendant that rested against my chest.

Aric reached out to touch it. "It is. That has to mean we're close."

He pulled back a large, bushy tree branch to reveal a cabin. There were so many horror movies that revolved around a cabin in the woods. I took a deep breath, hoping this wasn't one of them.

"That has to be her." He stepped back for me to get by the branch first. Though I wondered why he hadn't used his power this whole time.

After all, he could control this nature we were in the middle of, but he didn't. There had to be a reason.

"Ouch." I pulled the pendant away from my skin quickly, holding the rope that tied it around my neck with a finger and thumb. "This thing is hot."

Aric hurried in front of me, touching the spot where it'd sat against my skin lightly. "There's a red mark." Then he touched the pendant and pulled his fingers quickly back. "Here." He reached around to untie it. "I'm thinking it got hotter the closer we got to the seer. Like a warning of... something. It can't be powers because it'd always be hot with me around. Just hold on to it until we're done here."

I nodded then bunched the rope up in my hand, letting the pendant sway so I wouldn't burn anything else.

Aric balled up his fist and knocked on the door.

"Come in," a woman's voice called from the other side.

After glancing at me quickly, Aric opened the door and went through first.

Inside the cabin, we entered the main area. The living room was to the right, a table that would equate to a dining room on the left and at the back, a kitchen. But it was very open.

"I've been expecting you," she said once I'd shut the door behind me.

"'Expecting' us?" I asked, thinking someone had called to warn her.

The corners of her mouth turned up in what I thought was meant to be a smile. "I am a seer, dear."

Right. Yeah. She'd have seen us coming.

The seer wasn't the old, decrepit woman I'd imagined in my head. In movies, it was always an incredibly old woman with foggy eyes. That wasn't her. She was younger. Maybe in her forties and while there may have been silver in her dark hair, her dark skin glowed with youth and there wasn't a wrinkle on her face.

"Then you know why we've come," Aric told her.

She nodded once, but her gaze remained on the pendant. When she finally looked up at me, she held her hand out.

Slowly, I took the pendant to her.

"And I know who sent you." Her words were spoken very precisely, almost slowly, like she thought we wouldn't be able to keep up. "And I know why."

"So what can you tell us?" I asked.

Her eyes changed from the sparking brown to cloudy white and there was no doubt, she couldn't see us in front of her anymore. When the clouds dissipated, those sparkling, brown irises were directly on me.

"Can you tell me where my sisters are?"

"No." She shook her head just as slowly. Everything about her was purposeful. "I can see things. That doesn't mean I know all."

"Then what *can* you tell us?" Aric pushed.

"I can tell you your journey won't be easy," she said. I snorted, though I hadn't meant to, but yeah. It didn't take a seer for me to know that. She raised her eyebrow as I schooled my face. "I can tell you that your sisters are far apart but still in Michigan."

Glancing over at Aric, I asked, "Why wouldn't they take us out of Michigan?"

"If you weren't here," she answered for him, "your family wouldn't be alerted when you woke up."

Woke up? As if I'd been asleep my entire life? I guess I had been, but damn. What if I had moved out of state after I aged out? That surely would've put a wrench in the plans.

"I can tell you that there is an imminent danger. An element that will do anything to keep you from doing what you set out to do."

Keep me from finding my sisters and undoing the curse to save the world. Yeah, I figured that.

"Who's the danger?" Aric asked, though I assumed it was the witches who'd cursed little babies.

The seer shook her head. "That, I cannot tell you. To find your sisters, you must focus within. With enough focus, you'll be led right to them." She held the pendant out for me to take. "You should keep this. It will help keep you safe."

My shoulders clenched as I brought my arms tightly to my sides and blinked rapidly. If the pendant would help keep us safe in some way, that meant there was danger. We'd known that, but somehow standing in this cabin—dark and gloomy—made all of this more real.

"One last word of caution," she said. "When the left hurts, always look to the right to heal." Then she glanced down at my hands before bringing her gaze to lock with mine.

That didn't make any sense, but I guessed we were done here.

Then we had to make our way back through the forest. I wanted to mull everything over in my head before talking to Aric about it and he must've sensed that because he didn't try to talk to me.

We were almost back to the car when the pendant tried to light my hand on fire and I stopped right where I was. I turned to Aric with wide eyes. "It's hot," I told him.

If that heat had warned us about the seer, then it only stood to reason that it was warning us about something else.

Aric lurched forward like he'd been hit or pushed. Over his back, there was a group of five walking toward us.

"Aric." I hurried over to him. He was fine but pissed off.

"Witches," he said through clenched teeth.

He rolled quickly to his side and waved his hand, sending two of them flying back.

"We know who you are, Gorgon," one called out in almost a singsong voice. "You won't get away from us."

"If I told you to run, would you?" he asked as he got back to his feet.

"No." Because I wouldn't leave him there.

He sighed. "Didn't think so."

Then he started throwing whatever he could at them. I stepped back until I hit a tree. A small, pointy, cutoff branch dug into my wrist and the trickle of blood that followed, I ignored. Only I'd get hurt doing absolutely nothing.

Aric was fighting a few witches and I didn't even have my Taser anymore because I'd forgotten about it with everything going on to ask for it back.

Quickly, I looked around me to try to find something that I could fight with when a pair of strong arms grabbed me and I screamed, causing Aric to turn my way, which got him hit with something invisible. It had to have been a spell.

"It's not you we want, Gobel."

Aric hit the ground with a *thud* then hurried back to his feet. He came running for me, but whatever the witches were doing didn't allow him to get to me.

I fought against the large man who had me. Was he a witch? In my mind, witches were only women, but that was very sexist of me. Men could be witches and I wasn't sure what this one was.

As I struggled, I got my left arm free, the one that I'd hurt, but I didn't care and was able to swing at him, connecting with the side of his face. His hands tightened on my arms before they loosened as he screamed and steam came from the side of his face. My blood sizzled its way down to his neck as he gasped for air.

Had my blood killed him?

I didn't have time to think about it. Instead, I turned and ran for Aric. When I got to him, I said, "Don't touch my blood."

He didn't ask questions, instead grabbing my right arm and starting to pull me away. When he looked over his shoulder, he gasped then hurled himself over me, wrapping his arms around me like he was protecting me.

Then he slumped over, falling to the ground with me beneath him. There was chatter in the woods, but it faded away.

Once I was able to get Aric off me, I rolled him

onto his back. He was gasping for air like something was closing his throat.

I didn't know what to do.

"Aric," I screamed. "Tell me what to do."

His mouth opened, making the worst sound I'd ever heard. He reached up and touched the side of my face, but looking at him, I knew.

He was going to die. We'd just started this and he was going to die.

I couldn't let that happen, but I didn't know what to do, so I pulled my phone out of my pocket and hit Alyssum's contact.

Chapter Twenty-One

"Hey," she answered. "What'd you find?"

"Alyssum." Hearing her voice made the dam in me break. I'd been holding it together for the most part so that I could help Aric. He gurgled right after I'd said his name.

"What's wrong, Sloane?" There was now a sufficient amount of concern in her voice. "Where's Aric?"

"He's hurt," I choked out. "There were witches. I don't know what happened. What do I do?"

"I don't know. I don't know." There were sounds on the other end of the phone that I wasn't going to bother trying to make out. She was rustling through something. Saying something to someone I assumed was Jensen

"Did the seer tell you anything?" she asked in desperation. "Anything that could help?"

"No," I cried as Aric's movements became less. He was dying. "She said... a lot. I don't know, Alyssum. I don't know." Tears fell freely down my cheeks and I didn't care to wipe them away. "She said that if the left harms, look to the right to heal."

"What does that mean?" Jensen asked, which meant she'd put me on speaker.

"I don't know. I don't fucking know," I yelled, not caring if the witch who'd been left standing came back for me or that there was a dead man just feet from me. One that I'd killed—somehow.

"Wait." I sniffed loudly as Aric's eyes shut. "A man grabbed me. I'd cut myself. When my blood touched him, he let me go and he..." I glanced that way. "Died."

"Is that helpful?" Alyssum snapped. This was her best friend lying under my hand.

"Alyssum. The seer said that if the left hurt, look to the right to heal. If the blood from my left hand killed that man, does that mean that the right could heal Aric?"

There was silence and this was lasting too long. Before she answered, I searched around for a sharp stick then dug it into my right arm. I paused, though. What if I was reasoning wrong? What if my right side killed too? What if it wasn't my blood that had killed that guy?

It didn't matter because Aric was dying either way.

Swallowing hard, I let the blood from my right arm drop onto his mouth. When that wasn't fast enough, I held my arm to his lips.

It wasn't like a vampire movie. He didn't latch on to it and try to suck me dry. At first, nothing happened.

"What's happening?" Alyssum's voice was stark in the quiet forest. "Sloane?"

"I'm giving him blood from my right side," I explained. "She said when the left hurts, look to the right to heal. If my left side hurt the man, my right side should heal. Right?"

"I don't know," she whispered before clearing her throat. "Nothing's happening?"

My heart beat erratically against my chest as the worst feeling washed over me. It was a good reminder as to why I shouldn't care about people.

With the exception of Rhea, anyone I could've cared about had left in some way.

The blood continued to drip past his lips and I'd drain my entire body if that was what it took. Alyssum was quiet on the other side of the call, though there were small sounds that told me she was still there and likely crying just like I was.

Aric's head turned quickly toward me and his eyes popped open. I pulled my arm away from his mouth as he sat up then fell back onto my ass in utter relief. I would've kept falling if my back hadn't hit the tree behind me.

"Sloane." He hurried over on his knees toward me. "Sloane, are you all right?"

"Aric?" Alyssum called from the phone, then she sighed in relief. "Are *you* all right?"

"We'll call you back," he said, then he hung the phone up without looking over. He pushed his hands into my hair and ran his thumbs across my cheeks, pushing away the tears. "Sloane, are you all right? The last thing I remember is that man had you then I got hit. Fucking witches."

I couldn't stop the tears. If my blood had healed him, then there was a chance that I was more than a liability. That was, of course, forgetting that I was the reason he'd been hurt in the first place.

"Sloane," he pled. "You've got to say something."

But I couldn't form words. My mouth opened.

Sounds came out, but none of them made sense. Not until I knew I had to warn him. "Don't touch the blood from my left side."

He furrowed his brows. "What?"

I held up my left hand where the puncture wound was. The bleeding had stopped, but the wound was still there and I didn't know if it had to be actively flowing blood or what.

He reached down and tore at my shirt where it'd already been ripped then took the piece of cloth and tied it around my hand, careful not to touch even the dried blood. Then he did it again to my arm where I'd cut myself to save him.

"I don't know what any of that means, but we need to get out of here."

Aric helped me to my feet and then the rest of the way to the car.

I couldn't tell what, but something had changed. The pull that I'd already felt to Aric was so much stronger. Intense. Like a bond had formed when he'd consumed my blood. I couldn't explain it, but maybe he could once I told him about it.

When he got behind the wheel of the car, I said, "We have to call Alyssum back. You were dying and I called her. She has to know you're all right."

"I was what?" His voice dripped with confusion.

I held up a hand. "I'll explain everything, but I have to call her first. She's got to be out of her mind right now."

"You call. I'll find us a motel."

My hands shook as I pressed her contact. She answered on the first ring and I told her that Aric was all right. She wanted to know more, but I explained that we didn't understand it yet. As soon as we did, I'd call her. After confirming Aric was OK directly with him, she relented and said she expected more information soon.

Then I pressed my head to the cool glass on the door and waited for Aric to find a motel. It took a while because we were in a remote part of the state, but he did it. He went in to get a room on his own then came back out to grab our bags and get me inside.

"I need to shower," I told him. I was dirty and sweaty and it was a perfect place to be alone with my thoughts.

"I'll come with you." He moved like he was really going to get into the shower with me, but I held up a hand.

"I'm taking these cloths off and I don't know if I'll still be bleeding," I told him because there wasn't a chance in hell I was going to let him come into contact with the blood on my left hand. In fact, I shouldn't have let him tied the bandages around it in the first place. "Can you just grab the first-aid kit that I saw in the car?" Hopefully, bandaging my hand would be enough.

He nodded then watched as I went off to the shower.

Once the water was rushing over me, I realized that I hadn't acknowledged that Aric had knowingly sacrificed himself, just as he'd said he would. He hadn't hesitated to jump in front of whatever he'd seen coming at me.

He loved me and had said he'd do it, but seeing him do it was entirely a different story.

Worse yet was knowing that he'd do it again.

After quickly drying off, I went out the room so he could clean up in the shower and I could get dressed. I was in cotton shorts and a tank top when he came out. I assumed we weren't going anywhere else for today. Maybe to get something to eat, but I'd want to bring it back here.

The motel room wasn't anything special. It had one bed in the middle, a small table with two chairs by the window, and a dresser with the TV above it. The décor looked like it'd been at least twenty years since it had been updated, but I didn't care about any of that.

All I cared was that we were here and no one knew it.

I'd just gotten both injuries bandaged up—though they'd stopped bleeding—when Aric came out of the bathroom with a towel around his waist, his hard abs on display like they were trying to get me to forget everything that had happened today.

"What if I don't want to keep doing this?" I asked him as he pulled his towel away, leaving him completely naked for a moment before he slid his boxer briefs up his legs.

"Doing what? Because I know you're not talking about us."

"I'm not talking about us," I told him quietly. "This. Tracking down my sisters. Or alleged sisters because I'm not sure I believe it all. Though given today, I have to believe some of it."

"We have to. You know that. If we want to stop—"

"I know. But the Gorgons have never done anything for me. Why should I want to break their curse?"

He dropped onto the bed beside me, resting his

back against the headboard as I sat with my legs crossed under me. "Two reasons," he said. "The Gorgons may not have done anything for you, but your mother did." My eyes met his. "She gave you up when she didn't want to try to save you all. That has to mean something."

I sighed. He was right. "What's the other reason?"

"That there might be two other women going through what you are right now, only they don't have anyone to help them. To protect them."

My eyes filled with tears. That would be awful, but... "What if I don't want you to protect me?"

He shook his head and cupped my cheek. "You don't get a say in that. So..." He slapped his legs then stood up, grabbing a shirt from his bag. "I'm starving. I'm going to go get us some food, then when I get back, you're going to tell me what the fuck happened in the woods."

Seemed like the best compromise that I was going to get.

While he was gone, I called Alyssum again to explain everything that had happened. I told her about the witches, the man who'd grabbed me, the fact that I'd cut my hand and when I'd hit him, his skin had sizzled where my blood had touched him. I told her about the seer. Everything I could think of. Every detail.

When I was done, she was quiet for a moment before she said, "You really are a badass, Sloane."

"Stop." I rolled my eyes. "I'm not."

"You are. You figured out what the seer was trying to tell you, then you used it. Just all of it."

"But I'm scared," I admitted. "What if I touch one of you with blood from my left side? What the hell is that about, anyway? Blood circulates the whole body. How could one side kill and the other heal? It's all the same blood."

"I don't know," she told me. "It's probably something to do with the duality of life or some other bullshit, but regardless, you know it's there. And you saved my best friend."

Her best friend was the man I loved. I would've saved him, anyway.

"But I killed a man. How am I supposed to live with that?" The guilt had been gnawing at my stomach since it happened.

"It was self-defense," she told me.

I blew out a breath to keep from crying. "I know but he's still dead because of me and maybe that's something you're used to but I'm not."

Alyssum furrowed her brows. "I'm not used

to it at all. I just know that I only do it when there's no other choice. I'm not going to let someone I love die because I'm afraid of the guilt. You just have to remind yourself that if you hadn't done what you did, Aric wouldn't be out there with Jensen right now getting us something to eat."

I quickly wiped a tear away hoping that she wouldn't notice and nodded. She was right. I didn't have a choice and honestly, I didn't know it was going to kill him. Obviously I had a hunch it was going to hurt him based on what the seer said but kill? No. I'd learn to live with this until I didn't feel guilty anymore.

When I heard a car door outside, I hung up with her, figuring it was Aric with food. When he unlocked the door and came in, he had a few bags in his hand. But he made sure to lock the door before coming over to me.

He'd gone to a burger place and right then, I didn't really care what we ate, as long as we ate.

I was two bites in when he said, "Now that we're settled, tell me what happened. I remember seeing the green glow that the witch sent, so I knew it was going to be bad."

That must've been the spell that had done whatever it had done to him. "It hit you," I told him. "You wrapped yourself around me."

"That, I remember. I didn't want it to hurt you."

I scowled but kept going. "You went down. You were gasping for air. I have no idea what it did to you, but on my side, it looked like it was strangling you. So I called Alyssum. There wasn't anything we could do, but then I remembered what the seer had said. When the left hurts, try the right. And since I'd cut my hand on the tree then touched the man who'd grabbed me and it had killed him, I thought that was my left hurting. So that had to mean my right would heal, right?"

"It was a good assumption."

"I had to try it." I shrugged. "It could've killed you, but you were dying, anyway, and I had to do something, so I grabbed a branch and cut my arm then let the blood drip into your mouth."

"And I came back," he finished. I nodded then took another bite because I didn't want to talk about it any more than I already had. This would at least buy me some time. He reached over and kissed me gently on the lips. "Thank you," he whispered, as if it didn't matter that I had a hunk of meat in my mouth.

"At least we know it works," I told him.

"We do."

"Maybe it would've worked faster if I had known."

"I don't want you going around cutting yourself with sticks." He gave me a dark look. "You'll end up with gangrene, so we'll get you a little knife to hold on to."

That sounded like a good idea. In the woods, I hadn't even thought about it.

Once we were done eating, instinct told me to try to sleep. It wasn't fully dark yet and while I was emotionally exhausted, physically, I was wide awake. So I thought it the perfect time to work on something else the seer had said.

To find my sisters, I must focus within.

Focus within, as if I already knew where they were.

I closed my eyes to meditate. Wasn't that how you focused within? As I sat there, something soft crawled up my leg. It was human, so I didn't freak out, but I opened one eye just enough to see Aric's fingers trailing up my leg.

"Stop it." I lightly slapped his hand. "You're distracting me."

He kissed the spot under my ear. "That was the point."

I sighed and tried again, but then his lips touched my collarbone.

"Aric," I chastised without opening my eyes. Then he was kissing the spot that would've been burnt by the pendant. "Aric," I said again, only this time, I looked at him.

"You're distracting," he said, his breath causing a burst of goosebumps to spread across my chest.

"*You're* distracting," I told him, but that was probably the point.

There was so much going on inside of me that it'd take a good therapist a decade to unravel and I wasn't going to be able to do it alone in this motel room. I wasn't going to do it ever given that any therapist would think I'm actually insane if I told her about the supernatural things I'd witnessed. But I wouldn't make any progress of any kind in this motel room.

He chuckled against my skin, then pulled me into a kiss. His mouth moved against mine, his tongue stroking my lips until they parted. If I wasn't careful, I'd fall into this and forget about everything else.

Just when I was about to lie back, bringing him with me, he brought the kiss to an end then stood up.

"All right. Let's go."

I furrowed my brows. "Go where? I thought we were already going somewhere. But tomorrow."

He chuckled. "Can't distract you, right?"

I scowled. "You already were."

"Exactly. So let's go to the beach. Being in nature helps me focus when I really need to. I can ground myself out there and maybe you can too."

I pulled him toward me. "I'd rather stay here."

He ran his tongue over his bottom lip. "Yeah. So would I, but we have to do this." There was regret all over his face. Then he leaned down to kiss me one more time. "We can finish this when we get back.

He wasn't wrong. I was going to get dressed, but he didn't see the point. We weren't going to see anyone and he wanted me to be comfortable. So I slipped on some shoes and followed him out the door.

It only took a few minutes to get to the nearest beach and it wasn't near Pictured Rocks. No. I didn't want to be close to the seer because the pendant would've heated up and I wouldn't have been able to focus.

When we stepped out of the trees to see the beach, I was instantly more at peace. It was relaxing listening to the waves crashing into the sand.

Without anyone else there, nothing would distract me.

I pushed out of my shoes and walked to where the water came to shore, letting the frigid coolness cover my heated skin. Then I closed my eyes and held my palms toward the water and took a deep breath. Then another. If Aric was close, I couldn't hear or feel him. He was doing an excellent job of staying out of my way for this.

Nothing happened, so I reset and tried to ground myself the way I'd seen Aric, Alyssum, and Jensen do it. I pushed my bare feet into the sand and took a deep breath.

Something was different this time. Something serene passed over me as if I were suddenly one with my environment. A gentle breeze blew my hair off my shoulders and I knew. It was like someone spoke it into my heart and into my mind.

The obsidian would guide me if I listened, the seer had said.

Well, right now, It was guiding me to where I was sure one of my sisters were.

I opened my eyes to the darkening blue sky with hues of pink. I thought the saying was "Pink at night, sailor's delight. Pink in the morn, sailors be warn." Which meant pink in the sky at night meant for smooth sailing while seeing it in the morning meant rough waters.

Hopefully, it was true for us too.

After turning around, I found Aric not five feet from me, watching.

"Detroit," I told him. "We have to go to Detroit."

He gave me a proud smile and said, "Then we're going to Detroit."

Chapter Twenty-Two

Aric insisted that we not leave for Detroit until the next morning. It was a six-hour drive and he wanted to travel during the day because he said it would mean we'd see what was coming for us.

For me, it was fine because I was dead-ass tired. So tired, in fact, that I wasn't awake long enough for us to finish what we'd started when he'd been distracting me. For me to pass that up, I *had* to have been exhausted.

I got to sit back and enjoy the beauty of the Upper Peninsula while he drove. With the window down and the radio on, I could almost convince myself that we were just a young couple on a road trip. That wasn't the case, but it helped take my mind off everything. At least until I rested my head against the window and closed my eyes.

Something my time with Alyssum had given me was a huge fear of falling off something high. So when the car began to shake, I thought it was a nightmare.

Then I opened my eyes and found that I was living it.

Aric's knuckles were white against the steering wheel while he tried to control the car, but the earth below us was shaking and it wasn't a normal earthquake. It was like the earth below us was trying to crack open wide to suck us down.

"Aric?" I wrapped my fingers around the door handle, like that was going to keep me from falling.

"We're all right," he said, but I didn't sound convinced. The car lurched forward.

I pressed my back into the seat as my stomach hardened and the hair on my arms rose. It was happening again. I was going to fall a million feet again. Would I even survive it this time? Pinching my eyes shut, I prayed to whatever was out there that it would stop.

The car rolled and I wished I could just run away. I wished I had the ability to blink myself right out of this car.

But I didn't. All I could was hold on.

The car lurched again, this time coming off the ground then slamming down on my side. Glass sprayed across me as I screamed.

The Earth was a pinball machine and we were the ball.

After what felt like forever, it all just stopped.

"Are you all right?" Aric asked as we hung there.

"I think so." My voice was hoarse from all the screaming I'd done.

"OK. We have to get out of here." He looked around to try to figure out how to do that. "I have to break my window," he told me.

"Then break it."

He narrowed his eyes on me. "The glass is going to rain down on you, so I need you to protect your face. Especially your eyes."

Yeah. Right. I wasn't thinking. I crossed my arms over my face so that my eyes, nose, and mouth were covered. Then some glass shattered and tiny shards came down on me like frozen snow. Fast and painful. When it was done, Aric told me I could take my arms down.

While I stayed where I was, he used his hands to grip the sides of the now-open window and asked, "Can you undo my seatbelt?"

Yeah. I could. It was right there. When I pushed the button, I realized he would've fallen into the steering wheel had he not been bracing himself. Then he pulled himself up and out of the car.

Once he was out, he reached back in. "Your turn."

"No way," I told him immediately. "I'm bleeding."

"It'll be fine."

I pinched up my face and looked at him like he was nuts. There was no way in hell I was going to touch him while I was bleeding from my left side. Hell, I wasn't even sure that if the wounds were covered, it'd be good enough.

It was too uncertain.

"Sloane," he said, sounding frustrated. "We have to get you out of this car."

"I know." As if I didn't want out of here worse than he wanted me out. "But I'm not risking you."

He sighed and dropped his head. "All right. Hang on." The sound of him crawling off the car and dropping to the ground made my heartbeat erratic. He was moving away from me, but he wasn't leaving me. I knew that, but I couldn't stop the fear.

"Hold on to something," he called out, so I grabbed the door handle and the side of my seat.

Metal groaned as something hit the side of the car with a loud *bang*.

Swallowing hard, I had to remind myself not to hold my breath. Me passing out wasn't going to do anyone any good. The car groaned then moved a little. I was being pushed upright. After a certain point, the car fell back to the ground with a *thud*.

Fuck falling.

Aric hurried over to me and yanked the door open. It took a lot of effort due to the damage. Then he undid my seatbelt and tried to pull me out, but I recoiled. "Stop," I snapped. "I'm bleeding."

He stepped back with his hands in the air and let me get myself out.

"Are you all right?" he asked, folding his arms over his chest like he had to—otherwise, he'd touch me.

"I think so. I need the first-aid kit." Getting the blood from my left side taken care of was a top priority of mine.

Aric went to the trunk then came back with the first aid. I used the cleansing wipes to clear away the three scratches on my left arm, then I covered them with Band-Aids and waited to see if the blood soaked through.

When it didn't, my shoulders slumped in relief.

Though I was starting to look like something special. My hand was still wrapped and now I had three Band-Aids up my forearm. Then on my right side, I had a large gauze pad covering the wound I'd created to heal Aric.

Oh, shit. I hadn't checked my face.

Pulling out my phone, I hoped that I wouldn't find anything. With the camera, I inspected my face and I was in the clear. My arms had been covering it, so that was good. Then I looked down at the wipes.

"I need fire," I told him. To me, that was the perfect solution. I wasn't about to leave my harmful blood out here for some poor animal to find.

"What?"

"Fire." I blew out a breath. "Where's Alyssum when you need her? I need to burn these so my blood can't hurt anyone."

Aric opened his mouth like he was going to protest, but then he snapped it shut, like he realized how important this was to me. He held up a finger and went back to the trunk of the car. It wasn't until he was back with a red stick in his hand that I thought he was nuts.

"What am I supposed to do with that?"

"Nothing," he told me. "But I'm going to set those on fire like you want. It's a flame flare." He broke the thing apart, causing a flame to shoot out of it. I scrambled to my feet and he set the wipes on fire. The wounds hadn't been bleeding bad enough to drip in the car, so this was all we needed to take care of. "There," he said once they were fully engulfed. "We need to walk to the nearest town. I'll call Jensen on the way."

After Aric grabbed our bags from the trunk, it wasn't as long of a walk as I thought it would be. Aric called Jensen, who said Ash wanted him to bring us another car. It was just going to take a while, so we would hole up at another roadside motel. I wasn't even sure where we were.

This time, I was to stay inside the motel, even when Aric went to get us something to eat.

When he got back, he had a bag in one hand and a woman's arm wrapped in the other.

"What the hell?" I hopped up off the bed.

"Grab a chair." He nodded toward the chairs surrounding the table. There were two, so I grabbed one and brought it to an open part of the floor. "She's a witch," he told me. "I caught her when I was coming out of the diner." He dropped the bag on the bed. "There's food in there for you."

I wasn't even thinking about eating.

He pushed her into the chair then twirled his

finger so that the branches binding her wrapped around the chair. "I'll be right back."

Leaving me alone with the witch scared me, but her hands were bound in the branch and there was part of one around her mouth so she couldn't speak. She pled with her eyes, though. She was clearly afraid Aric was going to kill her and honestly, so was I.

He was back minutes later with something metal in his hands. He laid the bars out to encircle her, then he stood up to find my very confused face.

"One of the things Alyssum taught me," he began, "is that if you bind their hands and voices, they can't cast a spell." Glancing over at the witch, I found nothing had changed. "And if we circle them in iron, they also won't cast a spell, even when I release her mouth." He waved his hand and the part over her mouth slid away. It still amazed me when he was able to do things with the wave of his hand. "If she casts a spell, it'll stay in the confines of the iron with her."

Well, I was glad he'd read the email Alyssum had sent. I blew out a breath. At least we were safe for now.

"Did she attack?" I asked while he opened the bag, pulled out a container, and handed it to me.

"Not exactly." He pulled one out for himself. "Eat," he demanded. "We can talk to her while we do. I thought bringing her here might help us get some information."

"I'm not giving you any information," she said defiantly, her brown hair a mess, but her clear, blue eyes creeped me out.

"You might as well tell us something," he told her then popped a french fry into his mouth. "We've got a while."

Still, she said nothing.

After a couple of bites, I decided to try something else. Ask some things that maybe it wouldn't matter if she told me or not.

"Do you know about me?" I asked her. Her answer was her smiling slowly. "You do. So you know what happens if you come into contact with the blood from my left side, right?" That smile disappeared. "I'm not planning on touching you with it. I just have some questions."

She tightened her jaw but kept her gaze on me.

"Will that always happen? If anyone touches blood from the left side of my body, will they die?" Because I didn't want to chance it with Aric. As a matter of fact, with these cuts, I was thinking about not sleeping in the same bed as him.

"No," she finally said. "It won't always kill." Aric sat up and moved closer. "It's the amount that kills. If, say, a drop were to touch someone's hand, it would maybe numb their hand. A little more may incapacitate them. A lot, and they die." She nodded at Aric. "Try it on him."

"Never going to happen."

"Why not?" She tilted her head to the side. "You can just heal him if it goes badly, right?"

"That's true," Aric agreed. "Come on." He held his hand out to me.

After pulling the small knife out of my pocket, I pricked the end of my finger to release a single drop of blood. My stomach hurt at the thought of this. At the idea of hurting him in any way. But I did need to know how it worked.

So I let the drop fall onto his skin and pulled my hand back.

"Shit." He blew out a breath, so I quickly wiped the drop away. "It's like my hand is numb." It looked like he tried his hardest to clench his fist and couldn't do it. He glanced over to her. "How long will this last?"

She shrugged as best she could. "That, I don't know. But she can stop it with the other side."

So I repeated the process with my right finger

and let that drip onto him. Moments later, his hand closed.

"That's wild," he said, looking at me with wonder. "I'd suggest you do more, but I think you won't go for it."

My answer was immediate. "I won't."

"So... what do we do with a witch who won't talk?" He stared at her and honestly, he looked pretty scary. Like he was ready to end her right where she sat. There was a darkness that I didn't recognize.

"We can't kill her," I told him because I knew that was where his mind was. Not because he was some murderous, rage monster, but because she was part of the coven out to stop me.

"We can," he countered.

"*Aric.*"

We locked in a stare-down as we silently battled.

"She'd kill *us* if she had the chance."

"I really would," she added, which wasn't helpful.

"*Aric,*" I said again.

"Fine," he said. "If she proves a little more useful, we can leave her here once we're on our way. I can't just let her go."

It was at least a compromise.

"Please tell me what you know about the curse,"

I begged her. This was our best chance to find out anything and I doubted we'd get a second one. "Please."

My hope was that leveling with her on a human level would work. The two of us sat in silence as if Aric weren't even there. Then the witch sighed.

"I've only heard stories," she finally said.

"I'll take anything you give me."

She shook her head then swallowed hard. "Supposedly, a Gorgon broke a witch's heart. We can be known to be... vengeful." Aric snorted, which made her narrow her eyes at him. I sent him a look telling him to be quiet. She was talking. We didn't want anything to hinder that. "Anyway, in retaliation, the coven cursed the Gorgon people. She was betrayed, wanted vengeance."

"But why take that out on all the Gorgons?" I asked her.

"Because the Gorgons were too powerful," she yelled, then she closed her eyes. "Especially when their three goddesses showed up. They'd be... unstoppable. Anything the witches did, the Gorgon could undo. What we decided to hurt, the Gorgon could heal." She took a breath and gazed out the window. "The coven found out the three goddesses would be born in the next generation. It had to be done. Together..." She shook her head. "We've done everything we could to make sure the Gorgon goddesses never came into power. Everything. So many layers." She snapped her mouth closed for a moment. "I'm not telling you anything else."

She didn't need to. She'd already told us so much.

Someone had foreseen the three goddesses coming. That, apparently, was me and my sisters. Due to what she'd said, we'd be too powerful. But too powerful for what? There had to be something. We just weren't going to know now.

Pushing her right now wasn't going to do any good and we still had some time before Alyssum and Jensen arrived. Aric motioned his fingers for me to follow him out of the motel room, which I did. Outside, we could talk without the witch hearing us.

"Have you ever heard any of that before?" I asked as soon as I'd shut the door.

"No." He folded his arms over his chest and shifted his weight back and forth from foot to foot.

"What do you think it means? There has to be something they didn't want the Gorgons powerful enough to stop, right?"

"It would seem so."

I furrowed my brows. "What's going on? You usually would have more to say."

Aric scratched the back of his head as he looked out over the parking lot like he was scanning for hidden dangers. "I'm beginning to think that the witches are behind the rivalry between the Gremalians and us."

I furrowed my brows and folded my arms under my breasts. "Why would you think that?"

He sighed. "It's going to sound crazy, but as long as we were feuding, nothing happened. Our leaders think it's their power causing all of this shit and I think it is to some extent, but could it be them using their power after the feud ending? Is that one of the layers she's talking about? I don't know, but it makes as much sense as anything else."

He was right. It did make as much sense as everything else. "You're right," I told him. "She mentioned layers, so if we think back, everything was totally normal until you and Alyssum became friends, right?" I paced down and back in front of him as I spoke. "You two become friends, you heal the rift between your people. As soon as that happens, all the natural phenomenon starts and not to mention, I show up somewhere it sounds like I shouldn't have been able to go. Also, this fucking mark on my chest never appeared before now." I stopped right in front of him. "Does that mean I've never been around a witch or did it not activate until all the other pieces were in place?"

"Exactly."

"So... Fuck. Could we fix it by creating another rift between your people?" Though the idea didn't sit well with me. From my understanding, they'd been battling for a long time and neither side ever knew peace.

He shook his head. "I don't think so and I don't think we could do it, anyway. Everyone feels a lot safer right now. They won't want to risk that."

I snorted. "Right. Safer."

"They probably *are* back home."

Yeah. He was right again. Now there was one more thing we needed to discuss since we weren't figuring out the answer to that riddle any time soon. "What about the witch?"

His jaw tightened, that sexy, little muscle right at the curve moving. "We can't let her go."

I narrowed my eyes on him. "We can't kill her," I told him. "I killed that guy accidentally in the woods and have to live with that for the rest of my life." I shook my head.

"You had no choice."

"I know. Still..."

He rested his hands on my shoulders. "All right. We'll leave her here, but anything happens and I'm ending her. I won't risk you."

A shiver ran up my spine at the way he'd said that, leaving no doubt that he'd do what he'd just promised.

I just didn't want another life on my hands if we didn't need to kill.

When we returned back into the motel room, I went to grab the food he'd gotten me. Alyssum sent a text saying that they were almost to us and I wanted to finish because my stomach was going to stage a mutiny. I wasn't sure how they got to us so quickly. My guess would be that they weren't in Delaware when we'd called but I didn't know.

As I moved around the lead barrier Aric had created, my foot got caught on the bedspread hanging to the floor and I tripped, kicking one of the iron rods out of place and catapulting me into the witch, causing the branches to crack.

That was enough.

She ejected from the seat quicker than I could make sense of and lunged toward me. Aric grabbed her from behind to stop her and threw her across the room, hitting her head on the dresser.

The witch landed with a *thud* and didn't get back up.

"No," I whispered as I scurried over to her. Her head flopped to the side unnaturally.

I pulled the small knife from my pocket and sliced through the skin on my right arm, letting the blood drip into her mouth.

Nothing happened.

When this had worked with Aric, he'd been dying. He hadn't been dead.

But this witch... She was already dead.

Chapter Twenty-Three

The room was so quiet that my heart pounding against my chest was the only thing I could hear. I hadn't wanted the witch to die, yet here she was... dead. And there wasn't anything I could do to save her. Honestly, I was surprised Aric had even let me try.

Maybe he'd known it wouldn't work.

I slumped back against the wall, putting pressure on the tiny cut I'd made. I'd always been a good clotter and now I knew why. If my blood could heal others, then, at least on the right side, it could heal me. The wound I'd made to save Aric had healed quickly.

Aric came over to me and squatted down. "Come on," he said gently, reaching a hand out to me.

I didn't want to take it, but I knew that I couldn't stay here.

He pulled me to my feet, then wrapped an arm around me to lead me out of the room. Once outside, I saw that Alyssum and Jensen were there, leaning against another identical black car.

"There's a dead witch in there," I said without greeting them.

Alyssum shook her head. "We can't take you two anywhere."

I snorted. It was seeming to be the case now, wasn't it? "I didn't do it," I told her. "It was him."

Aric shook his head. "She was going after you. I don't regret a thing."

"What happened?" Alyssum asked while pointing at my hand clamped over the cut I'd made.

"I tried to save her." Our eyes met. "It didn't work."

"She was already dead," Aric said again. "Nobody can save the dead."

"All right," I said. It was a lot of information and Alyssum bobbed her head like she understood, but I wasn't sure she did. "Dead witch in a hotel room... we should probably go."

"Unless you can stay a minute," an unfamiliar voice said from my left.

Aric pushed me behind him while Alyssum held her hands out in a way that I knew meant she was pulling in energy.

"Hold on," the woman said, raising a hand. "I come in peace."

Aric growled.

"I do, big man," she said again. "Yes, I'm a witch, but not from that coven and I don't agree with what they're doing. I'd like to help."

"I'm not trusting a witch," Aric said, taking a step forward.

"Put the talisman on me," she told him. "Two things with that particular one. The engraving is embedded iron, so I won't be able to cast a spell. The obsidian will grow hot if I try anything witchy at all."

It took a moment before Alyssum turned to him. "We could use more information."

He didn't look over at her. Instead, he continued glaring at the witch. "The last time I tried to get information from a witch, she ended up dead inside a motel room."

The witch glanced through the motel window, but she wouldn't have been able to see anything.

"I'll take care of that," she said. "If it helps, my name is Tabitha. Witches don't normally give you their names, right? It's my olive branch. I'd like to stop what's coming."

That had to strike a nerve because Alyssum and Aric were born enemies who only ever had wanted to stop what was coming.

Aric turned to me then took the obsidian necklace off me before going over to her and putting it on her. I supposed we were going to try to trust her.

Alyssum said we should get out of the street, so we went to the diner where Aric had gotten our food, but we all only ordered a drink so we weren't sitting there loitering.

"Talk," Aric demanded.

"Well, like I said, I don't agree with what the coven is doing and they only did all of this because the heartbroken one went way, way, off the rails and the train plummeted off a summit. Like way off. They need to cover it up because the Gorgon couldn't fixed what she'd broken and everyone would know she'd broken it."

"What did she do?" I asked.

Tabitha shook her head. "If I tell you... I'll be betraying the coven more than I already am and they... won't take kindly to it. I do have to protect myself a little. So I'm not going to tell you all that, but I am willing to help how I can."

"Absolutely not," Aric said.

"Agreed," Jensen immediately replied. They didn't want her to help us.

"Where are we going to find another witch willing to do anything for us?" Alyssum whisper-yelled. "Seriously."

"No," Aric told her as he gave her a dark look. She was unfazed because she rolled her eyes.

"Then you two can scram," Alyssum said. "Sloane and I will talk to her."

"I'm not doing that, either," Aric said.

"You have to do one or the other," I told him. "You can stay and hear what she has to say or you can wait outside, but I'm talking to her."

His jaw tensed. "We're all going to regret this."

Brushing off that warning, without thinking, I relayed everything the dead witch had told us. Tabitha nodded her head as she listened then told us that as far as she knew, that was all accurate information.

"What about what the seer said?" I asked. "She said that my sisters are far apart but still in Michigan."

"They are, as far as I know," Tabitha told me. "I mean, they're adults now, so they could've moved. When the coven found out that your mother was having three babies, they immediately thought of the goddesses and wanted to end that. So your mother was ordered to sacrifice one of you. If she didn't, the coven threatened to kill you all."

So she'd given me up to save me. This was just more confirmation.

"What do you know about the Gorgons?" I asked.

"Not much." She took a quick drink of her water. "We aren't really allowed to know. It's *most Gorgons bad,* in all the covens. But I've seen what the covens have done and started to think that maybe I was being lied to."

"The other witch said that the coven's curse had layers. What layers?" I asked because that would be important to know.

"Honestly?" she asked. I nodded. "I don't know all of them. From what I gathered, they created mortal enemies out of two peoples who already were fighting."

Alyssum raised her hand. "That would be us. Gremalians versus Gobel."

"Yeah. I didn't know what people it was, just that the rivalry existed. The story was that they'd never reconcile. If by chance they did, there were backups.

The earthquakes, the tsunamis. Tornadoes, floods. I assumed when those started that meant whoever it was had reconciled."

"Which means they used the fact that the Gremalians and Gobel were already fighting over the cooper to their advantage. So the rift." Alyssum ticked it off her finger. "The natural phenomenon. What else?"

"It'd be sacrificing one, separating the others, the rift, the natural phenomenon. The mark that she has." She pointed at me. "That means the witches can feel when she's near. After that, I'm not totally sure, but I guarantee that's not all of it."

"What about the Gorgons scares the coven?" That had to be it, right? There was something about us they were afraid of. A power we'd wield or something.

She rolled her eyes. "The elders insist that the Gorgons have a duality. Or at least the three goddesses will. Something that would represent life and death."

The special blood in my body turned cold. That had to be what they were referring to, but it didn't sound like all witches believed it.

"Your blood," Alyssum said quietly.

"What about your blood?" Tabitha asked with wide eyes.

"The seer said that when the left hurts, to look to the right." I swallowed hard, my mouth suddenly full of saliva at the thought of telling her what I'd done. "I killed a man—I think a witch, but I'm not sure."

"He was with witches," Aric added. Until then, he and Jensen had just been silently watching.

"I killed him with the blood from my left side." I swallowed. "But then I was able to heal Aric with blood from my right side."

Tabitha's lips parted as she watched me. "So you're the duality. Do your sisters have that power?"

I shrugged. "I don't know. I haven't met them."

"We're trying to find them," Alyssum added.

This was all too much. I needed a minute. I told them I was going to the restroom then excused myself. Aric moved to get up which meant he'd follow me but I shot him a dark look and he sat back in his seat. I didn't want a babysitter in the restroom. Besides, I didn't actually have to go, but I did need to splash some cool water on my face. I was there, resting my hands on the countertop, taking deep breaths and blowing them out slowly when Tabitha came into the restroom.

"It's a lot." She started rubbing my back. "It's a

lot to take in, especially if you didn't grow up knowing about any of this."

I opened my eyes and turned to her. "I didn't and it is. Mostly, I didn't want to hurt anyone."

"Of course not." Tabitha's dark hair was pulled back in a ponytail, making her look around my age. Maybe she was older, I didn't know.

"I think that's why I didn't get more hurt, though." Then I realized that she wouldn't have any idea what I was talking about. "When the Gremalian and Gobel were fighting, I got hurt a couple of times. But it should've been more seriously. Maybe I healed myself. I think a human would've died."

"That's probably true." She glanced down at my newest bandage. "Is that where that comes from? Trying to heal someone?"

I nodded. "It'll be fine. Probably is now, but I clot quickly."

"That's good." She reached up and yanked the pendant off her, tossing it onto the countertop.

Tabitha swung her hand out, throwing me into the wall. I tried to scream, but nothing came out. She was murmuring something—a spell—that was holding me there and stealing my voice. My arms were plastered against the wall, fingertips facing down. She kept her hand in the air, pointed at me, like that was what was holding me in place.

"I'm sorry to have to do this," she said. "You seem nice, but this is an opportunity that I can't pass up." She pulled a thin blade from her back pocket and slashed it across my right arm. The blood flowed freely. Then she used the same hand to pull a vial out. "I assume that you don't need much to heal."

She held that vial to my arm as I tried to fight. Nothing worked. My blood filled the glass container, then she screwed a lid on top.

"Now that I'm thinking about it..." Her voice was too calm for the situation. "Maybe I want to be able to hurt, as well."

That thin blade slashed across my left arm, causing me to call out into a quiet, empty void. The burning was unreal. She pulled a second vial, this one not see-through glass, and filled it with blood from my left arm.

Shit. This hurt and the blood just kept flowing.

Only when she tried to put the cap on, her arm fell for just a second. It was enough to release me and I charged at her, not caring that I was leaving a flow of blood in my wake. But she hurried out of the bathroom, whispering another spell that caused me to drop to the floor.

There wasn't anything I could do about it, either.

Without being sure how much time passed, the door flung open and Alyssum gasped. I was bleeding worse from my right side than the left, but if she touched any of the left-sided blood, she'd die. Or become incapacitated. And it was impossible to tell which was which.

"Don't... touch... the... blood." I pressed my left arm into side for pressure as I sat up against the wall. The right one was deeper, though it was healing up, which meant the blood was slowing. On a whim, I let some of the right-sided blood drip onto my left arm. It couldn't hurt.

"Aric," she called out the door.

A moment later, the door burst open and Aric along with Jensen was standing there.

"What the fuck happened?" Aric yelled as he moved into the bathroom.

"Stop," I said, but I was so groggy from blood loss and maybe the witch's spell that I wasn't sure he'd heard me. "Stop!"

He didn't come closer but squatted down to look at me. "Why?"

"Some of this is left-sided blood."

His jaw clenched as he nodded his head, so I

knew that he understood. "We need to get you out of here."

"Yep." It took everything in me to move to my knees. Then I had to release the pressure so I could steady myself on the wall as I stood up. I could only imagine what my clothes must have looked like.

Aric's hands opened and closed like he was fighting the urge to touch me. The moment he'd tried, I moved away from him. Sure, he'd tried to touch my right side, but I had no idea if left-sided blood had gotten on that side. Did dried blood count? I didn't know. It was like I didn't know anything at this point.

"What're we going to do?" Alyssum asked once we were outside in the sun.

Aric glanced around. Luckily, this town was small enough that there weren't people everywhere and if there actually were, I didn't see them. "How about back to the motel? We still have it all night. We can go there so she can get cleaned up."

My stomach churned. The last thing I wanted to do was go back to where the dead witch was.

We crossed the street, he unlocked the door, and the four of us stepped in. The first thing I looked at was the corner where the witch had fallen, but she was gone.

"Tabitha must've kept her word on that," Jensen said.

Aric handed Alyssum the car keys so she could go get my bag, I heard him say, though I had no memory of the bag being put into the new car. Last I knew, it'd been on the floor in the motel. Then he followed me to the bathroom.

"You can't come in," I told him, though my head felt a little woozy. That bathroom had looked like a crime scene and the memory of it widened my eyes. "What about that bathroom? If someone touches—"

"I thought of that. I'm going to have Alyssum and Jensen do a little Gremalian electrical magic to sap it. It'll still be there or at least the residue will be, but the organic matter should be gone."

Nodding, I braced my hand on the counter and took a deep breath.

"Sloane, I don't think you can do this yourself," he said quietly. "What if you wash off your right arm, so I can at least touch that?"

Again, all I felt like I had the energy to do was nod while he grabbed a washcloth, wet it, and let me wipe all the blood away from that arm.

My eyes filled with tears as I did it. The idea that I could kill him or even hurt him was stabbing at my soul.

"Hey." He leaned down so his eyes were level with mine. "What's going on?"

"I just..." I blew out a breath. "This is all so much. And I could kill you. I don't want this. I don't want to be this."

"I know." He cupped my face and I remembered that there hadn't been any blood there. "How about you worry less when it comes to me and I promise to avoid your blood? Take that stress away."

I was about to agree, then he dropped his hand to my left shoulder, where I knew left-sided blood was and my eyes widened in horror. "*Aric!*" I screeched.

He stepped back. "What?"

My breath came in large huffs that hurt my chest. "Are you all right? What are you feeling?"

"I'm fine, Sloane." He furrowed his brows and watched me the way you would an injured animal.

"You touched my shoulder. There was blood on my shirt."

He pulled his hand up then turned it so that I could see there was nothing there and my shoulders slumped in relief.

"That's not taking the stress off," he said.

"Well, you weren't being careful."

He moved to get a better look at my shirt. "It's dried on your shirt. Maybe dried doesn't do the same thing. I mean, I feel nothing. I'm not even tingly." He glanced down at my left arm that had stopped bleeding. Dried blood streaked to my fingertips, but I looked at him with a warning. He'd better not—

Yup. He touched the blood on my arm, so I braced myself, ready to open a vein on my right to save him.

But nothing happened, so he continued touching the dried blood on my clothes and my skin. "We're good, Sloane. Dried blood doesn't hurt."

After letting out a long breath, I swallowed down the nausea. "OK. Good. But you almost gave me a heart attack."

"I didn't want to scare you, but we did need to know. Now, get naked and I'll clean off your clothes the best I can until we get to a washing machine. After you're done, we're leaving."

"I'm going to need to eat," I told him as I stepped under the water. Having someone bleed you like a medieval doctor trying to cure a cold took your energy. I needed to replace it.

"I'll send Alyssum and Jensen back to the diner for food. We can eat in the car."

Once I was out of the shower and had clean, blood-free clothing on, Aric tied my wet clothes up in a plastic bag. He must've really wrung them out because they weren't dripping from the bag. Then we piled in the car, Aric and I in the back, Alyssum and Jensen in the front with him driving, and got on the road to Detroit.

But something had changed. Shifted. The mood was even more tense than it had been.

"Is something wrong?" I asked Aric quietly, but we were in a confined space. Everyone would hear it.

That muscle in his jaw clenched. Yup. Something was wrong.

"Aric?"

"If you and Alyssum would've listened to us, you wouldn't have been hurt." *Oh.* Now that he knew I was all right, he was pissed.

"I'm fine," I snapped back. "And we got information that we wouldn't otherwise have gotten."

"But you might not have been fine!" he yelled back. "And that fucking witch has a vial of your blood. From both sides."

"Yeah." I couldn't disagree with him that her having those would be a problem. "Why did she do that?"

He looked at me with wild, wide eyes. "Are you fucking kidding me right now?" I assumed it was a rhetorical question. "'Why would she want that kind of power'?" Yeah. Even in my head, that hadn't sounded great.

She had a plan of some kind for sure.

Alyssum and Jensen stayed quiet in the front seat, though I caught her glancing back at us.

"If you wouldn't have been fine, I would've had to watch the woman I love bleed to death, Sloane. I'm not doing that. Next time you two don't listen to us or even consider what we're saying and you get hurt, I don't give a fuck what side of your body the blood came from. I'm helping you."

Which meant he would touch me, risking his life again to help me.

"We were wrong," Alyssum said loudly, causing Jensen's head to snap around to look at her, then he had to go back to watching the road.

"What?" Aric snapped.

"We were wrong." She snorted. "Yeah, I get it. It's shocking that I'm admitting I'm wrong, but we were. We were too focused on the information that we did eventually get, but we should've thought it through."

"Maybe from now on, we should rule by committee," Jensen offered. "Whatever the majority votes for, we do."

"What about a tie like today?" she countered.

He glanced at her again and from my angle, he was fighting a grin. "We'll have to think of clever ways to break a tie."

Though from the grunt that came from Aric's chest, I wasn't sure there was a creative way he'd even consider right now.

He was pissed, but it sure looked good on him.

Chapter Twenty-Four

We arrived in Detroit late, but I couldn't sleep. The four of us were in a single motel room again because it was decided that being together was safer. As I stared at the ceiling, I knew there was a better way to spend my time.

Carefully, I leaned over Aric to get my phone off the table, where all of ours were charging. Then I sat back against the headboard and opened up the search on my phone. If Gorgons had existed forever, there had to be something online about them.

So I searched. Though most of what I found right away was about Medusa and her sisters, which honestly, did sound a lot like what we'd been told. Though as far as I knew, I couldn't turn people into stone with my eyes and as of yet, snakes had not appeared in my hair.

The thought of which made me shiver.

So gross.

Though it was an added fear that one day Aric would look at me and become stone. I couldn't think about it. It was all too much.

"What're you doing?" Aric's tired voice whispered in the room.

Looking down at him, I said, "I couldn't sleep, so I've been trying to see if there's anything online about... I guess, me."

He pushed up. "I'll help you."

"No," I told him, setting my hand on his shoulder so I could encourage him to lie back down. "You were sleeping fine. Go back to it."

He shook his head. "I'm not just going to go to sleep while you're up working and worrying."

The light on my phone dimmed when I shut it off, leaving only a little moonlight in the room. "I'm not worrying," I whispered. "I've... come to terms with what I am. It's better to know that the left side of me could kill you, but the right could save you."

He chuckled quietly. "We did find out that dried blood doesn't do either."

I sighed. Yeah. That was good to know. I'd been

so stressed to make sure no one, not even a random animal, accidentally came into contact with my blood that this was a load off. "Come on."

Me lying down encouraged him to do the same and he wrapped me tightly in his embrace, not bothering to avoid the bandages on my arm. Even if the blood was dried, I'd keep my left arm covered until the wounds were fully healed. Never knew when a scab would break open.

At least I got a few hours of rest that was only broken by the weirdest dream. It didn't feel dream like. It was more like someone was speaking directly to me.

When I woke the next morning, I tried to shake it off, but the feeling lingered.

It had to be a message or a memory or something.

Once we were all awake, Jensen and Aric went to get us breakfast, leaving Alyssum and me alone in the room. I hadn't said anything about my dream, so I was glad to have her alone because I worried that it would make me sound crazy.

"I had a weird dream last night," I told her as we got dressed. I'd just pulled a shirt over my head.

"Did it have the hair snakes? Because that would creep me out."

I laughed because clearly, I wasn't the only one

who'd thought about the hair snakes. "No. And it kind of didn't feel like a dream. More like a message." I looked up at her. She'd paused with her shirt in her hand. "Does this make me sound crazy?"

"No. I've heard of weird things. Connections. What did it say?" She yanked a light-pink shirt over her head then sat down on the bed across from me.

"I don't know that it said anything." I groaned. "This is going to sound so weird, but I got the impression that the curse did start with a brokenhearted witch. That was the catalyst, but not the whole reason for it."

Her teeth sunk into her bottom lip as she listened.

"Like it was a deep, genuine love, but he betrayed her, so she wanted revenge."

"What did he do?"

"He betrayed her. Took a powerful talisman, I guess you'd call it. It's something that would protect the Gorgons, not only from the coven who used their power over them, but something else. I don't know what it is, but the witch's power was the only thing that would protect them. It was that and I have a feeling it was because the three goddesses hadn't shown up yet. So he took it and left without a word, causing the witch to want to seek revenge." I glanced down at the obsidian pendant hanging against my chest. "You don't think this is the talisman, do you?"

She shook her head. "It couldn't be, right? How would the witches still have it?"

"Yeah. That makes sense."

"So," she started, staring into the middle distance like she was trying to figure this all out in her head. "They curse the Gorgons because of the witch's heartbreak over him stealing something powerful. We don't know what happened to the talisman, but the curse is for the three goddesses to never show up or at least that's part of it. It's a good reason to want to sacrifice one of you." She held up a hand. "I didn't mean—"

"I know you didn't. Keep going."

"So the talisman could protect them, but talismans have finite power." She glanced up at me with those blue eyes. "We spent some time with Flora to learn whatever we could." She took a breath. "So she thought your combined three goddesses' power could break the witches' bonds to magic. Giving them yet another reason to curse you. But why not curse the Gorgons before that?"

I shook my head. "I don't know. Maybe there was a piece to the puzzle that they needed?"

"Maybe..."

"That means the reunion of the sisters," I said, as if I weren't one of them, "would threaten more than just the witch who cast the curse, right?"

She nodded. "It'd threaten the entire coven's hold on magic." Then she sat up pin-straight. "There was something Flora said her grandmother told her when she was little. Something about a power too great for any group to possess. What if the Gorgons were meant to inherit it and the witches are afraid of what happens to them once they do?"

"So they'd need the three goddesses to unlock it?"

She nodded. "It's just a hypothetical, but it would make sense." Both of our gazes went to the door when we heard two car doors close right outside the motel room. "We have to tell them."

"But we don't know anything yet," I told her.

She shook her head. "You heard Aric in the car. He was pissed that we overruled them and we agreed to share and come to decisions together."

She was right. Of course she was right, but it sounded insane and I hated the idea of telling him. But I would.

As soon as Aric and Jensen stepped through the door, I said, "I know how to find the first sister."

Aric furrowed his brows and set a box of donuts on the table. "What?"

"It's going to sound weird, but I had... a dream, I guess, and there's, like, this invisible bond between us. I'll be able to feel when we're close and I think I know where to start."

Alyssum's mouth dropped open as she put her hands on her hips. "You didn't tell me that part."

Snickering, I said, "We didn't get to it." Then I turned back to the guys. "Better grab a donut. I'm about to take you on a wild ride."

We all munched on our breakfast and had some coffee while I told them everything I'd just told Alyssum. I had to give them credit because they let me get it all out without stopping me and they acted like this was the most normal thing in the world.

It wasn't. But it was my normal now.

"Do you think her sister knows about all this?" Alyssum asked.

"I didn't," I said. "Why should she?"

She shrugged. "Are you nervous? I mean, it is your sister."

"No. Of all of this, meeting a birth relative doesn't really give me pause, ya know?"

"All right." Aric stood and tossed his empty coffee cup in the trash. "We should get going, then.

You said you think you'll be able to lead us. We should get this started."

While we cleaned up, we decided that Aric would drive and not me so that I could close my eyes and focus whenever I needed to. Probably for the best because as much as I'd said the idea of meeting a sister didn't faze me, my hands were vibrating almost imperceptibly.

As Aric drove, we went strictly on my instincts. When I said *turn left*, he turned left. All of this led us to a bookstore. Not where I'd thought we'd end up, but here we were.

The scenario in my mind had us pulling up to a seedy bar in the middle of the night. But it was daylight and a bookstore.

"Are you sure this is where we're supposed to be?" Jensen asked.

I shook my head as I looked back at him. "I'm not sure of anything."

"But do you feel a pull?" Alyssum clarified.

"Oh, yeah." There was an intense pressure in my chest unlike anything I'd ever felt before. Pressure and slight nausea. Which was great. If there had to be a bond, please let it be nausea, right?

Everyone stayed close behind me and let me do my thing. I moved in whatever direction increased the pressure until finally, I turned down an aisle with a woman who had my similar coloring but didn't look like me at all.

I supposed we weren't identical.

She was my height with brown hair cut into a stacked bob. Very trendy. She was reading the back of a book and rubbing her chest when I approached. If her chest was feeling anything like mine, I could relate.

"Hi," I said, sounding as awkward as I felt. She was wearing jean shorts and a tank top.

When she glanced up at me, I found that she had the same big, brown eyes that I did. "Hey." Then she went back to reading her book.

After swallowing hard, I took a deep breath. "This is going to sound ridiculous..." She looked back up at me and raised a single eyebrow. "Are you adopted?"

That eyebrow slammed down as she thrust the book back onto the shelf and turned to walk away.

"I told you it'd sound weird." I hurried over in front of her so she'd have to stop. When she turned to go the other way, Aric, Jensen, and Alyssum were at the other end. Probably not the best idea, considering she now looked trapped. I waved them back. "Like I said, I know it's going to sound insane. But... are you?"

"No, but why are you asking me that? And why are you and your friends trapping me in this aisle?" Her stance changed, like she thought she might have to fight me.

No? She would've had to have been... Wait. I hadn't been. Right. "I was raised in foster care," I blurted out. "Were you?"

She narrowed her eyes on me. "Yes. Again, why are you asking me this?"

"Listen." I took a small step forward. "I can't prove this to you, other than the intense pressure you're probably feeling in your chest right now, but you and I are sisters. Two-thirds of triplets actually."

"You're cracked," she said. "I'm not getting trafficked by you and your friends." She made her way around me, but I followed.

"Please stop," I begged. "I'm not trying to traffic you. I've been looking for my sisters and you're one of them. Please." I reached out and grabbed her wrist, but she snapped it right back. "Please. Can I buy you a coffee so we can talk?"

"What did you do?" she asked, looking at me like I held all the answers to all the questions.

"I haven't done anything. I swear." I even held my hands up to prove it.

"You... When you touched me..."

Right. My entire arm had gotten warm and if she was asking me, then hers did too. "You felt it, didn't you?" To me, it felt like a lock, sealing our connection.

She stood there like she was contemplating her *fight or flight* plan for a few moments before she sighed and said, "One coffee."

I led us to the café in the bookstore, we ordered then sat down in a table away from everyone else. Out of the corner of my eye, I saw that Alyssum, Jensen, and Aric ordered drinks and sat down as well.

"What's with your friends?" she asked.

"First..." I placed a hand on my chest. "I'm Sloane Reagan."

"Sabrina Levine."

"I'm really happy to meet you," I told her. "I grew up with no family, so this is a treat."

She nodded. "Yeah. Me too. So what about them?"

"I've only known them for a while. Alyssum... I helped her in a time she needed help and we've been friends since. The brown-haired man is her boyfriend and the one with darker hair is mine. His name's Aric. Her boyfriend is Jensen."

"So they're just here to help you find me?" She took a drink of her coffee quickly. "And you said we're part of a triplet set? How would you know that?"

I blew out a breath to try to keep me from cackling like a deranged witch. There was so much to tell her and not a lot of it is believable.

"Please remember that I told you this isn't going to sound real, OK?" I began. Sabrina nodded. "First, you feel the connection, right? Like you believe me when I say we're sisters."

She narrowed her eyes and set her jaw as she looked at me. "I don't know that I ought to, but yeah. I do."

"So, there is, apparently, a whole supernatural world out there that we've never known about," I said. The way her face dropped, I knew I was losing her. "I know. Trust me. I know. But Aric is something called a Gobel, which to us would be like a goblin."

She turned in her seat quickly to look at him. "He doesn't look like a goblin."

I snorted. "I know, right? Alyssum and Jensen are Gremalian—"

"Gremlins?" she whisper-yelled.

"Not exactly, but yes."

"So what are we?" she asked. When I didn't answer she continued. "That's what you're going to tell me, right? That we're something. What? Witches."

Now I did laugh out loud. "No. Definitely not witches. We're Gorgons."

She groaned. "That doesn't sound sexy."

"Clearly, it can be," I told her. "Look at us." That at least got a smile out of her. "But seriously, I didn't believe it at first, either. But there are things we can do." I glanced around quick and saw that some of the tables had these droopy, sad, almost-dead single carnations in a vase. "I can prove it. Come on."

She got up from the table with me. I went over, grabbed a flower, then headed to the bathroom. Because it wasn't empty, I went into the big stall with the baby changing table on it. That was where I set the flower.

"You can see this flower is almost dead, right?" I asked. She nodded with incredibly wide eyes.

I took the small pocket knife out of my pocket and pricked the tip of my right index finger, then pushed until a drop of blood appeared. Then I let it fall onto the flower.

Like magic, the flower grew and bloomed like it'd been given a second lease on life.

"Holy shit," she said under her breath. "It's like you—"

"Healed it. Yes. Blood from the right side heals." I was whispering as well because the bathroom was echoey and though I thought no one else was in here, I wanted to be careful.

"If the right heals, what does the left do?" Since I didn't know Sabrina, I couldn't tell if this was overwhelming her or if she wasn't believing it or what.

My face grew more serious. "Hurt." So I did the same thing to my left side, dropped the blood on the flower and watched it die.

"Shit," she muttered. "So you think I can do that?"

I shrugged. "I don't actually know. I don't know if this power is mine alone or if it's the same for all of us. But that's not the worst part. The worst part is that witches cursed the Gorgon. The curse kind of started to be broken when the Gremalians and Gobel ended their fighting. That's why all the Midwest earthquakes and shit are happening."

"So how does that involve us?"

"We have to finish breaking the curse so we can right what's going on with the environment. I don't completely know everything it's going to take to do it, but that's what we need to do. The next step would be finding our other sister."

"OK. So what do you need me to do?"

"Right now, I just needed you to believe me."

"I do."

And that was a very good thing. "So we have to find our other sister. We're something called the three goddesses. There's a lot to explain to you and I'd rather do it somewhere else."

"All right."

My heart fluttered at what I was going to say next. "We have a motel room not far. We could go there and explain everything, but I don't want you to think we're going to traffic you."

She snickered. "I don't think that anymore. I don't know why, but I believe every word you're saying."

"I think it's the connection," I told her as we made our way to the door. Before we left the room I dropped the flower in the trash. "I think it'd tell you if I was lying."

And for now, we were both going to have to trust that because we had another sister to find.

Chapter Twenty-Five

We weren't going to be finding that other sister today. There were no clues as to where she was so far. With nothing to go on, we headed to our motel. Sabrina followed in her car because even though there'd been some talk about going back to Sabrina's apartment, it was decided that there was a chance the witches would know about that place. Yet it was more unlikely they'd know about the hotel.

Once we arrived, Alyssum and Jensen left again to get us food. This was the kind of trip where you ate when you could, slept when you could, because you never knew what was coming next. Aric stayed here, I would guess because he didn't want me alone with my newfound sister. Or with anyone, really.

Given that witches kept trying to kill me at every turn, I couldn't blame him.

"Alyssum and Jensen will have drinks with them when they get back," I told her as Aric closed the door behind me.

Sabrina glanced at him then back to me. "I'm all right."

The awkward silence between us was loud as hell. "Why don't we sit down?" I sat on the edge of one bed while she hesitantly sat on the other so that we were facing each other. "I grew up in foster care," I told her to start. "Every couple of years, it was a new family. Some weren't great."

"Me too." Her shoulders visibly relaxed. "I didn't move every couple of years, though. I moved, but when I was thirteen, I was placed in this really nice home with some other foster kids. Three others and it was good. That's where I aged out of. The moms—there were two—still call to check up on me."

"It's nice that you had that." What she was talking about was like the unicorn of foster families. I'd heard they existed, but that hadn't been my experience.

"What's with him?" She nodded toward Aric, who was doing something on his phone while leaning against the wall near the door.

I let out a quiet snort and smiled. "He's very protective."

He's hot, she mouthed and I couldn't deny that, so I nodded in agreement, but Aric snorted, which meant he'd seen it all.

Rolling my eyes, I shook my head. "So." I slapped my hands against my thighs. "I told you I'd tell you everything, so here we go."

First, I went to my bag to grab the envelope with the information Ash had given us inside. Slowly, I pulled everything out. After all, this was all we had of our birth family. Then we went through each piece as I explained what we knew.

"So that's our mother?" she asked as she ran her finger lightly over the figure in the dark photograph.

"We think so. We don't know, though. It could've been someone else taking me there. Were you left at a firehouse, too?"

She shook her head. "Hospital."

"Do you heal quickly?" I asked her.

"Now that you mention it, I do. I broke my arm in fifth grade and was supposed to be in a cast for six weeks. But the doctor wanted to make sure I was healing correctly." She swallowed. "I didn't think anything of it, but when they took the x-ray at three weeks, it was totally healed."

"I do, too," I told her.

"How do we know if my blood does the same thing as yours?" Sabrina glanced from me to Aric then back. "I've bled on people before and none of them died."

"Yeah. I'd gotten my blood on someone before too," I confessed, making Aric's brows furrowed. At least he was doing a decent job of not interfering with our conversation. "None of them died." Now I looked at him and waited for an opinion.

He had so much more experience in this world than I did.

Aric cleared his throat then pushed off the wall. "Your abilities were probably blocked and the dam broke loose once the war between the Gremalians and us ended. My guess is that was part of the natural undoing of the curse. After all, you can't break a curse if you don't know it exists."

"Then how do we find out?" Sabrina asked. "If I can kill someone with my blood, I want to know. I don't want to become an accidental murderer."

"She's right," I told him. "We should know. She could hurt one of you if we don't."

Aric wet his lips and nodded. "Prick her finger."

My eyes widened as I started to shake my head. "No, Aric."

"What?" she asked, looking from me to him and back again.

"Do it." His gaze met mine and he was absolutely serious.

Aric wanted me to use him as a guinea pig to test Sabrina's powers. My stomach churned like a hurricane ripping through the gulf, volatile and unrelenting. This could hurt him, but if it was just a drop, maybe he'd be all right. Still, I didn't want to chance it.

"Aren't there any flowers around?" I asked as I pulled the small knife out of my pocket.

"There aren't any that are useful," he said quietly. "Just a drop." That was his reassurance that he'd be fine, but I was ready to rip open a vein to save him if that wasn't the case.

"What're we doing?" Sabrina asked.

"I'm going to prick your finger to get a drop of blood. Just a drop. We'll put it on his hand and if he feels something, then we know your blood works like mine."

Swallowing hard, I took her finger in my hand and quickly poked it with the knife. I'd have to keep this thing sharp so it didn't hurt as much when I needed to use it.

The red bubble appeared, reminding of me of

when one of my foster fathers would take his blood sugar, and despite everything inside me telling me to stop, I allowed it to drop onto Aric's hand. Then we waited. It should've been instant if something was going to happen.

"Anything?" I asked, but he shook his head, so we waited another few seconds.

"Still nothing," he said as he walked to the bathroom and dipped inside quickly before the water started to run. When he came out he was drying his hands. "So she doesn't have the blood thing."

"Right." I went to my bag to get the first-aid kit so that I could use one of the alcohol swabs on the end of the knife. Just because we weren't human didn't mean we couldn't get an infection... I didn't think. "So no blood magic."

"What powers do I have, then?" she asked as she wiped her finger on a tissue.

"Don't know yet. I'm sure we'll figure it out."

"And what about when we find the other sister? How do we break the curse?"

"Don't know that yet, either," I told her. "We're working on it, but we have to find her first."

Alyssum and Jensen returned with some food and the group of us situated ourselves around the small room. Those two were on the bed they'd be sleeping on while I sat on the one I'd be sleeping on. Aric was close to me and Sabrina sat in the lone chair in the corner.

"So how did you find the gremlins and goblins?" Sabrina asked, which brought groans from Aric and Alyssum, but Jensen and I snickered.

"I'm not really sure," I told her, but there was still laughter in my voice. "I was drawn to where they live, but I can't explain why."

Alyssum sat forward. "I think it was because Aric and I teamed up. It was like the first moment of each side coming together."

"Why did you two groan when I asked that question?" Sabrina continued and I loved that she asked whatever she was curious about. It was the only way she was going to learn and there was no possibility that I'd be able to tell her everything she might want to know without being asked.

Alyssum took a bite before answering. "We don't love being called 'gremlins' and 'goblins.' Yes, that is how the humans made sense of what we are, then it got bastardized for movies, but that's not us. I've had this conversation with him." She pointed at Jensen, who was doing everything he could not to laugh right at her. "And while we decided that I am small and can't eat from midnight to dawn. I'm definitely not a gremlin."

Jensen cleared his throat and said, "Definitely not."

After we'd finished eating, we spent some more time answering all of Sabrina's questions. At least until night set in. Then she left to get some sleep and we decided to do the same. Tomorrow, we had things to do, hopefully, including trying to figure out her powers so when the time came, she'd have them.

This would be a huge interruption to her life but she didn't mention anything that would stop her from going with us. She had a job but it was at a bar and it wasn't one she loved so she said she didn't care if they fired her. She lived alone but the rent was paid for the month and she could make the next one from her phone if necessary.

We'd agreed to meet here at the motel mid-morning. There was an empty lot surrounded by tall buildings that would make it more difficult for others to see us.

"OK," Sabrina said the next morning with her hands on her hips, like she was ready to get down to business. "What can you do?"

It took me several seconds to realize she meant Aric. "He controls nature. Is that the way to say it?" I asked him, but he shook his head, like he couldn't believe that was all I'd said. "Like the trees and grass and flowers."

Sabrina furrowed her brows. "That doesn't sound so useful."

"Oh, please," he groaned and honestly, I didn't think he'd be able to do much. We were surrounded by concrete.

Aric did his thing and things grew from the concrete as Sabrina and I both watched with awe. This wasn't something I'd seen. A tree wrapped around the top of the building to our left, covering us in shade as it blocked out the sun.

"Holy shit," she muttered, taking the words out of my mouth.

I was about to say as much when a voice I didn't recognize said, "You really shouldn't make yourselves so easy to find."

Turning to my right, I found a woman who looked to be around thirty with several others around her.

These people had to be more witches.

Aric pulled his hands back, which stopped the tree from growing more. "You and Sabrina get back to the motel." He stepped in front of the two of us. "Kill anyone who isn't us."

As I grabbed her arm, my stomach plummeted. Killing someone else wasn't really something I wanted to do, but to protect us, I guess I'd have to. Without arguing, I shoved Sabrina ahead of me and we hurried back. It was just around the corner.

When we got there, I got the door opened quickly then quickly shut it and locked both the doorknob and the deadbolt. I wasn't sure that would stop witches, but it was what I could do. Then I stood between Sabrina and the door with my pocket knife out and ready to use.

"Who was that?" she asked.

"I assume it's the witches who are looking for us."

"So that's all true?"

I couldn't risk looking away from the door. "Yeah. I told you it was."

There was a heavy silence before she said, "I don't think I totally believed you."

"Well, it's true." Hopefully, she was fully on board now. "And they won't stop until we find the third sister and break this damn curse."

"OK. What do we do?"

"Right now, we wait for the others."

Time was in limbo. It was like the moments when you needed help, so you called 911, and they got to you quickly, but even as quick as they'd arrived, it felt like forever. That was now. Not long could've passed, but it seemed like it was a hundred years before there was a knock on the door.

"Sloane," Aric called out. "It's us."

When I stepped forward to unlock the door, Sabrina grabbed my arm. "Are you sure it's them?"

"It sounds like Aric."

"Can the witches... I don't know, imitate voices?"

Well, shit. I had no idea. Was that something they could do to trick us?

Quickly, I went to the window and slowly pushed back the curtain so that I could see the three of them standing outside not looking any worse than they had when we'd left them. After unlocking the door, I took a step back.

"Can witches glamor or whatever to look like other people?"

Alyssum's eyebrows slammed down in confusion. "What?"

"How do we know you're you?" Sabrina asked.

Aric cocked his head to the side then closed the distance between us, cupped my face, and kissed me. My entire body relaxed as his mouth moved over mine and I pushed up onto my toes, completely forgetting that there were others in the room with us. Then he ended the kiss and whispered, "It's me."

Nodding, I ran my tongue over my bottom lip. "It's him." Then I blew out a breath. "What are we doing now?"

"We have to get out of here," Alyssum told us. "We have to go somewhere more secluded so we can figure out Sabrina's powers. Somewhere less populated."

"We think that witches can sense the two of you being near," Jensen explained. "That's how they keep finding us. They might still find us out in the woods, but it'll take them longer."

"We can also set up some alarms," Alyssum added. "But we have to go."

Sabrina nodded, but it looked like she was doing it absently. Like she didn't know she was. "So I have to leave with you?"

I turned around and took her hands in mind. "Just for a while. You can go back to your normal life once this is finished, but they aren't going to stop looking for you and if you're here alone... I don't think it'll end well."

"No, it's fine," she said, but her voice shook. "I don't like my job, anyway. I'll get another when I can come back."

But she needed clothes.

Aric offered to go with her to her apartment for her to pack a bag, but he didn't want me going. Staying with Jensen and Alyssum here was safer, he said. We weren't in the middle of the city, which was closer to where they were going. Though I thought that it'd be even safer if we were all together, I was outvoted.

Once Aric texted that they were done, the three of us got into the SUV, Jensen driving, Alyssum up front, and me in the middle seats, to go pick them up. No sense in Sabrina bringing her own car.

Twenty minutes later, we were all together, only Alyssum had climbed into the back so Aric could sit up front with Jensen and the three of us could talk like we'd known each other for years.

"So back in the lot, Aric showed his power," Sabrina said to Alyssum. "But you didn't show yours. What can you do?"

We'd been driving at least an hour and were on a country highway where we only passed a car once in a while.

"I can control electricity," Alyssum told her. "It's kind of cool."

"She and Jensen also have this energy-sucking

thing when they're together," I added. "That's horri-fying to see."

And I hated it every single time.

"Show me," she insisted.

Alyssum furrowed her brows. "The power-sucking? No way. Jensen's driving and Aric won't let me do it to Sloane, which means I'd have to do it on him. I've used him as a guinea pig enough."

Sabrina sat back. "I meant the electricity."

"Oh." Alyssum snickered. "I can, but it's going to piss Jensen off."

Knowing him, he wouldn't stay mad at her, though.

Alyssum shook out her hands and took a deep breath, the way I'd seen her do more than once when she was drawing in energy. Then she touched the metal on the door and sparks flew, racing toward the front of the car.

And the car turned off... Just no power whatsoever.

"Damn it, Alyssum," Aric said with a sigh while Jensen got the car off the road as it coasted to a stop.

"Yeah, my bad," she said but the humor in her voice told them she wasn't sorry.

Jensen shook his head then got out of the car

while Aric slid over into the driver's seat and popped the hood.

Sabrina was both in awe and trying not to laugh. "They act like that's a normal thing that happens."

I snickered. "I think it does with Alyssum around." Alyssum laughed quietly.

The car came back to life and the hood closed, but this time, Jensen came back to the passenger seat.

"Aren't you going to say something?" Aric asked him once he was inside the car.

Jensen shrugged. "What am I going to say?"

"You're scared of her," he accused Jensen, but I could hear the humor he was trying to hide.

"I mean... yes, but in this case, it was an easy fix," Jensen explained. "I try to pick my battles."

That's when the three of us women got lost in a fit of laughter. He wasn't wrong. Jensen loved Alyssum, but he'd fight with her if he felt it was necessary. This just wasn't something that made it necessary.

Jensen turned in his seat, dropping his heavy gaze on her. "Just please don't do it again until we get where we're going."

"Promise," Alyssum told him, but we couldn't help but laugh again.

We arrived at a cabin on a lake that The

Gremalian owned a couple of hours away from Detroit. It wasn't really Ash's but more like inherited by the next leader. By the time we got there, Alyssum, Sabrina, and I were bonded like sisters. Better yet, we had a plan.

Figuring out Sabrina's powers was of the utmost importance, but so was finding the third sister.

We'd work on both at the same time. Aric and I on powers. Jensen and Alyssum on figuring out where to go next. I'd also work that part because I planned to look within again like I had before, which had led us to Sabrina.

If I'd done it before, I could do it again.

Chapter Twenty-Six

The cabin Aric and Jensen had brought us to was in the middle of nowhere with solar power for energy. Given the thick woods we'd driven through, I thought there was no chance the solar would work, but it turned out to be in a clearing that got plenty of sunlight and Aric moved his hands. Branches cracked and creaked as they moved away from us, creating an opening toward the sun. The sound of furniture moving across a wooden floor echoed through the trees.

It wasn't furniture. It was Aric literally bending the trees to his will.

Inside the cabin looked like it belonged to a magazine, though it could have used a good dusting. Surprisingly, I figured it'd be more rundown, but the

wooden beams comprising the ceiling gave it charac-
ter. The rustic furniture wasn't overdone and I could
picture a couple using this place as a getaway.
Sitting in front of a warm fire in the fireplace, backs
against the couch, snuggled under a blanket in the
winter.

But that wasn't why we were here. We were here
to be safe.

We'd barely gotten into the place when Alyssum
and Jensen said they were going to get us some
supplies in the nearest town. It would probably take
a while, given how far we were from everything.

Aric came over to me and put his hands on my
shoulders. "I'm going, too."

"To get supplies?" That didn't make sense. In
what world would he want to leave me alone?

"No." He shook his head. "I'm going to use
nature to create a barrier around us. Make it harder
for anyone to get through."

"Oh. Yeah. That makes sense."

He cupped my face and ran his fingers over my
cheeks the way I knew he liked to do. I liked it too.
"I'll be close." Then he leaned down and pressed his
lips to mine. His kiss flooded my body with warmth,
making me feel all mushy inside.

Once he'd ended the kiss, he gave me another

small one before leaving the cabin as I watched him go.

"Damn," Sabrina muttered, causing me to turn toward her. "I've never had a man look at me like that, let alone kiss me like that."

"Like what?" I asked, closing my arms around me.

"Like..." She waved her hands around. "That. I don't know. Like you're the most important thing in his world." My cheeks heated at the description. "He must really love you."

"Yeah." I moved closer to her after deciding to be honest. "It scares me. I mean, I love him, too, but I know for him that means he'll put himself between me and danger."

"And you don't want that?"

I shook my head and held off the ripple of fear that came over me. "He'd die for me. I don't want him to die."

"I understand." She shrugged. "I mean, I understand the words. I've never had that with anyone, so I don't know."

"I just..." I blew out a long breath. If there was anyone who could understand what I was feeling, it had to be her. She'd been through the same kind of thing I had, grown up basically the same way. The rest of them had a loving family at least for a little while. I couldn't relate to that. "I'm a little scared of that kind of love," I admitted for the first time to anyone.

"Why is that?" She sat on the arm of the couch in the living area, though this was one big area.

"You know," I told her, but she just waited, which meant I was going to have to say it. "I'm afraid of being left alone again. My worry goes beyond losing someone I love. I'm literally terrified that I'll be all alone in the world again." Now that I'd found this little family and it was so different from my relationship with Rhea, I was scared to lose it. That was tough to admit.

"That, I understand. Even though the last years I had a solid family to live with, I haven't forgotten all the years before it. But if we figure out my powers, I can help stop that from happening."

"Right." I stood up straighter. "But how do we do that?"

"How did you figure out your powers?"

A flash of the blood dripping from my hand... Me pushing the man away. Him screaming.

The scream echoed in my ears even now.

"I didn't." Well. That wasn't exactly true now, was it? "I mean I did, but it was on accident. I cut my hand on a tree, then I tried to push the guy attacking me away from me. He died. It reminded me of something a seer had said, which is why I tried using the other side of my body's blood to heal Aric."

"You know that if anyone heard us talking right now, they'd think we were crazy."

I snorted. "Yeah. They would. I think we're crazy, but I know what happened and can't deny it. So... The seer I met said that we're a trio. The maiden—that's me. I don't know why, though. I'm still new to this. Maybe it's a birth order thing? A crone would be old, right? Maybe."

"So that would make me..."

"Either the mother or the crone. I don't know how we'll be able to tell."

Before we could hypothesize any more, Jensen and Alyssum came through the door, each carrying too many bags.

"You know, we could have helped. Made more than one trip," I told them.

"Eh." She set the bags down hard on the counter, though Jensen was carrying at least twice as many.

"Someone doesn't like to make more than one trip," he told me.

That was when Aric joined us and as the five of

us put everything away, I asked, "How do we train Sabrina to figure out her powers?"

"Oh, shoot," Alyssum said as she snapped her fingers and hurried over to her bag. "I meant to go over this with you already, but we haven't had time." She pulled an old-looking book, with a cracked spine and wrinkled pages, out of one of her bags. It wasn't super big. "I found this in the library before Aric totaled the car."

"*I* didn't total it," he said right away. "The earth did that."

Alyssum rolled her eyes but didn't respond as she brought it over to the table where Sabrina and I were. "I found this in a place it shouldn't have been, but I think everyone thought this was just kind of rumor. Fairy tales. Dark fairy tales, but we wouldn't have known it's real. It talks about the Gorgons. But more than that..." She pointed to a drawing on the first page.

I wrapped my hand around the pendant hanging around my neck. The drawing looked exactly like this one, which meant this pendant had been meant for the Gorgons all along and this book... It was about us.

Aric and Jensen had just finished putting the last of the groceries away then said they were going to make us all some sandwiches. The way the cabin was set up, the three of us women took a seat at the table, but the men would be able to hear everything.

"What does it say?" I asked.

"It talks about the legend of the three goddess. Again." She held her hand up. "I can't say that this is accurate at all, but someone must've done some research or something because there're too many similarities."

"We need information, Alyssum," I said gently. "We won't hold it against you if it's wrong."

She sighed. "I wasn't thinking that, but good."

Alyssum went on to read that the legend, or whatever you wanted to call it, said that the three goddesses would be born to keep the supernatural world in check. Basically as a power balance to the witches, who, at that time, had been seen as the most powerful.

I mean... If they could cast whole curses on us, then it seemed to me they were indeed the most powerful.

"The maiden signifies innocence and youth, which feels like you, Sloane," Alyssum said. Yep. Put that together myself. "The mother shows nurturing and creation with her mind. Entire worlds that aren't there."

"What the hell does that mean?" Jensen asked.

None of us really knew, but Aric said, "Could it be something like illusions? Create entire worlds that aren't there. That would be an illusion."

"Could be," Alyssum agreed. "And the crone is the elder. Wisdom and death with the metal gaze."

"'Metal gaze'?" I furrowed my brows. "Does that mean the whole Medusa, *turning people to stone* thing?"

"It has to, right?" Alyssum went back to reading. "It says here that it's a gaze that she alone can cast, but that her sisters can undo."

"Which means…" My eyes went to Sabrina. "That Sabrina could turn us all to stone right now."

"No," Sabrina said after she'd snorted.

"Yeah. If you're the crone."

"Hang on." Alyssum held her hand up. "If the sisters can undo it, then she wouldn't be able to turn you."

"Oh, OK," I said with a humorless laugh. "Just the rest of you, then."

"We don't know I'm the crone," Sabrina countered.

"I know. But how do we figure it out? I had to *kill* someone to figure out my powers."

"Before we resort to murder," Alyssum continued, "it should be noted that it does say in here that ending the Gremalians and Gobel conflict was the first step in breaking the curse. So we were right there."

"If the curse is meant to be broken by the three sisters, maybe you gremlins and goblins should stay back," I told them as my stomach tightened painfully. Their responses would be predictable and I didn't want any of them angry with me. At the same time, I wanted them safe. They'd become my family.

"Fuck that," Aric said right away as he watched me. "If you think you're doing this and I'm going to fuck off back to Phoenix, you really are crazy."

Sabrina, Alyssum, and Jensen watched us back and forth.

"I'm actually not," I snapped. "I care about you three. I just—"

"It doesn't matter," Alyssum said, cutting me off. "You're literally in this because you saved my life. I wouldn't have been able to heal with the amount of blood I was losing, Sloane. I get it. It's dangerous. We all know that and we're going to be here, anyway."

Aric's dark gaze bore into me like a drill. I didn't have to look at him because I could feel it. Me suggesting they stay back had pissed him off and I didn't feel bad about that. Him getting hurt or worse worried me. The image of him in the woods the day he'd almost died haunted me.

That night, when we went to bed, Aric was quiet, as he had been since I'd suggested that he, Alyssum, and Jensen go back once we found the third sister. My intention hadn't been to hurt his feelings, but apparently, I had.

"You're mad." There was no question to it as I sat on the bed where we were supposed to sleep. Though I'd heard that you were never supposed to go to bed angry because you never knew what could happen in the night, I wasn't sure it applied here. We didn't know what would happen in the night, but most likely nothing. It was tomorrow we had to worry about.

He let out a long sigh. "Yeah, I kind of am."

"Because I want you to be safe?"

He turned to me with a pinched expression and narrowed eyes. "Not because you want me to be safe, but because you keep trying to make me leave." He dropped down onto the bed with a heaviness that made me lean toward him.

"I'm not trying to make you leave."

"You are," he snapped, though he kept his voice down so the entire cabin wouldn't hear us. "Every time you say that we should stay back, you're trying to make me leave you to deal with this shit alone. You know how fucked up that is, right?"

"I just—"

"No, you don't have to explain." He adjusted himself so that he was sort of facing me. "I understand the feeling, but I'm telling you wild hogs wouldn't be able to make me go. I'm not going to go be safe while you're in danger and it's insane that you think it's even an option."

"OK," I finally told him because arguing with him wasn't going to help anyone. There wasn't anything that would make me leave him, so why did I expect that they'd do it? I'd have to learn to accept that, no matter how much I didn't want to.

Actually, I knew the answer. I'd always been left on my own to figure things out. In the human world, I'd been the only one looking out for my safety and I guess I kind of expected that of them too when I knew damn well this was different. *They* were different.

I'd never been loved before, other than by Rhea and Charlie by extension.

"I won't say it again," I promised as I climbed onto his lap so that I was straddling him. He adjusted again so he was sitting fully with his back against the wall and his big hands grabbed my hips. "I've never had anyone who cared this much," I whispered as I leaned down and kissed his neck. "I don't know how to handle it."

Aric cupped his hands around my cheeks, his fingers lacing into my hair. "I don't just *care* about you, Sloane. I love you and that is going to keep me here to make sure you're safe."

"I know." My words were still quiet so that he wouldn't be able to hear the tears in my voice. I could control them from my eyes, but there was no doubt my voice would crack. Then I swallowed hard.

I wasn't the one who usually initiated things between us. It was my shyness in this area that kept me from doing it, but tonight, with no idea of what tomorrow would bring, I had to do it.

My hands rested on his bare shoulders as I leaned in to kiss him. I'd kissed him plenty of times—it was what came next that I'd never done first. As he took over that kiss, I slid my hands down between us and didn't stop until I slipped them into his boxer briefs. It was an odd angle, but when his breath hitched as my fingers touched the head of his cock, I didn't care.

Aric's hands moved from where they'd been holding my bed to trail down my arms to my hips. Slowly, he pushed those hands under my shirt.

But he was taking too long for me and I sat back, breaking our kiss, to yank my shirt over my head. My bare breasts hit the cooler air, causing my nipples to harden. He pulled me toward him so that my bareness pressed against his.

He was warm and his chest hard as he held me tightly, wrapping his arms around my back. His kisses were wet as he trailed them down my neck, making my toes curl as he trailed his lips across my chest. I wasn't sure how he did it, but when I lifted my hips, he was able to get his boxers past me then continued until they were off.

Aric was everywhere, touching and squeezing as I stroked his erection. He squeezed my ass with his big hand then brought me closer to him.

I wanted him. Needed to feel closer. Needed to, just for these few short moments, block out everything we still had to do. With the threat of danger around every corner... I had to have moments like this because I didn't want to waste a second. When he brought one hand around to the front of me to circle my clit, I thought I was going to explode right then.

In our time together, I'd figured out that I was pretty easy to orgasm, but I thought that was him.

The way he touched me, the way he handled me... It was him.

Again, summoning a bravery that I hadn't known I actually had, I grabbed a hold of his cock then lifted myself and placed him at my opening.

"Sloane," he grumbled from his chest right before I dropped myself onto him. His hands tightened on my hips. "Condom." He said it clearly, but it sounded like he was struggling with something.

My eyes widened. I couldn't believe I'd just done that. I gasped. "Oh, my god. I'm so sorry. Caught up in the moment."

"It's fine. I'm fine," he said through clenched teeth. "I want you to know."

I swallowed hard then thought about it. I'd had my IUD for two years—as soon as I'd been legally allowed to make that decision myself—because while I hadn't been having sex then, if it happened, I hadn't wanted a kid. Aric had used a condom the times we'd been together and that was the smart thing to do. But maybe... just this once...

"I'm covered," I told him, sounding a little breathless. "IUD." Because this one time, I didn't want anything between us.

Aric paused for only a second then threaded his

hand into my hair, fisting at the back of my head, and covered his mouth with mine.

Was it reckless? I didn't think so because I was covered, as I'd told him.

Since I had no idea what I was doing, Aric helped guide my hips and at this angle, I felt so full. Maybe it was just because it was different. Maybe it was him—I didn't know. But I let myself get lost in it. With one hand, he gripped my hip, and the other came back around the front to tweak my sensitive area.

It didn't take much for me to tumble down that hill of ultimate pleasure and I collapsed against his chest while still riding him. Thankfully, he came right after me and brought my body to a halt so I could lean against him and catch my breath. He wrapped his arms around me and just held me there as long as I needed.

Then I sat up and moved back so that he could fall out of me and smiled up at him shyly. That whole thing had been so unlike me, but what did I know? I was still exploring this side of me and what we'd just done... I'd loved every minute of it.

"I'm going to go out to the bathroom," he said, his voice low. "I'll bring back a washcloth for you to get cleaned up, then you can go out there after you get dressed."

I nodded tiredly as he gently moved me off him so he could get up.

If only everything could be just like this moment. There was a lot we still had to do, but when it was done, I was going to demand more time like this.

It was the security I found with him that I craved. Him... yes, of course, but the only reason I could be with him this way was because he made me feel safe and secure and loved.

If I lost that, I didn't know what I'd do.

In the morning, I woke up long before I'd had enough sleep and stretched out my tired muscles while remembering everything from last night. A smile crept over me as I glanced at a sleeping Aric next to me. When he was asleep, there was no worry wrinkling his face. He was relaxed and if I didn't think I'd wake him, I'd run my finger over the line that formed between his eyebrows whenever me being in danger came up.

There was movement out in the main area, so I carefully got up and headed out there. I'd put my pajamas back on last night, so I didn't have to do it today.

At the table, Sabrina sat with a cup of coffee in

front of her, one leg pulled up to her chest and Alyssum's book in front of her.

"Not a fan of sleep?" I asked as I got a glass of water.

"I am, but it's not always a fan of me."

I felt that. Sometimes, sleep wasn't easy to get. I blamed it on the years of trying to do it in loud houses.

"Listen," she said as she shifted toward me. "I found something in this book. I think it's a lead on the third sister." We didn't usually refer to the three of us as sisters yet. It was still too new. "Right here."

I leaned over and read what she was pointing at, then slowly sat in the chair. It talked about a specific place just outside of Ann Arbor. There was only one place I could think of. "I think you're right. Near Brighton?"

She nodded. "It's outside of Ann Arbor. But it sounds like someone in Alyssum's group was set to find us, so this has to be more recent of an entry. Things got heated with the Gobel and whoever it was had to stop looking." She took a drink from her cup. "There are warnings about what we'll face, but nothing specific. Why would they even look for us before the gremlins and goblins made peace?"

I shrugged. "I don't know. Maybe they thought

they could stop the aftermath? Maybe Alyssum knows."

"We better wake them then, right?"

I nodded. We were going to have to grab a quick breakfast and then get on the road.

This feeling of dread filled me. We had a sister to find and that was the priority right now. But the danger was so high and real that everything in me said to run the other way. Figure out something else to stop what was happening.

The problem being... there wasn't anything else we could do.

Chapter Twenty-Seven

It was only going to take about an hour to get to Brighton. When we got closer, I'd try to look within myself again to help us find her the way that I had with Sabrina. Hopefully, the pendant would talk to me. Otherwise, we'd just be walking around until Sabrina or I got the sister vibe, which I noticed had gone away since I'd first found her. There was still a tingle telling me she was near, but that intense, nauseous feeling hadn't come back.

Yesterday, I had promised Aric that I wouldn't mention him leaving us to finish this. That didn't mean I wouldn't be worried about his safety. Actually, I'd probably have an ulcer before all of this was said and done, given the amount of stress and worry I had specifically for him.

Maybe it was crazy, but I didn't want to live through losing him.

In the SUV that Aric was driving with Jensen up front, Alyssum and Sabrina sat in the middle seat while I had climbed into the third row. I needed some distance to spiral now so I wouldn't do it when we needed me to be on my game.

I pushed on the pocket knife in the pocket of my shorts just to remind me it was there. All of my previous cuts had healed to where you couldn't even tell that they'd ever been there.

"Alyssum," I called out quietly. When she looked back, I waved her over.

She undid her seatbelt then quickly climbed back with me and put another one on. We all were being diligent about always being buckled up, given that we never knew when the earth was going to rumble.

"What's up?" she asked quietly, as if she knew that I didn't want everyone in the car to hear this.

"I'm curious about something," I told her.

"Go ahead."

I bit my lips together quickly to calm my nerves. "I want to know how you do it."

"Do what?"

"Deal with knowing that Jensen could be hurt...

or worse." It was hard speaking my biggest fear out loud. Every time I did, it was hard, but this was different. I wasn't just saying that I worried about this, I was looking for a way to accept it and live with it.

"I don't think about it much," she told me quietly. When I scrunched my face up like I didn't believe her she said, "I don't. Maybe it's growing up in this life, but I assume that he'll protect himself."

"And that's it?"

She nodded. "That's it."

"But you know he'd protect you first and disregard his safety. That means he'd die if it meant saving you, right? That's the part I'm talking about."

Her face softened as she watched me. "It does mean that, but I'd do the same thing. This is how I was raised. It's like..." She paused, as if she needed to find the right words. "It just is and we all have to live with it. I know that sounds cold, but again, this is how I grew up."

"So what I'm hearing is that I need to push this fear down as far as I can and forget it exists."

She snickered, then put a hand over her mouth to quiet it. "I don't know that's possible, but if you can, yes. And let's not forget, you have us on your side.

Jensen and I will Wonder-Twin power the shit out of people. We're going to be fine."

Alyssum and Jensen could join hands and suck away all of someone's energy... Their basic will to live would be gone. It didn't kill them, but it made them wish it had. That would give us time to act, but had they ever tried it on witches? No. They hadn't, so we didn't even know if it would work or not.

When I glanced out the window as I tried to figure out how in the hell I'd just make myself not worry about Aric the way that I was, dark clouds rolled across the sky. "What the hell is that?" This, I asked much louder, causing Alyssum and Sabrina to move closer to the window.

We couldn't do anything but watch as the wind swirled. I'd seen this in movies before. "Tornado," I whispered. Then I cleared my throat. "Is that a tornado?"

"Not until it hits the ground," Alyssum said, pushing herself back. "We need to get out of here."

"It hit the ground." Sabrina tapped the window. "Holy shit. There's more than one!"

It took me a second, but she was right. The tornado we saw forming had split into three.

"Go!" Jensen yelled and Aric hit the gas.

You couldn't outrun a tornado, so I watched to

see which direction it was headed so that we could go the opposite. "Right!" I called out. "Turn right, then the next left."

Aric hit the gas as hail began to fall, pelting against the metal of the SUV. I closed my eyes and took a deep breath. It sounded like a freight train out there.

"Nope," Aric said, slamming on the brakes, then throwing the car into reverse.

No, no, no. That was back *toward* the tornadoes. Then the car lurched forward again. I looked back to water flowing toward us. I had no idea if there was even a river or other body of water around, but whatever it was, it was flooding.

Aric hit the gas again to get us out of there while Jensen turned the radio on and searched for a station. Finally, he settled on one that was covering the current weather.

There was talk of how the three tornadoes had come out of nowhere and the announcer was calling them "the three sisters." Sabrina looked over her shoulder at me.

Yeah. The irony here wasn't lost on me.

I gripped the seatbelt tightly when Aric hit a bump, assuming that I was about to fall again. But I didn't. After what felt like forever, the hail ended, the clouds cleared, and we were in the sun again.

"That was..." Sabrina shook her head, like she didn't have the words. Yeah. I understood that.

The car was quiet until we got just outside of Brighton.

Brighton wasn't a big city. It was rather small, in fact, but this was my cue to try to look within myself like I had at the beach in the UP. But nothing was happening. The radio played and even when I drowned that out, I focused on other people's breathing.

"Could we find somewhere to stop?" I asked. Aric looked into the rearview mirror, where he'd be able to see me. "I need to find somewhere to look within myself." Sabrina gave me a curious look. "It has to be away from distractions."

"Got it," he said, then he took another left.

Aric found a patch of trees and drove down the trail to get me somewhere quiet I could focus. Once he was at a stop he thought would work, I climbed over Alyssum to get out the back door while he climbed out of his.

"I was with you on the beach," he said as he settled his hand on my lower back. "I won't bother you, but I'm not letting you go out here alone."

Nodding, I told him, "I know. I'm fine with that."

We walked away from the car a little. Not too far. We could still see it and the others could still see us, but I needed distance. Then Aric stepped away from me too. I sat down on a log that was there, closed my eyes, and took a couple of cleansing breaths. I must've been better at it this time because soon, there were flashes of a scene before my eyes.

It was a restaurant. Not what I'd call a diner. There was a woman who looked familiar taking orders. The feeling that I had when I'd been in that bookstore to find Sabrina washed over me. I had to brace myself on my knees, the nausea was so intense.

"Sloane, are you all right?" Aric asked quietly.

I held up a hand but kept focused on what I was looking for. Was this restaurant here in Brighton? That was where the book had led us. It had to be, right?

The wind kicked up, at first just blowing my hair off my shoulders, then gaining in intensity.

"We have to go," Aric said with a new urgency.

"Just another—" I searched harder, but everything was getting farther and farther away.

"We don't have any more time." He grabbed my arm and yanked me up then hurried to the car with me in tow. Once I was inside, he climbed in as leaves began to pelt the car.

"More natural phenomena?" Jensen asked.

"No idea," Aric told him. "But I'm not waiting to find out."

He put the car in gear and hit the gas, causing the tires to spin before jetting us forward. He quickly turned around, intending to follow the same path out that we'd come in, but something happened. The path changed. Then it changed again, making him take a sharp turn.

He rolled his window down and stuck his hand out to move some of the brush.

A tree to the right moved and I called out, "Aric! On the right." He swerved to avoid it.

"Are you doing this?" Jensen asked, but I already knew the answer.

"Fuck no." Then Aric had to slam on the brakes because the path was completely blocked by a wall of trees that looked like they'd been carefully woven together.

He waved his hand, making the trees grow away, then slammed on the gas pedal.

Almost right away, he had to bring us to a screeching halt.

"This is ridiculous," Aric said, then he undid his

seatbelt and jumped out of the car. "Alyssum," he called out.

She scurried out of the SUV while Sabrina and I followed her. Jensen was right on our tails.

Aric grunted as he used his power to try to clear the path. It was working, but they were moving slowly. "Zap it," he told Alyssum.

Alyssum held her palms out to draw in the energy, then she released it on the woven trees. The sound of branches cracking vibrated around us like thunder so loud that I had to cover my ears.

"This has to be a trap," Jensen called out over the noise as he too began zapping tree limbs to break them apart so Aric could move them quicker.

They were so focused on the patchwork blocking our path that they didn't see the quick-moving white fog headed our way. Now maybe I'd seen too many movies, read too many books, but there was no world in which this kind of fast-moving fog was a good thing.

"You guys!" I called out as I watched it. They ignored me at first, but then I said, "Look!"

That got their attention.

Fuck. We were going to have run toward it to get into the car.

"Come on." Aric grabbed my hand and we

started running. Alyssum and Sabrina got in at the same time Jensen and Aric did. "Roll up any windows." Aric pressed his button but couldn't make it go fast enough.

Some of the fog got in the car.

I was fine. I felt fine, but Sabrina gasped then coughed. Out of nowhere, she burst from the car back into the mist and left the door open.

Without thinking about it, I jumped out after her, pushing the door closed as I did. Then I ran after her. She wasn't fast and I was starting to slow down as I choked on the fog. Once I got my hand around her arm, I pulled her back.

Then I ran into what felt like a brick wall that almost sent the both of us to the ground.

Luckily, Aric and Jensen each had a hold of one of us and pulled us through to the car. Aric pushed me in one side while Jensen pushed Sabrina into the other and slammed the doors. Then they got back in the front seat.

"Here," Alyssum said, handing each of the guys one of the copper-soaked cloths that I'd made with Fern from the first-aid kit under the seat.

Good. They'd heal. But I looked down in horror at the way my skin bubbled.

The guys coughed like they were gagging, so

Alyssum gave them each a vial of her mother's concoction. Another thing I'd thought to put into all the first-aid kits. Plus there was copper in this car. They'd be fine.

Sabrina and I, however... might not be as lucky.

Alyssum turned her attention to us, using whatever she could to make us better, but we didn't heal from the copper the way they did. She poured water from a jug in the back on our arms, which did make the burning stop. Then Sabrina and I both drank some, which seemed to calm our throats.

"We're going back to the cabin," Aric said.

"No," I said, then I wished I'd been quieter. "Just take us somewhere we can have a minute."

The look on his face said he didn't want to do it, but finally, he nodded, punched something into his GPS, and got us out of the trees. It shouldn't even have been big enough to be considered a forest.

He drove while I laid my head back to rest.

The next thing I knew, the car door opened and Aric was standing there with his hand out. He clearly wanted me out of the car. Sabrina got out the other side with Jensen's help and Alyssum was behind us.

"What was that?" Sabrina asked as she leaned against a brick wall.

We were in a park near some baseball fields and she was leaning against the dugout. There was no one here and no one driving by would see us. They'd know we were here but wouldn't be able to tell that Sabrina and I were in the shape that we were.

My lungs no longer felt like they were on fire. That was a good thing. Alyssum led me over to the bleachers so that I could sit down.

"Are you insane?" Aric yelled, making me look up at him. "What were you thinking?"

"I had to get her," I told him.

Alyssum glanced at me then looked at him. "Maybe this isn't the best—"

"I don't need your opinion, Alyssum," Aric said, fully dismissing her. I would've thought she'd fight that, but she didn't. She also didn't leave my side. "*I* would've gotten her."

Jensen brought Sabrina over to sit down because she looked like she was about to collapse.

"That's what I didn't want!" I yelled back.

"What the fuck, Sloane? You know that I'll heal faster than you do with the copper." He took two steps closer. "If anyone has to get hurt, it should be me. Or Jensen. Or Alyssum." Jensen grumbled under his breath. "Because we can heal fast. We will be better quicker. Don't do that again."

I didn't care that everyone was watching us right now. "I *will* do it again," I snapped. "I'll do it every time because I told you I don't want you getting hurt because of me."

"It wouldn't have been because of *you*, it would've been because of her. You're so damn stubborn that you're going to get yourself killed."

I snapped back like his words had bite because they had. "I'm not going to get myself killed."

"Yes. You are." He squatted down in front of me so we were more the same height. "Do you forget that you can heal me? Your blood could heal any of us. Can it heal yourself?"

That, I couldn't answer because could it? If I cut myself and then dropped right-side blood on me, would the wound heal quicker? Logically, I didn't see how that would work, but none of this was logical.

"That's right," he said when I didn't answer. "You don't know. So you're going to have to let us do some of this shit."

After snapping my mouth closed, I resolved myself not to continue this argument. Mostly because he had some really good points. I could heal them. I could probably heal Sabrina and now was a great time to find out.

"We should try to heal you," I told her.

Sabrina's eyes widened. "How?"

"With Aric, I made him drink my blood. But we could try doing it like the flower. Where I just put a drop on you. At least to start."

She blinked a whole lot before she nodded. I couldn't blame her. It was kind of gross.

I took my pocket knife and pricked my finger, letting the blood pool there. Then I dropped it on one of the sores on her leg that the fog had caused. It sizzled and she winced, but then the sore rapidly healed. I grinned.

"Well," I told her, "looks like we have to do the others."

There weren't many sores, but one by one, I dropped a little blood on them and they healed up. She looked as good as new twenty minutes later.

"See?" Aric said gently. "Everyone is fine except you."

Yeah. I did see. Mine were starting to heal, I could feel it, but it would take longer than the others. I did try to drop some of the blood from my right finger onto my left side, but nothing happened. I couldn't heal myself that way.

"If the witches want us dead, why don't they just

kill us themselves?" Sabrina asked as we sat there, waiting for me to feel better.

"They tried," I told her. "They just weren't successful.

"Yeah, that had to be witches." Alyssum rubbed my shoulder soothingly. This shit wasn't the worst, but it was painful. I would've pulled away from her, but any blood was dried and we knew that dried blood didn't have the same effect. "They wouldn't be able to kill you themselves which is why they keep trying to kidnap you and attack the rest of us."

"Why the hell not?" I asked. It seemed like the easiest solution to their problems.

"Because if you're part of the natural undoing of their curse, they can't kill you themselves. That's why they didn't when you were babies, I assume. And I don't think they're trying to kill you. Most likely, they're just trying to stop you." She shrugged. "And maybe kill the rest of us."

"Well, I know they weren't close by for this," I told her. "The pendant didn't get hot and I don't think my mark showed up. Sabrina would probably have one too and I know nothing showed for her.

"Why would they want to kill all of you?" Sabrina asked her.

"We're helping you," Aric told her, but he never

took his eyes off me while I avoided looking directly at him.

Everything he'd said had been right. I could heal any of them of almost anything. If it was internal, they could drink my blood, as disgusting as it sounded.

But if Aric had gone into that fog longer, it could've been worse. What if something like that killed him before I could heal him?

"And you know that pesky Gobel bond." Alyssum bumped my shoulder with hers.

"No," I told her. "I don't."

"I think I told you. Once a Gobel becomes your friend, it's like a bond. You can't get rid of them unless you break the bond, which is super hard. So Aric is lifelong."

Now I did bring my eyes up at him. "Is that true? Are you doing all of this because of a bond?"

He shook his head and folded his arms over his chest. "I'll be their friend because of the bond, but no. It doesn't require I put myself in harm's way." Then he squatted down again, causing Alyssum to put some space between us. "And what I have with you is much stronger than a friendship bond."

So now I worried that he was putting himself in harm's way against his will. Though if I would've thought about it, I would've known right then that a bond wasn't what he was talking about.

It was because he loved me and I probably should've stopped fighting his need to protect me. Going forward, I needed to remember that we were all working together and I needed to stop working against him.

Chapter Twenty-Eight

Once I was feeling semi-able to function—which took another twenty minutes or so—we headed toward Brighton. We'd been hovering on the outside of the city limits and hadn't ventured in yet. As we approached, Aric—driving again—made a sound and then the car shot off the road into a field of tall grass. He got the car to a stop without anything bad happening.

Every time there was an issue, I expect to fall down something or be turned over since that was what happened most of the time now.

"What's going on?" Jensen asked him from the front seat.

"I don't know," Aric told him. "It was like I was on a track that took us over here."

They both undid their seatbelts before Aric turned and met my gaze. "Can you three please just wait here?"

I nodded because this one time, I was going to listen.

The guys got out, leaving us three to watch them try to figure out what was happening. Aric walked toward the city and then... just stopped. Jensen tried and the same thing happened.

"I'm going out there," Alyssum said, then she opened the door and hopped out.

Sabrina and I looked at each other then followed her. Alyssum was already almost to them, so we both jogged to catch up.

"What's going on?" she asked them when we were close enough.

"Not sure," Jensen told us. "It's like there's something stopping us from going into the city."

I furrowed my brows as I walked toward this barrier they were talking about and yep. I slammed into an invisible wall.

"What the hell?" I asked.

"Yeah, we don't know." Jensen glanced over at me then back to the invisible force field keeping us out.

"Maybe we should try another area." I took off at

a jog to go down a little farther, but halfway to where I wanted to go, my toe caught on something and I freefell to the ground.

"Sloane," Aric called out as I turned over onto my back. I knew there'd be some kind of falling involved. "Are you all right?" He reached a hand out for me to take then lifted me off the ground.

"Yeah. I'm fine." I'd gotten some of the long grass on my face, so I brushed it off. "I tripped over a rock, I think."

Alyssum dropped onto the ground to search for the rock. When she found it, she pulled the tall grass away and muttered, "Oh, shit."

"What?" I hurried over and got down beside her so I could see what she did. "Wait. Could someone get the envelope from the car?"

Jensen moved before Aric had the chance and was back quickly. I took the envelope from him and found the picture of the cloth with all the runes on it.

"Look," I said as I handed her the picture.

"Yeah. You're right."

Sabrina threw her hands up in the air. "Do either of you want to include the rest of us?"

"Oh." I stood, brushing my legs off. "Sorry. It's one of the runes that's on the cloth in the picture."

"What does that mean?" she asked and at first, I

was just going to tell her that I didn't know, but I wasn't sure that was true.

Why would this rune be here and not the others? That was what I wanted to figure out.

"What if the city is surrounded by the runes?" Alyssum asked. Once our eye connected, it was like we were the only two out here and suddenly, we had a really good understanding of each other.

"Keeping us out?" I asked.

She shrugged and looked back at the photo. "What if it's to keep *all* magic out?"

My eyes widened. "That would make sense. It would stop all of us from getting here.

"No," Aric countered. "How would that make sense? She's in there. She's magic."

"Is she, though? Sabrina didn't get the tinglies until we met. No power ever came out for her and we're still working on that."

"But *you* could."

"No. I don't do anything. It's inside me. So, like... I don't do breathing. I don't do making blood. And I've bled before and no one died, so even that was latent and didn't come out until after the first step to break the curse happened."

"She's right," Alyssum said, looking from the photo to the rock again. "These runes were put on the blanket for a reason. Now, they're here. It has to be something like this. Maybe to keep out new magic? I don't know, but it's keeping us out."

"I have a thought." Sabrina raised her hand. "I've been here before. We stopped in Brighton to pee on the way somewhere else. I had no problem coming in. So I'll try. If I can't get in now, then we know that at least some parts of this are true."

"Do it," I said right away. It wasn't like she'd get hurt, especially if she didn't go running at it like a maniac.

Sabrina slowly made her way over to where the barrier should have been. At first, she was fine and then *bam*. She hit the wall the same as the rest of us.

"Nope," she said, stepping back. "Can't get in."

"Then there have to be more runes surrounding the city," Alyssum told us. "We have to find them and break the runes' hold."

"How do we do that?" Jensen asked.

She took a breath and shook her head. "I'm not sure, but I'd guess it has something to do with blood. Curses are usually sealed with blood. It would make sense for the runes to need the same to break." She wet her lips and looked uncomfortable. "I think it'll have to be a lot of blood, though."

"I'll do it," I said right away.

"No," Aric said immediately.

"Yes," I countered. He was going to argue, but I held up my hand. "I'm not going to fight with you about this. I'm doing it."

Aric's jaw hardened.

"I can do it," Alyssum said.

"What? No." Jensen stepped closer.

"I don't think it has to be Gorgon blood," she told him.

"I'll do it," I said again. "This is all because of me—for me, whatever—so I should do it."

"What if we split it up?" Sabrina asked. "There're five of us. It looked like there are five ruins. There were five ruins on the fabric in the picture as well. We each take one. That way, none of us gets drained."

"I'll go first," I said right away because if this didn't work, I didn't want any of them making this kind of sacrifice and have it not work.

I went over to the rune and squatted down, then took the pocket knife out and opened it. At least it was sharp and I didn't seem scar from any of the previous cuts. At this point, I needed a spigot on one of my veins so I didn't have to keep wounding myself. I put the blade to my skin and drew it across. The red blood was stark against my skin. I used my arm and not my hand because using the hand was dumb. I'd keep reopening it every time I moved it. And I used the left arm just to give it a little more juice.

The blood flowed over the rune and I wasn't sure if I was hearing things, but to me, there was a sizzle.

"How will we know when it's enough?" Aric asked as he paced.

"I don't know," Alyssum said.

So the blood just kept flowing as I made sure to cover the entire rune. "Wait," I said. "Do you see that?"

There was a line that almost looked like a trip wire shimmering in the sun.

"That's got to be the sign," Alyssum said, so I pulled my arm away. Aric stepped forward with a rag to tie it around me, but I grabbed it from him. "It's left side."

He raised his hands in defeat and stepped back. Clearly, he would've chanced it by putting the rag against my arm, but I wouldn't. That could kill him.

"That's more blood than I thought," Jensen said and I couldn't disagree. It wasn't like a whole pint, but it sure as hell wasn't a prick of the finger.

We were able to follow the line to the next rune. This time, Alyssum stepped up to do the ritual, but when she did, nothing happened. No line showed up.

"Stop," Jensen demanded. "That's enough." It had been more blood than I'd needed to give.

And that's when I realized... It had to be my blood. "It's me," I told them. "It has to be me. I have to do them all."

"That's too much," Aric said, wrapping me in his arms.

"It doesn't matter."

"What about Sabrina's blood?" he asked, looking desperate for there to be another answer.

I shook my head. "She doesn't have the left/right thing going on. Her blood hasn't hurt anyone. It has to be me."

So I pushed away from him, took the knife, and cut myself in the same spot as before, letting out a squeak that I tried to muffle. But it hurt. I couldn't deny that.

Once enough blood was there, the line showed up and we repeated the process. Aric stayed closed to me, but each time I had to reopen the wound. It was still better than creating a new one each and every time.

Finally, we made it to the last one, but by this point, Aric was carrying me more than I was walking. The only saving grace was that I'd make more blood. If I lasted that long.

It was so much to break the runes.

When we got to the last one, Aric sat me on the ground, but for me, it wasn't solid. It was tilting and I didn't have the energy to bring the knife to my now-even-paler skin.

"I need you to do it," I told him as I closed my eyes and focused on my breathing.

"Sloane," he said quietly as he pushed my hair away from my face. "I can't."

"I can't," I told him as tears filled my eyes. "I need you to do it."

"We've come this far, Aric," Alyssum said, but it sounded like she'd been crying. "If we stop now, this was all for nothing."

"What if she doesn't make it?" he snapped back.

"If you get me to the third sister, she and Sabrina will be able to break the curse without me. All we were told is the three of us need to reunite."

"Sloane," he said again softly. When I summoned enough energy to look up at him, his eyes shimmered, like he was holding back tears. "Please don't make me do this."

So I nodded slowly. "Alyssum." I wasn't even

sure I'd said it loud enough for her to hear me, but she was there and took the knife.

"I've got it, Sloane." She cleared her throat and sniffed. I must've really looked bad for everyone to be so upset.

As gently as she could, Alyssum pulled the knife through my already tender flesh. I couldn't help but cry out. It was the last time. We weren't going to have to do it again. Aric hissed air into his lungs at the sound that I made.

The blood was slow to drain. I wasn't sure there'd be enough as my heart pounded harder than I'd ever felt it before.

"I'm so sorry, Sloane," Alyssum whispered as she held my arm against the rune.

My vision tunneled as I began to see black spots and the sound of a rubber band snapping made me wince.

"It worked," Alyssum said, pulling my arm away from the rune. She was going to wrap it, but I wouldn't let her. Instead, I used the last of my energy to get it covered so that I wouldn't inadvertently kill any of them.

And then my world turned black.

"Yeah, but what the fuck do we do about it,

Alyssum?" Aric said in a gruff tone, like he wanted to yell but couldn't.

"I don't know, Aric. She wanted to break the runes and she's still breathing. We have to find her sister. It's what she wants."

"Fuck what she wants," he spat. "I never should've let her do this in the first fucking place. Now, we figure out how to make her better, *then* we go find the third sister."

Someone was holding my hand and I turned my head to see who, but before I could, I was out again.

This time when I woke, it was because Alyssum was rubbing my head. "She's hot. The blood loss must've caused a fever." She put something cool against my head. "Sloane," she said a little louder. "We have an idea."

That got me to open my eyes, though it was hard. So hard, in fact, that I wasn't sure I'd be able to hold them open very long.

"We think Jensen and I can take some of Aric's energy and give it to you."

"Which we've not successfully done," Jensen muttered. He was standing behind Alyssum with his arms folded and I was on a bed. Where in the hell had we gotten a bed?

"Doesn't matter," she snapped. "We're going to take some of his energy and give it to you. Sabrina's going outside so that we don't accidentally get hers." She leaned closer so that I could see her better. "We don't know how this is going to feel, so just hang with us."

I closed my eyes but could still hear everything going on in the room.

Alyssum dropped my hand and moved away, her feet shuffling against the carpet. "Are you ready?" she asked and it was until Aric said that he was that I knew she'd been talking to him. "All right. Let's do this."

A sizzle that reminded me of Jensen and Alyssum sucking the energy from Laken in the workout room bubbled against my ears. Aric grunted and something hit the ground. Then Alyssum said, "Grab her hand." And a hand grabbed each of mine.

I assumed one was Alyssum's with her thin, dainty fingers, and the other Jensen's with his strong, much bigger hands.

And then I was filled with fire, making me cry out. It ran through me, ran through my veins, scorching a path over me. With all of this, I should be a vampire when I woke up.

Finally, after forever, but what had probably been seconds, they broke the connection and I fell back to sleep as I heard Jensen say, "Let's get him on the bed."

When I woke again, my body told me that I hadn't gotten enough sleep, but I felt better than I had when I'd woken before. A simpler way to say it was that I didn't feel like I was dying. I also wasn't alone in the bed.

Aric was asleep next to me. He had a relaxed look on his face. As I watched him, his eyes opened slowly. "You're awake."

"I am. But I need more sleep, I think." I brushed my fingertips over the curl falling onto his forehead. "Are you all right?"

"I'm great." His voice was exhausted. "Just lost a little energy, that's all."

"I think it worked," I whispered. "I don't feel as bad."

"Good. We just need your body to replace the blood."

I nodded slowly. "Where is everyone?"

"We're here," Alyssum said in the dark. "We didn't want to be in separate rooms so that we could keep an eye on you."

That must've meant we were in a motel, which would explain the bed.

We'd broken the runes and were one step closer

to finding the third sister and righting all that was going on with the Earth right now.

I just needed a little more sleep.

In the morning, I still moved slowly, but I felt much better than I had the day before. As much as I tried to hide it, one look at Aric told me that he knew I wasn't back fully yet and I wasn't sure he was, either.

But that wasn't going to stop me from finding my sister.

Chapter Twenty-Nine

WE STARTED the day slowly for Aric's and my benefit. His energy wasn't fully back and that made me worry over how much they'd taken. While I was feeling pretty good, I didn't think all of my blood had been replaced yet. Jensen went to get us food and eating helped a little. When I looked in the mirror in the bathroom, I wasn't as pale, but since I'd almost drained myself completely of blood, it was probably going to take a while to get back to normal.

But we didn't have time to rest anymore. I was well enough to look for our other sister. Hopefully, no one would need me to heal them or kill them because I wasn't sure I'd survive the blood loss and I was absolutely certain that Aric wouldn't let me do it, no matter who it was.

"Are we ready?" I asked when it looked like everyone was finished.

"We absolutely have to do this, right?" Sabrina asked without looking at me.

"I don't think we can turn back now," I told her. "Not with everything that's happening and everything we've been through." What I'd done yesterday couldn't be for nothing.

"Then I'm ready."

The five of us piled into the black SUV with Jensen driving slowly so that I could look for what I'd seen in my vision. He looped around and that was when I saw it. It was a restaurant with a diner vibe and though I didn't pay attention to the sign, I instantly knew it was the right one.

"Here," I said quickly, slapping the back of Jensen's seat, making him take a sharp turn into the parking lot.

"You sure?" Aric asked.

"Yeah. It's exactly what I saw."

The five of us went in, but Aric, Jensen, and Alyssum took a seat at the first table near the door to watch as Sabrina and I looked around.

"Table for two?" a young woman who looked to be around our age asked. She had bright-red hair and a fake smile that told me she'd rather be anywhere but here.

"Not yet. We're looking for a waitress, I think," I told her. "She might look sort of like us..." That was about all the information that I was willing to give her.

The waitress, whose name tag said Indira, narrowed her eyes as she looked at us. Then they sprung open wide. "Oh." She snapped her fingers. "You're probably talking about Stella."

S-name? Yeah. That was probably her.

"She's not in today," she told us.

"Do you know where she is?" I asked while Sabrina hovered at my side.

"I'm not telling you where she lives." Indira frowned. Yeah, I hadn't expected her to. "But it doesn't matter. Barry, our weirdo town cop, took her in right before her shift started this morning."

I furrowed my brows as my stomach tightened. Jail meant that we wouldn't be able to get to her. All of what we'd done had been for nothing in that case.

No. We'd figured everything else out. We'd figure this out too.

"So she's in jail?"

Indira shook her head. "Not really. He wanted to talk to her about something, I guess. But we don't have a jail. We've got one cop who has a small office that he likes to treat as a jail, though."

"Where is it?" Sabrina asked her, speaking for the first time.

"It's over by the edge of town, toward Brighton."

Maybe that was why we'd been led to Brighton, even though we were technically outside of it. All of this area would have been included in the runes' protection.

"Thanks," I told her, then Sabrina and I hurried toward our group.

We left the diner before I told them what I'd learned. Jensen hopped behind the wheel again and drove us in the direction Indira had mentioned. He drove slow while I concentrated, though concentration wasn't what I needed when then nausea slammed into me, almost causing me to lose the breakfast we'd just had.

"Did you feel that?" I asked Sabrina.

She rubbed her stomach and winced. "I felt it."

"It's got to be there." I pointed to the small building we were passing so that Jensen would pull in.

My mouth watered the way it did right before you threw up. "She's got to be in there."

The five of us filed out of the car, but I turned to them. "I think only Sabrina and I should go in."

"Absolutely not," Aric countered. Understanding his need to be near me didn't mean it was the best idea. I wanted to be close to him. We could protect each other, but that wasn't going to work.

"I think five of us going in there is going to be more suspicious," I told him. "You three wait out here and help if we need it, but I don't think we will." I swallowed down the gross feeling that was getting worse as Sabrina's fingers dug into my arm. She had to be feeling it too. "But if we don't get in there soon, we're both going to lose our breakfasts."

"Go," Alyssum to us. "I'll make sure we all stay out here." Then she gave Aric a pointed look.

Sabrina pushed her arm through mine as we hurried through the door on that building. Inside, it was kind of like an office, but there was only room for one desk, on which sat a computer and a phone. Behind the desk was a hallway and two doors, from what I could see.

But there was no one in sight.

Then we heard a toilet flush followed by a sink running before a man walked out. He was taller than us, but not very tall, and a little stout. His hair had been cut into a buzz so short, I couldn't really tell what color it was supposed to have been.

"Can I help you?" he asked, resting his hands on the belt that held his gun, like he wanted to remind us that he had it if we did something stupid.

Small town cops were sometimes the worst. Some of them were bored and looking for a reason for what they called "action."

"We're looking for our sister," I told him. "Stella?"

He pursed his lips and snorted. "Well, you'll have to wait until I'm done with her."

That sounded so gross that I couldn't stand it.

"What do you mean?" Sabrina asked.

"What I mean is I think she has some information that I need and she's going to stay here until I get it."

"That doesn't sound legal," Sabrina muttered.

"Can we just talk to her?" I asked. "I don't think you're actually allowed to keep her here just to get information." Though I didn't know the law, so I could've been totally wrong. "We just need to talk to her."

He eyed us suspiciously. "I've never heard of Stella having any sisters." Then he scanned the both of us. "But you all do look related."

"Right. Can we talk to her?"

He sighed and shook his head. "You've got five minutes."

Then he waved his hand for us to follow him. He took us down that short hallway to another that we couldn't see. The right side was all wall, but the left was a small room with some kind of glass window. Sitting inside was our third sister. She was lying down on a cot with her eyes closed until the officer banged on the window, startling her.

She looked over and pinched her brows together. Obviously, she didn't know us, so it'd be weird that strangers were coming to see her. Then he dropped open a small latch that had holes in it. I guessed this was how we'd be able to talk to her.

"Your *sisters* want to talk to you," he told her, like he didn't believe us, but we did look alike. Sabrina had the short, brown hair while mine went past my shoulders. Stella's hair was the same color, though she had streaks of purple in it and it was cut into a super-fashionable bob.

Clearly, Stella was confused, but she just got up off the cot and walked coolly over to us like she'd known us her whole life.

Unfortunately, the holes to talk to her through weren't big enough for us to make contact.

"Thanks, Barry," Stella said, which caused him to grumble. My guess was calling him by his first name wasn't the respect that he wanted. "Who are you?" she asked quietly. "Don't talk too loudly," she said, keeping her voice down.

Nodding, I stepped closer to the little area meant for our voices to travel through. "I know this sounds crazy," I told her, keeping my voice down as she'd instructed, "but I'm Sloane and this is Sabrina. We're your sisters."

First she looked me over then did the same to Sabrina. "I don't have any sisters."

"Yeah, I know you think that." I sighed. "I thought that too. So did she, but you grew up in foster care, right? Or you're adopted."

She narrowed her eyes on me. "How do you know that?"

"Because we did too. We're triplets," I said. Her face didn't change with the news. "We need to get you out of here. There's something much bigger going on than whatever he's trying to get out of you. I have some friends outside. Once we get you out, I can explain everything."

Stella folded her arms over her chest. "Explain a little, at least."

After glancing at Sabrina, who shrugged, I said,

"OK. The condensed version is that three of us are Gorgons. The three goddesses, to be exact, and we need to be together to break a curse that a coven of witches put on us."

Stella chuckled but still kept the volume down. "I don't believe a word of that, but if you say you can get me out of here, I'm in. I don't care."

I sighed in relief. Just standing here was so draining that if I had to do too much to convince her, I didn't think I'd stay on my feet.

"You don't look so good," she said, looking at me without concern.

"She's not," Sabrina told her as she wrapped an arm around my waist.

"I'm fine," I said once I caught my breath. "We're going to go outside and be back."

Stella nodded then stepped away from the window. Sabrina and I turned back down the hallway, calling out a quick thanks to the officer and made no mention of the fact that we'd be right back. That, we wanted to be a surprise.

All the three of us needed to do was be together and complete a circle. Assuming I understood anything in Alyssum's book. That would mean the three of us would join hands. All hell would likely break loose, but we'd be on our way.

I had to assume everything would still happen to undo the curse if the three of us weren't together after that. Although we needed all three of us to break the damn thing, anyway. Not getting to know Stella at all kind of sucked but there just wasn't anything else I could do.

It took us a minute to get back out to the other because I was so slow-moving. I would've thought I'd have felt better by now. Aric took one look at me and rushed over, taking me in his arms then basically carrying me to the car, where he opened the door and lifted me into the seat.

I couldn't say it wasn't welcomed.

"She's in," I said, though I sounded a little out of breath, though I hadn't done anything. "We just have to get her out."

"Jensen and I have a plan." Aric cupped my cheeks as he looked at me with concern. "I want to take you to a hospital."

"Absolutely not," I told him. "How would we explain anything? I'd be there forever with them poking around to figure out how I'd lost so much blood. Maybe they'd put me on suicide watch, which involves alerting police. No. We need to do this." I reached out and touched his cheek, making him slowly close his eyes and lean into my hand. "I don't have the energy to argue about this."

He opened his eyes slowly, but there wasn't any less concern there. "All right. But you're going to take a break." His tone told me that I wasn't going to argue with him. Besides, I didn't have the energy to. "Jensen and I are going in there. Alyssum is taking you back to wait at the first rune."

It wasn't far and they'd be able to hurry over to meet us. There was only one thing. "You have to take Sabrina with you. That way, Stella knows you're with us."

He nodded. "That's fine." Then he leaned in and pressed his lips to mine. It was quick, but he did linger a moment. "Put your legs in."

I did and he shut the door.

They talked outside the car while I laid my head against the window and closed my eyes. I could use a nap already. Then the front door opened and Alyssum slid in behind the wheel of the SUV.

"You still with me?" she asked. I nodded, but she wouldn't have been able to hear it.

"Yeah," I told her, keeping my eyes closed as she pulled out of the parking lot and took us over to the runes. I didn't have anything to say, really, and the quiet was nice.

Then she brought the car to a stop and got out again. After Alyssum rifled through the back of the SUV, she closed the back and opened my door. Luckily, I'd sat up before she'd done that.

"Drink this," she said, holding out one of the vials with her mom's concoction in it.

"Why? Copper doesn't heal me." Though I had started to feel better since Aric had put me in the car.

"Just drink it," she insisted. "It'll taste like ass, but there are other healing properties to it than just the copper. You know this."

I did, but I'd never considered it might help me. So I downed the entire vial in one swallow. She was right. It tasted bad, but none of that would matter if it helped. Maybe it was the placebo effect, but I did immediately feel slightly better.

"If nothing else works, it'll help keep you hydrated," she said.

When I'd learned to make the medicine with Fern, she'd told me that some of the ingredients had hydrating properties. I should've remembered that before and taken this earlier.

"I have to say, I feel a little better already." I handed the vial back to her.

"We'll give this one a little time, then you're getting another one."

"No way," I countered. "These for sure heal you three. I'm not using them all up."

"I don't care what you say." She cocked her head to the side and narrowed her eyes. "I'll pour it down your throat if I have to. If it helps you, then you take it."

Understanding where she was coming from didn't mean that I wanted to use up all of the one thing that would heal them from the worst injuries they could get. The guilt of using it while one of them died would be too much.

"Besides," she said, "once you're better, you can heal us."

Well, shit. She did have a point.

"Why are you here with me and not with them?" I asked her, though I thought I probably already knew the answer.

"To protect you." She scanned the field as she spoke.

"I can protect myself."

"Aric doesn't want you using any of your blood. Not until you're better."

"He worries too much," I muttered.

She glanced over at me then leaned against the car next to my open door. "He loves you. Of course he's going to worry about you."

"I know," I told her. He did love me. That was clear. But he also needed to give me the space to do what I had supposedly been born to do. There wasn't anything Alyssum could do about any of that, though, so there was no point in talking about it right now.

"Listen, I—" Her eyes widened and whatever she'd been about to say gurgled in her throat as she fell back.

"Alyssum!" I called as I swung my legs out of the car to hop out to help her.

Before I could get out, a zap of electricity shot toward me. I threw myself down onto the seat, so it missed me. Then the sound of thunder rattled me and the car. I slapped my hands over my ears to muffle it. It was so loud. Like a train three feet from me.

When I opened my eyes, I couldn't see out of any window. My body shook, my heart raced, and the hair on my arms was standing on edge.

The front window was covered in branches and leaves. That would have been Aric's power. *What the fuck?* Were the Gobel attacking us? No. The electricity have been first—that would have been the Gremalians. None of this made sense and I was sure I'd be wasting time just sitting in this car.

But someone had attacked us. I had to do something.

First, I hurried to the back row of seats and yanked the first-aid kit over the back. I grabbed another vial and drank it down. If the first one had helped me feel a little better, then this should help more. I was going to need any energy I could get, but my arms and legs still felt so heavy.

I tried to open the door, kicking with everything I could, but it didn't budge.

I was trapped and there was nothing I could do.

With only the sound of my breath in the car, I tried to think of *something* I could try. Alyssum had the keys, so I couldn't even try to roll a window down and drop some death blood on the trees. There was nothing I could do but sit here and worry about what was going to reveal itself.

Then the branches started to snap. Someone was coming. There was a crack and a sizzle as the branches fell away. That weird pulse of electricity that I'd felt when I'd first gotten to Delaware prickled over my skin.

Please be Aric and Jensen. Please be Aric and Jensen.

Then the door was yanked open and I pushed myself as far away from it as I could.

"Sloane, it's me." Aric was breathing heavily, like he'd been running, but I knew from experience the man could go for a long time without breaking a sweat.

That was fear. He was breathing like that because he'd been afraid.

I hurried over and with the last bit of energy I had, I threw myself at him. He wrapped those strong arms around me and held tightly as he pulled me out.

"Are you all right?"

I nodded as I searched the area for Alyssum. Jensen was on the ground, leaning against the car with her in his arms.

"Is she all right?" I asked. He didn't answer and I knew she wasn't going to be.

After pushing out of Aric's arms, I took many unstable steps to get to her all while pulling the knife out of my pocket. I dropped down beside them and brought the blade to slice through my skin on my right arm.

Then I tried to place it against her mouth. "Help!" I screamed at Jensen.

He took my arm and put it to her lips. Then we waited.

Not long after, her eyes flew open and she sat up,

spurting red liquid from her mouth. That was my blood. Not hers.

She looked up at me. "What the hell happened?"

"I don't know. We'll figure it out, but I need to complete the circle."

Stella and Sabrina were standing nearby, holding hands, with their eyes wide and their mouths open in evident surprise. Sabrina knew about my blood. Stella didn't. But seeing all of this was a lot for both of them.

"Aric." I reached for him. "Help me."

He put his arms around me and lifted then shouldered most of my weight as we went over to my sisters.

While he held me up, first I took Sabrina's hand and then Stella's and the ground rumbled. "Hold on," I told them.

The wind whipped around us, causing my hair to fly everywhere as the three of us gripped each other harder. A green mist of energy burst up from the three of us and shot upward.

Was that the witch's magic leaving our bodies?

I tightened my grip on both of them as much as I could because the weakness was getting worse. Aric was behind me holding me up, but I wasn't sure it'd be enough.

And then everything just fizzled out.

"Is that it?" Sabrina asked. "Did we do it?"

They were looking to me for an answer that I didn't have, so I closed my eyes, wrapped my hand around the pendant, and looked for the answer.

The pendant never go hot, though I would've thought it would have, considering we were messing with witch magic.

But the answer was clear.

"It didn't work," I told them. "I'm not strong enough."

To break this next part of the curse, the three of us had to be full of our power. I wasn't. I was weak and we hadn't even figured out what their powers were yet.

Even with that, it all came down to me not being strong enough to undo the ruins and unite with my sisters. The ruins had taken too much from me.

Chapter Thirty

"WHAT DO YOU MEAN, it didn't work?" Sabrina came toward me as I leaned more heavily against Aric.

"I'm too weak. We need to be at full power. Have to have the circle complete, which it wasn't because of me."

All of that was true. But one thing I thought our combined power had done was start to heal me. With each second that passed, a little more of the weakness fell away, leaving me feeling stronger and stronger.

I was about to say that to them when something exploded in the middle of us, sending everyone flying back. I hit the ground with a painful *thud*. Yet it almost didn't hurt. Almost.

Finding my sister just might have healed me.

Shit. Aric had been behind me and now he wasn't. "Aric!" I called out over the noise. He was on the ground not far from me. I quickly crawled over to him, but he didn't respond. "Aric." I slapped his face gently a couple of times, hoping to rouse him.

I wanted to give him my blood just in case, but the knife was somewhere near where Jensen and Alyssum had been. Now, I didn't see them.

His eyes popped open, scaring the shit out of me, then he sat up. "What's going on?"

"I don't know." I got to my feet and brought him with me as we tried to figure out what had happened.

"Witches," he said as he pulled neckline of my T-shirt aside. "It's glowing."

Fuck. How did they keep finding us? That was something I knew the answer to, actually. The mark made it easier for them to track us. I swore right there that when we were done with this, I'd cut the damn thing off my myself if I had to.

Alyssum and Jensen ran up to our side and I let out a breath of relief that she was all right. That hadn't been guaranteed.

"We have to fight," she said and I wanted to know where the noise was coming from.

"Not you." Aric pulled me back. "You're too weak right now."

"I'm not," I told him. "I was. I think my sisters' magic healed me. I feel great."

"Be careful," he said before quickly kissing me.

Alyssum and Jensen threw electricity while Aric worked on building a natural wall between us and them. I didn't get a good look, but there were quite a few of them and only six of us, and my sisters didn't know their powers yet.

This didn't look the best, but Alyssum and Jensen were going to be the key. With their power-sucking ability, the numbers shouldn't matter. From what I understood, they needed to pull in enough energy to be able to drain anyone else. But they also need to be in contact—holding hands, from what I'd seen. And right now, they were throwing more energy than they were taking in until the wall Aric was building was finished.

"It's not going to hold long against them," he said when he'd joined me again.

"Stella, Sabrina!" I called out as I reached my hands out for them to take. If I was right, I had enough power to complete this.

Stella grabbed my left hand and Sabrina my right and then they took each other's.

An instant bolt went through us, straightening all of our spines. The green light shot out from the circle that grew in intensity to the point that it was almost painful. Like a million tiny needles piercing my skin until the force pushed us apart and disappeared.

"Is that it?" Sabrina asked.

I yanked the burning pendant off my neck and held it in my hand as I closed my eyes and concentrated as best I could. "That's it. Now, we can fight."

"I don't know my powers," Stella said as we headed to where the witches were tearing the wall apart. Alyssum, Jensen, and Aric were already standing guard there.

"What better time to figure them out?" I gave her a reassuring smile. Mine had come out in a time of need to save my life. Maybe theirs would as well.

Stella took a deep breath and turned to me. "Tell me what to do."

I had no idea, but I couldn't leave her with that. "Concentrate," I told them. "Pick one witch and try to look within yourself. That's how I know we're united now. I looked within."

They both nodded and took a couple of steps back, closed their eyes, and blew out a breath. Sabrina was supposed to have illusions. We thought.

We weren't sure. That meant that Stella would have the metal gaze.

Metal gaze... Metal gaze.

Shit. I took off in a run toward them.

"I can't explain it all. But the crone would have a metal gaze. Stella has to be the crone. The metal gaze must be Medusa's gaze."

"As in *turn people to stone?*" Stella asked with confusion. I nodded. "Is my hair going to turn into snakes?"

"That, I don't know. But be careful with it. I think it won't work on Sabrina or me because we are one-third of you. But the others..." I couldn't let Alyssum, Jensen, or Aric be turned into stone.

"I'll try."

While I wanted to watch what they were going to do, I had my own things I could contribute.

"I don't have my knife," I told Aric as soon as I got to him, slightly out of breath.

"Good."

"I can't just stand here and do nothing." And if I couldn't use my blood, I had nothing to do.

A loud crack tore through the air and part of the wall collapsed.

He tensed his jaw and flared his nostrils as he pulled a small knife out of his pocket. "I'll give you this, but you have to promise only to use it if you have to. I can't have you dying on me out here."

I wrapped my hand around the knife, but he didn't let go. "I promise," I told him and he finally released it.

When the wall collapsed, everything happened at once. Aric pushed me behind him despite my protests. Alyssum and Jensen pulled in energy and clasped each other's hands, taking down most of the witches.

"We'll hold them as long as we can!" Alyssum called over.

And then this field in the middle of nowhere turned into a beautiful island paradise, causing the witches to stop, as if they couldn't see us.

"Who's doing this?" Alyssum called out.

At first, I didn't know. Then I swung my gaze to Sabrina. She had her hands held up with a red, translucent vines coming out of her palms. She was creating an illusion to confuse the witches who weren't moaning on the ground.

"Keep it up as long as you can." That was what was meant by *worlds that didn't exist.*

"We can't see them!" Jensen yelled, though he and Alyssum kept their grip on one another tight. "We won't be able to hold them off forever."

The illusion affected everyone, it seemed, except the three of us. Handy.

The two witches who had led the charge were looking around and trying to make sense of what they were seeing. Which was perfect. Because they never saw me coming. When we got closer, I held up my left arm and put the knife to it without breaking the skin.

"If you move, I'll cut," I told them. Hearing my voice made them shake their heads and their eyes widen. They couldn't see through the illusion, but they could now see Aric and me.

One witch chuckled. She was tall with long, dark hair that I'd almost call black. Though she was beautiful, her eyes were so dark that I couldn't see the pupils. "Sorry. Cutting yourself won't hurt us." She pulled her hand back, ready to cast a spell.

"I'm a Gorgon," I said in a hurry. "I heal from the right, but I kill from the left. Sound familiar?"

She dropped her hand but held it in front of her like she was at the ready.

The cries from the downed witches intensified.

"This will continue unless their lives are sucked from their bodies," I explained as Aric called up some branches to wrap around the two witches who were still standing. He forced their arms to their sides and I hoped that without their hands, they wouldn't be able to cast anything. "Tell us what we want to know."

"And what's that?" the dark-haired one asked.

"Tell us how to break the curse."

"No." Aric squeezed his hand into a fist, tightening the branches around them at the same time Alyssum and Jensen drew more energy in, which meant they could suck more energy out.

The screams intensified and the illusion faded.

When I turned to Sabrina, she mouthed, *Sorry*. But I shook my head. She didn't need to be sorry. She'd done what she'd had to do.

"Tell us," I called out. "And this will stop."

Did I know that it would stop? No. But I needed them to tell us what we had to do next.

"Three are three things needed to break the curse," she struggled to get out. Aric had the branches pretty tight.

I glanced up at him. "We thought two."

She shook her head, but it barely moved. "No. Three. Warring factions must unite in the place they both possess, but one controls."

"That's us," Aric told me. "We knew that."

"The Gorgon triplets reunite."

Yup. We'd done that.

Her face contorted into a creepy smile. "There must be a great sacrifice. You must lose the thing that completes you."

"Fuck that," I said right away. "I'm not losing Aric." Since he was the thing I loved the most, it had to refer to him. Then again, though she'd said *you*, maybe she hadn't been talking about me.

Damn riddles.

I was about to ask her another question to clarify when a giant rubber band snapped against my skin, causing me to cry out.

Alyssum and Jensen were both leaning with their hands on their knees, panting like they'd been running for miles.

That snap had to have been them.

And I realized there were no more cries.

All the witches, except these two, were dead.

We were standing in a sea of dead witches.

I swallowed hard as the rest of our group joined us. "What's the great sacrifice?" I asked. When neither answered, I yelled, "What's the sacrifice?"

Both of their skin turned pale and they didn't answer. Aric had squeezed the branches tighter.

"You killed them!" I raged at him.

"I had to, Sloane. We couldn't let them go."

"But we needed answers."

"We'll get the answers." Alyssum rubbed up and down my arm. "We'll go back to Delaware and talk to Fern. Maybe visit the seer again. We'll figure it out."

"Delaware?" Stella asked. She was pale and fighting with the hem of her shirt. Today had been a lot and we hadn't even explained it all to her.

"Not the state. A town up north." It was the best way I could describe it. "That's where they're from. We'll be safe there to figure out your power."

Though the idea of a metal gaze—Medusa's gaze—scared the crap out of me. If she could turn people to stone, what was to stop her from turning one of my friends to stone accidentally?

"So we're leaving?" Stella asked.

I nodded. "We'll explain everything on the way. You're sure you don't care about your job?"

"No," she emphasized. "I'm a waitress. I can get another easy. This feels more important."

Though I meant we'd only explain what we knew because even I didn't know everything. And time was of the essence. If we didn't do this soon, the world was never going to recover.

In a sense of relief, my sisters and I joined hands again and I didn't think anything else would happen. But the green mist was back, only this time, it was thick and unforgiving as it swirled around us, glowing brighter and brighter with each passing second as the earth began to rumble. It was like the final bindings of the curse were unraveling when I thought it already had.

The wind died down and the earth stilled. For a moment, there was silence—the peaceful calm after the storm.

We were left breathless.

Sabrina let out a long sigh, her shoulders dropping in relief. "Was that the last of it?"

"It has to be," I told her. My soul told me that this part of the curse was finally broken.

"That wasn't so bad." Stella grinned, wiping the sweat from her forehead.

I snorted. Yeah. Not so bad.

As I looked out over the witches, their bodies melted into the ground. It made me think of a show I'd seen once that had talked about a place of great power being where a large number of witches had died and I wondered if there was any reality to that.

But something still felt... off. My skin prickled as I glanced down at my hands. I shouldn't have been feeling anything, but right now, it was like something was crawling up my arms. It wasn't painful, but it wasn't comfortable, either.

Something had changed. Something was happening.

"Sloane?" Aric's voice came from behind me, soft with concern.

I opened my mouth to tell him that I was fine, even though I didn't know that I was, when a sharp jolt shot through my body. My legs gave out beneath me, and I collapsed to the ground. My hands throbbed with heat as panic rose in my chest.

"Sloane!" Aric rushed to my side, dropping to his knees as he took me in his arms. "You're hot. What's happening?" He looked to my sisters, but they didn't know any more than I did.

"It's OK," I managed to get out, though I wasn't sure that even I believed it. Sabrina and Stella were at my side, on their knees across from Aric.

"What's happening to her?" Stella asked, panic slipping into her voice.

"I don't know," Alyssum muttered, staring down at me with an intensity that made my skin crawl. "I don't think this is part of the ritual."

While they debated what this could have been, memories—no visions—flooded my mind. Scenes I didn't recognize but had a deep connection to. Faces flashed before me: our mother—she looked like us— the witches, and then... three women that resembled us. Only it wasn't us. They had powers I couldn't fully understand.

The visions disappeared as quickly as they'd come, leaving me gasping for air.

"What did you see?" Sabrina's voice was sharp, cutting through the haze, like she knew for sure that I'd seen something.

"I-I'm not sure," I stammered as the heat faded from my body. "But... I think I saw the thing that completes us."

Stella's face darkened. "We don't even know each other. How can one thing complete all of us?"

Alyssum gasped and met my gaze. "Your mother?"

I glanced between my sister, the weight of what I had seen pressing down on me. "I think so."

"Our mother is the thing we have to sacrifice?" Sabrina asked quietly.

"I think so."

But that would mean we had to find her.

I clenched my hands, the slight burning fading slowly, yet I felt stronger than before. "We have to find out what happened to our people. And then we have to kill our mother."

Thank you for reading THE GORGON CURSE!
I hope Sloane & Aric took you for a ride.

If you're reading this book first, you can go back and
read about Alyssum & Jensen!

The Gremlin Prince

The final book in The Empowered Series - THE
GODDESS SACRIFICE is coming soon!

Being a Gorgon was never on my to-do list—hell, I
didn't even know they existed. Growing up in foster
care, I had no idea I was one third of a powerful trio
of sisters—the three goddesses. And while I may be
the maiden and not the crone, this newfound family
isn't exactly what I had in mind.

Breaking the curse that's hung over us without our
knowledge, is a little more complicated than we'd
hoped. First, we have to find the mother who
abandoned us for our own good.

Then, we have to sacrifice her. You know, as one
does.

And as if that wasn't enough, there are witches lurking around every corner, just waiting for their chance to stop us. The clock's ticking, the Earth is rebelling, and the stakes? They couldn't be higher.

This isn't just about survival anymore. It's about freedom, loyalty, and breaking free of a destiny we never asked for. But the hardest part? The only way out of this mess is through the one person I never wanted to meet.

Ready or not, Mom, here we come.

The Goddess Sacrifice is the final book in The Empowered Series. You can expect danger, adventure, and steamy nights with a Goblin who's more worried about her safety than is own.

Preorder THE GODDESS SACRIFICE!

Being the daughter of my people's leaders, I should understand protocol and appropriate behavior. Problem is, I understand both, I just don't follow them.

But I have a different plan.

There's a boy... now a man, who is supposed to be powerful. I want him on our side.

What I didn't know is that together, he and I might be unstoppable.

Now I just have to find him.

START READING THE GREMLIN PRINCE TODAY

START READING KISSING THE PLAYER TODAY

Do you love rock stars?

FOREVER GRAYSON

Forever 18 Book 1

One night three years ago is coming back to haunt me.

It was supposed to be one night then I'd never see him again. One night at a dive bar where I met someone who could scratch an itch.

He wasn't famous then.

Now he's a rock star.

A rock star whose manager just hired me to be the band's stylist. It's a dream job to me but it could be a nightmare.
Is it worse if he remembers me? Or worse if he doesn't?

START READING FOREVER GRAYSON NOW

START READING DAISY NOW

Cross *Courting Chaos Book 1*

When a sexy drummer mistakes me for a groupie and tries to kick me out of the venue, I'm willing to chalk it up to mistaken identity. Usually everyone knows me but I shouldn't assume. Now Cross wants to make it right ini the hope that my father won't kick his band off the tour.

In trying to make amends, Cross becomes my surprise protector when I accidentally snap some pictures of his bandmate in a bad situation and he wants them deleted.

Cross being my protector has me wanting something I've never wanted before... A sexy drummer.

Growing up with a famous father has taught me many things but the number one rule has always been NEVER FALL FOR A ROCK STAR.

I guess I want to break the rules.

START READING CROSS TODAY

**After living under my father's rule, I'm
about to break free.**

My father has kept me on a short leash my entire life.

The Orin comes for me.

Finding out what he is... scares the hell out of me.

Finding out I'm his supposed mate... I don't know
that I'll recover.

START READING MOONSTRUCK TODAY

I'm a witch. Or so they tell me.

Finding out I'm a witch isn't even the weirdest part of my day. Having the guy who hated me in high school stand before me to tell me that I am, is.

Somehow, I'm supposed to learn spells and how to ground myself to the elements, fight the fact that I want him like I want air, and not freak out that my parents are part of a shadow coven trying to pull me over to the dark side.

Yeah. No problem.

START READING CURSED MAGIC TODAY

THE HARBOR POINT SERIES

A new adult contemporary romance series

Meet Gio and Sal.

Two damaged men who meet the woman who can set them right.

Then there's Cash.

He's not damaged but he's ready to do the healing when he meets Gemma.

START READING LOVE BY THE SLICE TODAY

THE FALLOUT SERIES

A new adult romance series

Coming home is hard.
Finding out the boy you loved had a baby with your
former best friend... heartbreaking.

*START READING LAST GOOD THING
TODAY*

GAMBLING ON LOVE

A new adult romance series

Desperate times call for desperate measures so
Flannery Tate is selling her virginity.

START READING HIGHEST BIDDER TODAY

I you'd like to just keep up with my sales and new releases, you can follow me on BookBub!

Bookbub: https://www.bookbub.com/authors/
heather-young-nichols

Heather Young-Nichols is a USA Today Bestselling author of contemporary and paranormal romances. She writes swoony heroes and snarky heroines with a heap of romance.

When she's not writing, she's binging a show with her kids, watching baseball, or snuggling with her cuddly animals.

Find Heather on Social Media or by visiting her website.

heatheryoungnichols.com

facebook.com/heatheryoungnicholsauthor

instagram.com/heatheryoungnichols

amazon.com/Heather-Young-Nichols/e/B00KKTM54A

bookbub.com/authors/heather-young-nichols

tiktok.com/@heatheryoungnichols